Brick-a-Breck

Written by **Julia Donaldson**

Illustrated by Philippe Dupasquier

A & C Black • London

For Jerry – J.D.

First published 2003 by
A & C Black Publishers Ltd
37 Soho Square, London, W1D 3QZ

www.acblack.com

Text copyright © 2003 Julia Donaldson
Illustrations copyright © 2003 Philippe Dupasquie.

ISBN 0-7136-6438-X

A CIP catalogue for this book is available from the British Library.

A&C Black uses paper produced with elemental chlorine-free
pulp, harvested from managed sustained forests.

Printed and bound in Singapore by Tien Wah Press (Pte) Ltd

Bowl One

Stephen Rice loved cereal.

This was a typical day's menu for
Stephen …

Breakfast – Cracklewheat

Playground snack – Corncrunch

Packed lunch – Sunnysnaps

Teatime – Toastyoats

Suppertime – Sultana Stars

Bedtime – Choc-o-not-hoops

Choc-o-not-hoops? What are they? you might be wondering. Well, Stephen's mum could tell you – she worked in a cereal factory. (Lucky Stephen!)
The company that Mum worked for was called Sunfield, and their most famous cereal was called Choc-o-hoops.

Mum's job was to watch the Choc-o-hoops coming out of the machine and pick out any broken ones. She was allowed to take these ones home. They were the Choc-o-not-hoops.

The only snag about
the Choc-o-not-hoops
was that they didn't
have a packet.
Stephen loved
cereal packets
almost as much
as the cereal itself.
Sometimes they
had free prehistoric
pencil-tops in them.

Sometimes they had
tokens to cut out,
so you could
save up for
something
really useful
like a glow-
in-the-dark
skeleton warrior.

What's more, the packets were great
to read.

All in all, Stephen Rice was a happy
boy – until the dreadful day that Sunfield
closed down the factory where Mum
worked.

Bowl Two

Suddenly they were poor. Mum was out of a job. There were no more free Choc-o-not-hoops. In fact there wasn't any cereal, except for porridge, which didn't count.

The only way Stephen could ever eat any cereal or read any packets was to get himself invited to friends' houses.

It was at his friend Bruce's breakfast table that Stephen read about the competition. This is what he read, on the back of a packet of Choosli …

DESIGN-A-CEREAL
Sunfield are inviting you to invent your own cereal and think of a name for it. If we like the winning idea enough we'll start making it. The winner will receive a lifetime's free supply of the cereal.

There was a form for you to fill in.

Name:
Address:
Name of cereal:
Description of cereal:
Drawing of cereal:

"Can I cut this form out?" asked
Stephen.

"No, my mum won't let us till the packet's empty," said Bruce.

"That's not a problem," said Stephen, and poured himself out another bowl of Choosli. Three bowls later the packet was empty and Stephen took the form home.

Bowl Three

Stephen chewed his prehistoric pencil-top. He closed his eyes and hoped that a good idea would float into his mind. It didn't.

"Ricy Robots … Brontosaurus Bran …"

"Too difficult to make," said his mum, who was a bit of an expert.

"Snowflakes," he murmured.
"That sounds like a washing powder,"
said Bruce, who had come to tea.
"Well, you think of something, then,"
said Stephen.

But Bruce just suggested silly things like
Soggylumps and Grottygrain.

The closing date for the competition
drew near. Two days before it, Stephen
went to his school's Summer Fair.
He spent most of his pocket money
on Fibreflake flapjacks and was just
nibbling one when Mum appeared,
clutching a purple vase.

"What a colour!" said Stephen. "Did you fish it out of a trough of Ribena?" "No," said Mum. "I bought it at the bric-a-brac stall."

Then, "What's the matter?" she asked,
for Stephen was punching the air as if
he'd scored a goal.
"That's it!" he said. "Brick-a-Breck!"

Bowl Four

Stephen's mum sat in front of the television. The presenter of *Kidsnews* was talking.

"Eight-year-old Stephen Rice heard this week that he is the winner of Sunfield's Design-a-Cereal competition. Can you tell us about Brick-a-Breck, Stephen?"

"Yes. They're shaped like little bricks," said Stephen. "So you can build things with them before you eat them. Like this." He held up a picture. A cereal bowl with a castle in it filled the screen.

"Well," said the presenter, "Sunfield liked Stephen's idea so much that they've actually made some sample Brick-a Brecks – or should I say Breck-a-Bricks? – and here's Stephen with another idea."

Stephen appeared again with a bowl
in which was an igloo made of cereal
bricks. "These bricks are white because
they're coconut-coated," he said, "so I
thought an igloo would be a good idea."

"And what's the next step, Stephen?"

"Destruction," said Stephen, brandishing a milk jug. He poured milk on to the igloo and it collapsed. Stephen was getting rather carried away. Some of the milk splashed the presenter's tie.

"But aren't you sad to see your work destroyed?" asked the presenter.

"Oh no," said Stephen. "I just love eating cereal, you see," and he started tucking into the collapsed igloo.

"Stephen Rice, thank you very much," said the presenter, wiping his tie. "And now on to the Brazilian rainforest …"

Bowl Five

Stephen's mum wasn't the only person watching *Kidsnews*. A man called Jasper saw it too. Jasper was the director of a film company which had been hired to make a TV commercial advertising Brick-a-Breck.

"That's the boy! He'll be perfect!" cried Jasper when he saw Stephen waving his spoon about.

And that was why a month later Stephen and his pretend sister were sitting at a breakfast table in a television studio. The pretend sister was a rather annoying girl called Clare.

"What other commercials have you been in?" she asked. "None," said Stephen.

"I have," said Clare. "I've been in Supersoup and Great Big Softy toilet paper. This one's going to be easy peasy Japanesy."

It did sound quite simple. The children had to pour milk on a Brick-a-Breck castle and ship and then eat them, while a little muscle-man made of Brick-a-Breck did press-ups and danced on the table.

The script was:

Clare: *Castle–ruin*

Stephen: *Ship–wreck*

Brick-a-Breck man: *Build 'em up with Brick-a-Breck!*

There was a lot of bustle in the television studio. Some people were scurrying around arranging things on the table, while others fiddled about with the big bright lamps.

Stephen was getting fidgety. This was taking ages. Even though he had eaten a fair bit of Brick-a-Breck during the rehearsal, he was beginning to feel hungry again.

At last Jasper was
ready for Take One.
A girl clapped a
clapperboard.

Clare, smiling
sweetly, placed
the last brick
on her Brick-a-
Breck castle and
said, "Castle."

Then she picked
up the milk jug,
poured milk on it
and said, "Ruin."

29

Now it was Stephen's turn. He placed the last brick on his ship and said, "Ship," then poured milk on it and said, "Wreck," as it collapsed.

After that, both children picked up their spoons and started to eat the cereal from their bowls.

"Cut," said Jasper.

Clare put down her spoon but Stephen finished eating his shipwreck. It was delicious.

Everyone else was crowding round a television, ready to see how Take One had turned out. Stephen joined them. One thing was puzzling him. "Where's the Brick-a-Breck man?" he asked.

"Don't be silly," said Clare. "He's a cartoon – they add him later."

Otherwise, everything looked fine to Stephen, but Jasper wasn't happy. "We need more shine on the orange juice," he said.

So a lighting man made one of the lights brighter, while the props people rearranged the milk jug and cereal packet and brought a brand new castle and ship to the table.

"Take Two," said Jasper, and they went through it all again.

Afterwards, when Stephen had eaten up the shipwreck plus Clare's ruined castle which she didn't want, he joined the others round the television screen. "Heaven," said Jasper as his eyes lit on the gleaming orange juice, but as soon as Stephen's face appeared he put his hand to his head. "That nose won't do," he said.

Clare giggled rudely.

"Too much shine," said Jasper.

Apparently, the light which had made
the orange juice shine so brightly had
had the same effect on Stephen's nose.
Stephen sighed as the make-up lady
dabbed his nose with a powder puff.

"What about Clare?" he asked.

"I'm not a red-nosed reindeer like you,"
said Clare. Stephen was getting fed up
with her. He hoped Take Three would
be the last.

Bowl Six

Two hours later, Stephen was hoping Take Fourteen would be the last. This is what had happened …

Take Three:
Stephen knocked the cereal packet over.

Take Four:
A man from Sunfield arrived
late and said there should
be a bowl of fruit on the
table to give a more
healthy look.

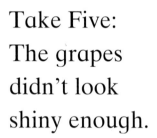

Take Five:
The grapes
didn't look
shiny enough.

Take Six:
Someone said the purple grapes didn't
go with Stephen's red T-shirt. Some
green grapes were found instead.

Take Seven:
Stephen's ship
collapsed before
he had poured
the milk on to it.

Take Eight:
Clare wasn't
smiling enough.
(Stephen was
pleased that
she had done
something
wrong at last.)

Take Nine:
Clare kicked
Stephen under the
table and some of
the milk splashed
into the fruit bowl.

Take Ten:
Jasper said
the table looked too
crowded and decided to
remove the orange juice.

Take Eleven:
The man from Sunfield
said he wanted the
orange juice back
and that it would be
all right not to have
the fruit bowl after all.

Take Twelve:
Stephen
wasn't looking
happy enough
while eating
the cereal.

Take Thirteen:
Stephen wasn't looking rosy enough –
in fact, he was looking slightly green.
Jasper got the make-up lady to rub
some red stuff on his cheeks.

"I think they should have got Simeon Jay
to act your part," Clare told Stephen.
"He was in Great Big Softy toilet paper
with me and he was brilliant."

Just at that moment, Stephen wished
that Simeon Jay, or anyone, could take
his place. There was a reason for his
greenness: he had eaten a whole fleet of
Brick-a-Breck ships and was feeling sick
– or seasick, maybe. His stomach, which
Mum always called a bottomless pit, now
felt more like a stormy sea.

"Take Fourteen," said Jasper.

As Clare did her bit, the storm in Stephen's stomach grew stronger. He placed the last brick on the ship, smiled as brightly as he could, and picked up the milk jug for the fourteenth time. Just then, his stomach gave a gigantic heave, and instead of pouring milk on to his ship, Stephen was sick all over it.

There were no more "takes", except for taking Stephen home.

In the studio, Jasper asked to see Take Two again – the one in which Stephen's nose had been too shiny. This time, Jasper said, "I like that shine! It's healthy, it's natural, it spells childhood! That's the one!"

Bowl Seven

Brick-a-Breck was a big success. Shops, cereal bowls and tummies all over the country were full of it.

This was such good news for Sunfield that they were able to re-open the factory in Stephen's town and give his mum her job back.

Actually, it isn't quite the same job. Instead of checking Choc-o-hoops she has to check Brick-a-Brecks, and make sure they are all properly brick-shaped.

This means that instead of bringing back bags of Choc-o-not-hoops she could bring back bags of Breck-a-not-bricks. But she doesn't … because Stephen, as the winner of the competition, receives a lifetime's free supply.

For some reason, though, Stephen has gone off Brick-a-Breck. In fact, he has gone off cereal altogether …

His latest craze is for pasta – shells, quills, tubes, spirals, he loves them all.

At this very moment, Stephen is poring over a packet of Romeo's Pasta Ribbons and reading aloud …

INSIDE THE BOX

My life *with* Test Match Special

PETER BAXTER

Quiller

Copyright © 2009 Peter Baxter

First published in the UK in 2009
by Quiller, an imprint of
Quiller Publishing Ltd

British Library
Cataloguing-in-Publication Data
A catalogue record for this book
is available from the British Library

ISBN 978 1 84689 062 8

The right of Peter Baxter to be identified as
the author of this work has been asserted in
accordance with the Copyright, Design and
Patent Act 1988

Design, layout and typesetting by
Andrew Barron/Thextension

Printed in Malta by Gutenberg Press Ltd.

Quiller
An imprint of Quiller Publishing Ltd
Wykey House, Wykey, Shrewsbury, SY4 1JA
TEL 01939 261616 FAX 01939 261606
E-MAIL info@quillerbooks.com
WEBSITE www.countrybooksdirect.com

INSIDE
THE BOX

———

CONTENTS

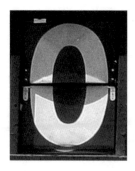

FOREWORD

I FIND IT RATHER EMBARRASSING NOW TO LOOK BACK and remember just how hard Peter Baxter had to persuade me to apply to succeed Christopher Martin-Jenkins as BBC cricket correspondent. It was during a stroll through Perth's beautifully manicured Queen's Gardens that Peter finally convinced me that my future lay in broadcasting, rather than writing for the tabloid *Today* newspaper. He was right, not least because *Today* went bust a few years later!

That meeting took place in February 1992 and marked the beginning of sixteen years of successful teamwork and great friendship, to the extent that we were each best man at the other's wedding.

The relationship between BBC cricket producer and correspondent on long tours away from home is unique. The newspaper writers all operate independently of one another, while Peter and I were a double act, each with our own specific roles. We worked together all day and then, inevitably, met in the bar for 'a sharpener' every evening before moving on to eat: I do not suppose that anyone knows me better than Peter, and vice versa.

It has not always been a barrel of laughs. The moment we were held up by armed bandits on the highway between Calcutta and Jamshedpur was only matched by the sinking realisation at Harare airport that we were about to be led to the cells for the night to await deportation. I was sitting next to Peter when the captain of an eventful Indian Airlines flight announced hysterically that we had landed only 'by the grace of God' and, of course, we share many painful memories of watching England being stuffed in Australia.

I learned quickly that it was wise to maintain a low profile on the day before a Test match on the subcontinent. It would always start promisingly enough as I waved Peter off to the stadium, rather like a mother at the garden gate seeing her child off to school. Darkness would inevitably have fallen long before a crumpled figure returned with tales of woe and utter frustration having battled with local technicians to establish a broadcasting circuit with London. Miraculously, on virtually every occasion, contact was established the following morning, the only memorable exception being a Test match in Calcutta in 1993 where, as Peter gently noted afterwards in his letter of thanks to the local All India Radio office, the broadcast might have been even more successful had just one of the several engineers they generously supplied been able to speak English.

Too often in life one realises how very special something was only after it has gone. Peter's gentle (although not necessarily always calm) and low-key attitude to production was such that, once on the air, *Test Match Special* under his care just seemed to happen by itself. Peter would appear merely to be tinkering about at the back of the commentary box, adjusting the rota or searching for CMJ, but this was his greatest skill. Peter had the nous and the confidence to allow the broadcasters freely to express themselves and to allow their true characters to emerge and to blossom. This probably comes only through experience – and Peter was also blessed with a group of established and formidable cricket commentators in his formative years – but he encouraged the informal and welcoming atmosphere in which a rather quirky, and definitely niche, radio programme flourished and developed into a broadcasting institution.

It is a mark of the closeness of the family of *Test Match Special* how keenly we all felt the loss of Bill Frindall early in 2009. He was the one member of the team who had actually been there even longer than Peter himself and the commentary box will not seem the same without him commanding his corner.

Time marches on, of course, and I know just how painful it was for Peter to hand over the baton. He leaves behind an army of grateful and loyal listeners who, with an equally determined correspondent, will strive to ensure that Peter's legacy is merely the beginning.

Jonathan Agnew
The Vale of Belvoir, February 2009

THE END

IT IS 19 JUNE 2007. I AM STANDING ON THE OUTFIELD of the Riverside Ground at Chester-le-Street, County Durham, on a chilly late afternoon that feels more like autumn than high summer, and my time as the producer of *Test Match Special* has only minutes to run. In fact, it may already have run its course, because Shilpa, my assistant, has told me that I have to be here for some vague reason when, as the programme producer, I would normally be upstairs keeping an ear on the output and an eye on the clock, to bring the programme off the air smoothly at the right time.

However, this, my final Test match in the *TMS* saddle, has been full of unexpected happenings. There was a presentation from the International Cricket Council, no less, and Jonathan Agnew ambushed me for an 'A View From the Boundary' interview. Now on my way down to the field of play, where the presentations for the end of the Test series are about to be made, I have had a remarkable number of handshakes and good wishes. To tell the truth, I am getting a little emotional about it all.

Probably the most touching comment of all has been from Nasser Hussain, one of about twenty-five England captains I have dealt with in my time in office, who has gone out of his way to come over to say, 'Thank you for all you've done for cricket.' I was really just the producer, getting the programme on the air – somehow.

Aggers is clutching the radio microphone and his few notes, with Vic Marks at his side, and now he is introducing the official presentations, as the Wisden Trophy is handed to Michael Vaughan for England's decisive victory over the West Indies in the four-match series. Then, after Vaughan has come across to us for an interview, he, too, makes a presentation to me on behalf of the England team.

Finally, I try to get Aggers to present the magnum of Veuve Clicquot for the Champagne Moment. I thought that Paul Collingwood had won it for the moment he reached his century on his home ground, but no, Aggers presents it to me. The Champagne Moment is the moment they get rid of me!

The signature tune, 'Soul Limbo', starts up and we are away. Back in the London studio, the announcer, Andy Rushton, credits the commentators and says, 'The producer ... for the last thirty-four years ... was Peter Baxter.'

And it's over.

But how did it happen?

FIRST ENCOUNTERS

LATE IN THE SUMMER OF 1966, I FIRST SET FOOT IN the *Test Match Special* commentary box. I had not quite completed a year on the staff of the BBC when I was sent to the Oval. My task was to carry out the production role at the ground, the job referred to in those days as the 'No. 2'.

I cannot remember the first moment I heard *Test Match Special*, but it would have to have been pretty much at its start in 1957, because by the end of that decade I remember doing what must have been excruciating imitations of John Arlott.

The earliest definitive memory I have of a specific commentary is of me sitting on a splintered wooden step in the Wellington College cricket pavilion in 1963, listening to the closing stages of the Lord's Test, when Alan Gibson described the tension as Colin Cowdrey came out to save the match with his left forearm in plaster.

Now here I was inside the little hut on the Oval pavilion roof, whose outpourings I had been glued to for years.

John Arlott was there, a legendary figure to me, and with him were Robert Hudson and Roy Lawrence to commentate, and Norman Yardley and Freddie Brown to add their expertise as former captains of England – the Trueman and Bailey, or Marks and Selvey, of the 1950s and 1960s.

The Test match itself was a memorable one. England had appointed Brian Close as their new captain, after a disappointing series against the West Indies had already been lost under Mike Smith and Colin Cowdrey. Tom Graveney and John Murray made contrasting centuries, but the West Indies were finally sunk by a record last-wicket partnership of 128 from John Snow and Ken Higgs.

Even for a nineteen-year-old, working at the match was not quite as daunting as it might have seemed. I had already been in the Radio Outside Broadcasts Department for eleven months, after a three-month spell with Forces Broadcasting in Aden, and earlier in the summer I had been sent out on my first 'OB' with no less a person than Rex Alston.

Rex was sixty-five by then and had left the BBC staff, which he had joined during the Second World War, but in his time he had been a sports broadcaster of the stature of Desmond Lynam today. Meeting him in the old radio commentary box at the back of the Warner Stand at Lord's on 4 June 1966 had been quite a moment for me.

Rex had come to the BBC during the war as a schoolmaster, with an impressive sporting pedigree in cricket, rugby and athletics. Some enlightened soul recognised that he had a perfect radio voice, and he made the transition from wartime billeting officer, his biggest breakthrough coming during a cricket match at Abbeydale Park in Sheffield in 1945, when he was trailing the father of cricket commentary, Howard Marshall. Marshall was summoned to London to rehearse his commentaries on the post-war victory parades, while Rex became inked-in to do the commentaries on the Victory Tests of that year.

There remained an air of the schoolmaster about his commentary, as in his words to the scorer in the first ever *Test Match Special* at Edgbaston in 1957, when Peter May and Colin Cowdrey were compiling their massive 411 partnership: 'Now, Jack Price, here's a problem for you. What's the highest partnership by a couple of Englishmen in a Test match in England? Can you work that one out … quietly … while Sobers starts the fresh over.'

A low-key county championship match, with occasional reports and snatches of commentary as part of the Saturday afternoon's *Sports Service* on the Third Network, with someone as relaxed as Rex Alston, had been the gentlest of introductions for a novice. I cannot remember us being over-taxed by broadcasting demands, although I do recall that at one stage the studio producer announced down the line that they were handing over to us shortly for an update when Rex had popped off down the corridor to relieve himself. For a minute or two I feared I might be about to make my broadcasting debut, but at the last minute a relieved and unruffled Rex returned.

Rex Alston was always 'Balston' to Brian Johnston, a nickname which arose from a session of county cricket commentary. In those heady days, for some reason, Edgbaston's hours of play were always a quarter of an hour behind the rest of the country. So, when Brian reached the close of play in the match he was describing at Lord's, there were still a few overs to go in Warwickshire's game. Brian explained this to the listeners and handed over 'for some more balls from Rex Alston!' Typically, Johnners continued to enjoy his own gaffe for many years afterwards.

He lured Rex into perpetrating a worse one in 1962 at Lord's. The Pakistan touring team that year had a player called Afaq Hussain, the first part of the name a commentator's nightmare in its correct pronunciation, with the 'aq' to rhyme with – shall we say – 'duck'.

Rex was covering the Pakistanis' match against the MCC in May and Brian had gone along to familiarise himself with the tourists before the First Test. He came into the radio box in the Warner Stand.

'I say, Balston, this chap Afaq's a bit of a problem. Let's hope he doesn't get into the Test team.'

'Don't say that name,' said Rex. 'I don't want it in my mind.'

That was too much of a challenge to be resisted and Brian left the box saying, 'Afaq, Afaq, Afaq ...'

The damage was done and as the Essex all-rounder, Barry Knight, prepared to face the next over, Rex was always alleged by Johnners to have come out with, 'There's a change of bowling and we're going to see Afaq to Knight from the Pavilion End – what am I saying, he's not even playing!'

In 1985 Rex attended a splendid dinner to celebrate sixty years of the Outside Broadcasts Department. That night he was taken ill and as a precaution moved to hospital. By a remarkable coincidence his obituary for *The Times* had just been updated by his old friend, John Woodcock, the cricket correspondent of the newspaper, and somehow the new version, instead of being restored safely to a filing cabinet in *The Times* office, found its way into a current tray and into the morning paper.

So Rex was woken in the Westminster Hospital to be greeted by reading his own obituary. He confounded that announcement by having his second marriage announced in the same paper the following year. His wife, Joan, used to recall their meeting at a dinner party, when, following discussion round the table on the subject, she asked him if he was interested in sport.

She reported him responding, 'Madam, it has been my life.'

For the MCC's Bicentenary match in 1987, I thought it would be a good idea to mark the occasion by reuniting three of the original *TMS* team, John Arlott, E. W. Swanton and Rex Alston. Eventually, John decided he could not make the trip from his retirement in Alderney, so we interviewed him on the telephone during the tea interval, but there was a delightful session in the afternoon when the years rolled back and it was commentary by Alston, with summaries by Swanton.

Back in the summer of 1966, when I was sent to the Oval as a producer for the first time, I had a pretty good idea of how these operations worked. I had been in the office that handled all the bookings for radio outside broadcasts, which was a link between production requirements and the technicalities of realising them and, following my earlier visit to Lord's, I had been drafted into the effort that went into the staging of the football World Cup.

My role for that was an extension of my day job in the OB Bookings unit, operating an office to channel the demands of the myriad foreign broadcasters. I shared a small room in the half-constructed extension to Television Centre in Shepherd's Bush with Paul Wade, who was eventually to move on to the BBC World Service as a sports producer and later became a sports correspondent at Capital Radio and a travel journalist.

Here we tried to satisfy the facility needs for commentaries, reports and other broadcasts. Thus the office was a lively, noisy, chaotic place as we battled to understand and fulfil all the often passionately expressed requests.

The various commentary teams from South America gave us the most headaches, though their arguments seemed to be mostly among themselves, rather than with us. Paul had the unlikely combination of a phlegmatic air of calm, and a reasonable command of Spanish, both of which came in very handy, as did his sense of humour. We had one extraordinary evening during the tournament, when he and I walked round the corner from Television Centre to help the Uruguay commentary team with their coverage of their country's match against France at the old White City stadium.

The stadium, once the home of British athletics – and more regularly of greyhound racing – is no more, long since demolished and replaced by a glass and chrome extension of the cash-strapped BBC. Before that fate befell it, my only other visit there was to a rugby league international, more memorable for me as the occasion on which I first met Don Mosey. But that is another tale.

On this occasion, we witnessed an extraordinary three-generation family performance of commentary by a father, son and grandson. One generation did the running commentary, with another providing the expert comments, and the third getting through as many advertisements as he could whenever the opportunity presented itself from a pile of cards, which he kept rotating. The whole thing was conducted at top volume, the trio sharing only two lip microphones between them, so that by half time they were awash with saliva. It was just as well it was all in the family.

My experiences during the year stood me in good stead when I joined the *Test Match Special* team for the first time. After working so recently at the World Cup final, this was comparatively straightforward. In those days we had only the main commentary box, with no other reporting position. Today's demands at a Test match will see – in addition to the *TMS* commentary – a box for Radio 5 Live, and others for the World Service, the Asian Network, Radio 1, Local Radio and, depending on who the visitors are, maybe various World Service language networks or a foreign broadcaster to whom we are offering assistance.

In 1966 the cricket producer for more than ten years had been Michael Tuke-Hastings. He had originally been Michael Hastings, but had acquired the 'Tuke' (a family name) because of a clash of names in the BBC. He was once announced at a reception following a quiz programme he was producing as 'Michael, Duke of Hastings,' a title which seemed to sit fairly easily on his shoulders.

By this stage he was not greatly enamoured of cricket and felt that he was better placed in the studio, where he could listen to the commentary and compile the highlights tape for posterity as he went along. For the Test matches outside London that was no problem, because for the regional outside broadcasts producers, putting on a Test match was something of a high spot amongst their duties. For Test matches at Lord's and the Oval, however, someone had to be found to do the production at the ground. It was a popular task, of course, but in a busy summer schedule it might not be too easy to find a fully-fledged producer. Young 'what's his name' – Baxter – from the OB Bookings office would have to do.

I had met most of the engineers, so there was an early welcome from the small shed-like control room across the flat roof behind the commentary hut at the top of the pavilion, where the microphone levels were balanced and contact with Broadcasting House was established.

The commentary box at the Oval in those days was a wooden hut alongside a similar one used by BBC Television, who would have their 'in vision' position with members of their team talking direct to camera on the same flat roof in the open air. In that area there was at least one friendly face and someone who was to have a huge influence on my career – Brian Johnston.

Ours was a pokey shed, with a desk built along the front and a wooden slatted bench along the back on which the off-duty commentators and I, as the No. 2 producer, would sit. I wore headphones into which Michael Tuke-Hastings would bark orders along the lines of, 'Tell Arlott he's talking rubbish'. It was an early lesson in which instructions not to pass on.

If that was my first encounter with the great John Arlott, I had at least come across Robert Hudson in the corridors of Broadcasting House, without ever getting to know him very well at that stage. Ironically that came four years later when he left regular commentary duties for administration, becoming Head of Outside Broadcasts. He was probably the best-prepared commentator of any that I worked with and had played an important part in the creation of *Test Match Special*.

Radio cricket commentary had been going successfully in Britain since the early 1930s, thanks to the brilliance of the pioneering commentator, Howard Marshall, and the vision of two administrators, Lance Sieveking and Seymour de Lotbinière. Even in 1948, when Don Bradman's invincible Australians toured England, although the BBC mounted full commentary on every ball of the Test series, it was done for the Australian Broadcasting Commission. BBC Radio only joined the commentary for various extended spells. By the 1950s two networks – the Light Programme (the forerunner of Radio 2) and the Home Service (now Radio 4) – were sharing the burden of taking the commentary periods, but these fell well short of covering the whole of a day's play.

In these days before Local Radio, the Home Service also had periods when the English regions – North, Midlands, South East and West – would carry their own programmes. In the summer these opt-outs included periods of commentary on county cricket. In the late summer of 1955, Robert Hudson was at Scarborough to cover Yorkshire's game against Nottinghamshire. With forty-five seconds of the commentary stint to go, Fred Trueman was on a hat-trick and Bob was watching the unforgiving clock tick those seconds down as the new batsman took guard. At last Trueman bowled and Poole, the unfortunate batsman, obliged with a catch to short-leg. Bob had just time to shout, 'It's a hat-trick! Back to the studio!'

As the North of England's Outside Broadcasts producer, inspired by this experience, Bob spent the next few months launching a campaign to create Test match coverage of every ball. To do this he proposed the use of the Third Network (later to become Radio 3), which was then a more loosely assembled schedule, though still the home of classical music. The fact that it took eighteen months to come to fruition suggests that there was probably quite a bit of resistance from the classical music lobby, which connoisseurs of BBC politics over the years would easily recognise.

It may well be that a useful nudge was given by Jim Laker in 1956, when he helpfully took nineteen wickets in the Old Trafford Test match. Wherever the final push came from, Hudson's vision was realised on 30 May 1957, when the whole of the First Test at Edgbaston was covered on a combination of the Third Network and the Light Programme with the slogan 'Don't miss a ball – we broadcast them all' under the new programme title *Test Match Special*.

Bob Hudson had joined the staff of the BBC in Manchester in 1954, after making his debut broadcasting rugby commentaries on television in 1947, and before that he had held a wartime commission in the Royal Artillery. The television producer who put him on the air was the man who took the same decision with Brian Johnston – Ian, later Lord, Orr-Ewing – who could therefore claim a substantial impact on radio broadcasting.

It was on television, too, that Bob first commentated on cricket, including his first Test match in 1949. He would always come to a commentary having seen as much as he could of all the players involved. He would have a book of notes on them and during the day's play he would be based at the back of the box during everyone else's commentary in order to avoid repeating any of the others' trains of thought.

The lightness of touch in his delivery rather belied this meticulous preparation. Anyone who remembers his description of the closing stages of the Ashes Test at the Oval in 1968 might recall phrases like 'the second short-leg from the left', as the close fielders gathered in a ring around the Australian tail-enders for Underwood's bowling.

I was No. 2 that day as well and I have a vivid memory of the rain hammering on the roof of our little wooden commentary hut so loudly that at one stage I suggested we all keep quiet with the commentary microphones open, while the studio announcer said to the audience, 'Listen to this'. It seemed impossible that any more play could happen, but Colin Cowdrey, the England captain, mobilised people from the crowd to help with forking the turf and mopping up so that Derek Underwood could bowl out Australia against the clock in the evening.

With so much care taken over what Bob said on the air, the gaffes were rare, but one that he would dine out on happened when a New Zealand touring team was being presented to the Queen at Lord's. 'This,' he declared, 'is a moment they will always forget!'

Although elevation to the leadership of the Outside Broadcasts Department in 1969 brought a hiatus in Bob Hudson's sporting commentaries, he still covered some of the great events of state. But for his six-year period at the helm he had a big nettle to grasp in the context of BBC internal politics, as he brought about the amalgamation of the two warring departments which handled sport on the radio: Outside Broadcasts and Sports News.

The huge Sports Department of today, with Radio, Television and the World Service Sport all together, might have happened anyway, but it could be regarded as Hudson's legacy. So, too, could the quantity of sport available on the radio. In 1969 a document had been published by the BBC called 'Broadcasting in the Seventies' – a blueprint for the next decade. The word 'sport' was nowhere to be found in it, a state of affairs that Bob found an affront and started determinedly to redress.

In his brief period as Head of Outside Broadcasts, in which his quiet efficiency was in sharp contrast to his flamboyant predecessor, Charles Max-Muller, amongst other major projects Bob had to mastermind radio coverage of the Commonwealth Games in Edinburgh, the World Cycling Championships in Leicester and the 1972 Olympics in Munich, to all three of which he took me along to work on the planning side.

Bob had only another eighteen months on the BBC staff following the end of the 1972 Olympics. In his retirement he would do talks on his time in broadcasting, concentrating on the royal tours on which he went in the 1960s, including tours to several Commonwealth countries, state visits elsewhere, and the steady procession of independence ceremonies as the British Empire shrank. He was also called back to commentate on rugby union internationals as a freelance. In cricket, I was able to give him a few county matches to report on and he did regular Sunday afternoon commentaries on BBC Radio London, though he used to tell me that the fee barely covered his cost in doing it.

He also continued to be used – quite rightly – as the principal commentator on the major state events. During the time he was Head of OBs and for quite a time afterwards he would do the annual radio commentary on Trooping the Colour, the Queen's official birthday parade. For several of these years I had the task of recording and shortening the commentary for broadcast on the World Service. I would sit in a studio at Bush House in the Aldwych with a studio manager and we would record the hour-and-a-half's parade with its sounds, music and Bob's commentary. We then had half an hour to reduce it to a half-hour programme.

The trick was to know the running order of the parade inside out and to plan the cuts ahead of time. Most of the military marches are fairly repetitive and it was therefore straightforward enough to cut out the middle of them – provided Bob was not speaking at the time. From the safety of my studio I would curse him for talking across the point at which I was hoping to make a cut.

In those days before digital recordings, we were doing this all on giant reels of quarter-inch tape and obviously at the end had no time to listen through. We would run the edited tape through the timer on the machine, though these were unreliable enough that I would feel the need to do that exercise on all three machines in the studio and take an average timing. The other trick was to leave plenty of the music from the Household Cavalry's ride-by which always ends the parade, so that the programme could be faded out to time when it took the air.

Once Bob asked me how I got on with this nerve-jangling business.

'Not too bad,' I said. 'You tend to say the same thing at the same point every year, so I know what's coming.' I think he was horrified.

I was to work with him quite a bit on various state occasions, surely the biggest being the Prince of Wales' wedding to Lady Diana Spencer in 1981. Spectacular though the day itself was, the spine-tingling moment I remember most clearly came the afternoon before. Painstaking as ever in his preparations, Robert Hudson was in St Paul's Cathedral filling in his notes for the big event and I was there, too, in the centre of the cathedral, checking the names on the seats in the prime places, so that when we were covering the arrival for the service we would be able to tell exactly who was who. It was important research because our broadcasting position was looking right down the aisle from the west door, with the congregation facing away from us. Bob would need to recognise the backs of people's heads, so we needed to plot a chart of the place names.

I was looking up in some awe at the great dome through which Christopher Wren had been lowered in a basket to inspect the construction work – a dizzying thought. The choir was rehearsing an anthem in one of the transepts and I noticed an anonymous young woman in a denim skirt and T-shirt going round casually inspecting the inscriptions on some of the memorials. The choir came to the end of their anthem and the conductor turned and beckoned this girl across. She mounted a small stand and sang, like an angel, 'Let the Bright Seraphim'. I had to sit and listen to this amazing sound. It was the first time I had heard Kiri Te Kanawa.

Under the dome the sound of choir and soloist in the near-empty cathedral was wonderful. While the music the next day was excellent, it did not quite achieve that electrifying acoustic quality. I was in prime position with Bob inside the cathedral, while outside, perched on Queen Anne's statue to describe the arrivals, was Brian Johnston. In the build up, as each commentator down the route was setting the scene for the procession, Brian told his audience that, when the carriage reached his position, Earl Spencer and his daughter would probably wave to the crowds and then go 'up the steps into the pavilion ... I mean, St Paul's!'

It was a wonderful event to be involved in. I had worked with Bob on several other major commentaries, sharing the intimate vantage point in St George's Chapel, Windsor, for Field Marshal Montgomery's funeral and the Queen's sixtieth birthday service, and the roof of the continental booking office at Victoria Station for various state arrivals, but this seemed to be his crowning moment as he made all his carefully worked notes and phrases come alive from the cramped writing on a stack of cue cards arranged in front of him. Radio has certainly not yet come up with anyone to touch him for such descriptions.

Robert Hudson taught me much, but the biggest influence he had on my life came in March 1973, when his secretary came and asked me if I had a moment to pop along to his office. I could not think what I might have done wrong, so I was intrigued rather than worried.

'Would you like to take over as cricket producer?' was his opening remark.

I did not hesitate.

Over a cup of tea in Bob's office, I took over the production duties involved with getting cricket on BBC Radio. That, of course, meant responsibility for *Test Match Special*.

The main thing I remember about that chat was Bob's briefing that *Test Match Special* was, above all, company for people. He told me then that his philosophy while doing commentary had always been to imagine that he was speaking to one person at home. I rather think he used the expression, which would be thought of as very out-of-date and un-PC now, 'the housewife at her sink'.

It was suggested to me some considerable time later that the final push towards Bob being prepared to risk this brave appointment of a twenty-six-year-old had come from Brian Johnston, with: 'Give young Backers a go. I'm sure he could do it.' It does seem probable that Brian might have wanted some influence and may not have been too happy with at least one of the probable alternatives. However, he was just leaving the staff of the BBC at the age of sixty – a fact which may have helped to prompt Michael Tuke-Hastings' decision to give up the production of cricket.

I have to confess that I was never a great cricketer. I enjoyed a brief period at my prep school when I started bowling unplayable leg-breaks from a strange, angled run-up to the wicket. But a master took me in hand to coach this talent and, inevitably, I lost it. Later on in my school career, I used to bowl endless and only moderately useful slow-medium rubbish in the nets to get batsmen back into form, though on one extraordinary day, in steady drizzle on a pudding of a pitch, this bowling took eight for 18 with balls that skidded off the wet grassy surface and, I think, a master umpiring who was only too keen to get back quickly in the dry.

In my early BBC career I played some very bad cricket in a scratch wandering side whose main aim was to keep the game going on a Sunday evening until the pubs opened. That was quite an ambition in those days of 7 p.m. Sunday opening and I am quite ashamed of the number of times we failed to make it and had to hang around in a car park, waiting for the doors to open on our first pint. My first wife, not normally given to cruelty, did venture the opinion that it embarrassed her to watch me play.

This may not seem like the ideal CV for what some might imagine to have been part of the fabric of bringing the great game of cricket to the nation and, indeed, the nation to the great game. In my defence, I can only plead a great enthusiasm for what is simply the best of all games.

OPENING THE
INNINGS

FOR MY FIRST SEASON AS CRICKET PRODUCER, I WAS
given a desk in the office of my predecessor, Michael Tuke-Hastings.
We shared the room with his splendid secretary, Brenda Davies.
She was a feisty Welsh girl, who took no nonsense from her boss.
To some he might have been a domineering figure, but Brenda's
spirit could frequently be overheard down the corridor with a cry
of 'Oh, for God's sake, Michael!'

She was forbidden to waste any time helping me sort out the administration
surrounding my new responsibilities, having to devote herself to Michael's quiz
programmes, but, as he liked to get in early and leave early enough to beat the
rush hour, I was offered her assistance from four o'clock in the afternoon. She
would wish him a safe journey home and then put his stuff to one side and say,
'Right, what needs doing?'

If I was pounding my way through commentators' contracts or *Radio Times*
billings on the typewriter (all carbon paper and correcting fluid in those days,
remember), this was always a very welcome offer.

My first big occasion in the new post was the annual departmental cricket
meeting. At that time there was an outside broadcasts producer in each of the
English regions and, in the case of the North region, two. Don Mosey was the
main man there, based in Manchester; Dick Maddock had the Midlands

patch, with his office in Birmingham; and the South West was looked after by Tony Smith from Bristol. London and the South East came under the London based producers, but for everywhere outside that area, they needed to talk to the regional producer, because borders had to be respected.

I eventually inherited a large wall map of the country which showed the BBC's regional boundaries and was therefore a crucial aid. It would reveal, for instance, that the border between the South East and the West actually ran between Brighton and Hove, making Sussex's county ground a Bristol OB. This was obviously ridiculous, because in those days if engineers were needed for coverage of a match at Hove, they would come up from Bristol and probably stay overnight. Applying some common sense to that one was a battle that it took me quite a while to win.

Tony Smith, the producer in Bristol, would go on later to become Brian Johnston's producer on *Down Your Way*. Dick Maddock in the Midlands, with a regional responsibility that took in most of East Anglia and spread to the Welsh border in the west, was a good friend, whose voice became familiar to *Test Match Special* listeners in the 1970s and early 1980s, when he used to do a great deal of the studio announcing for Test matches.

He had at one time been a television announcer and told of dashing for a bus straight from the studios in full make up and attracting strange looks from his fellow passengers. His office in Pebble Mill commanded a fine view across the rooftops of Edgbaston towards Birmingham University and on his wall was a print of a Canaletto painting of Venice which bore a remarkably unlikely similarity to the view from his window, with the famous Campanile echoed in the university clock tower; a view that came back to me when my daughter, Claire, entered Birmingham University.

Dick Maddock often used to find the Edgbaston Test match clashing with another of his big events, the Royal Show at Stoneleigh, so that I would be invited to handle that Test on the ground, rather than sitting in the studio in London, as I would normally do for Tests outside my patch. His other Test match ground, Trent Bridge, however, he kept very much to himself until his retirement, so that I did not go to a Test match there until 1983.

When doing the *TMS* studio job, we would have up our sleeves the standby music in case rain intervened. This was carefully selected with one crucial criterion in mind. There must be no rights to pay if we used it. The composers had to be long dead and the performances were all by foreign radio orchestras. Most of the pieces we played in such breaks were therefore not too well known. However, on one celebrated occasion, Dick Maddock proudly introduced 'The Breton Shepherds' Dance' when what came out was the all too recognisable 'Sabre Dance' by Katchachurian. Down the line from Lord's, I enquired of Dick what the Breton shepherds had been drinking.

As I have mentioned, the North region boasted two OB producers. Soon after I joined the department, the senior of these at that time, Tony Preston, made way for his second-in-command – Don Mosey.

On balance it is fair to say that Don did not like me much. We first met at the White City stadium in the late 1960s, when he was producing a rugby league international (that being considered, in BBC politics, a northern game) and I was sent along to lend a hand. I arrived to be welcomed by an incoherent rant against everything generally and everything south of the River Trent in particular. It was so ridiculous that I realised that he had to be joking and dutifully offered a laugh. That just about sent him into orbit in his fury, so that I kept my head down for the rest of the evening.

My next encounter with Don was when I became involved with the quiz programme *Treble Chance*. It was produced by Michael Tuke-Hastings and in 1968 he found himself short of someone to sit next to the question master and do the scoring. He asked me and I travelled around for a series of recordings of the programme in which university teams pitted their wits against a resident panel. When we visited Scarborough, Don was there to make sure that all went smoothly and the following day gave Michael and myself a lift to catch the train back to London from York.

Having spent his latter years, before he joined the BBC, covering Yorkshire's cricket for the *Daily Mail*, Don was very keen to become a *Test Match Special* commentator and spent most of that journey cursing Brian Johnston, who in his view had kept him out by dint of wanting only ex-public schoolboys on the team. Michael let Don's invective flow and I kept quiet again, realising that Don and I were unlikely ever to be bosom pals. In later years I used to remember this when Don would assert that Brian was his greatest friend. (Although he refused to take part in the tribute programme on the day that Brian died, on the basis that I was presenting it.) I knew, too, that Brian would have been horrified to have overheard this conversation and I never told him of it.

It was on one of these quiz programme trips that Brian gave Don his nickname, 'The Alderman'. After recording a show somewhere in Don's fiefdom there was a reception in the mayor's parlour. Brian caught sight of Don across the room holding forth to a group of councillors and felt that he looked a bit aldermanic and the name stuck, to the extent that Don called his somewhat bitter autobiography *The Alderman's Tale*.

Brian, for his part, seemed to get on very well with the Alderman, with whom he used to play a word game at the back of the commentary box. Brian's less ambitious choice of words was generally a winning ploy. When *The Alderman's Tale* was published in 1991, venting Don's spleen across its pages, it was obviously divisive. I arrived in Birmingham on the eve of a Test match, thinking it would be difficult to share a dinner table with Don. But Johnners made it easy.

Before I had even broached the subject, Brian informed me, 'I've told the Alderman I can't take salt with him because I'm with you.'

He had declared his position on the book.

The year that I was appointed cricket producer, we were without a BBC cricket correspondent following Brian's retirement, and Don was pushing hard for that job. In the event it was Christopher Martin-Jenkins who was appointed at the end of the 1973 season, in which he had made his *TMS* commentary debut, in time for England's winter tour of the West Indies. Don's fury burst around Robert Hudson's ears – not to his surprise.

The ultimate cause of Don Mosey's hatred of me came in the summer of 1982.

In 1981 he had been to the West Indies to cover an eventful England cricket tour. Ian Botham was the captain, which was newsworthy enough on its own, but added to that a Test match had to be cancelled because of Guyanese government objections to the arrival of Robin Jackman, a man with links to the then ostracised South Africa. Then there was the sudden death of the coach, Ken Barrington, and allegations of extra-marital indiscretions. The News Department were not happy about Don's coverage of these major stories for them.

That tour was followed by the extraordinary summer of 1981, when Botham emerged from a disastrous spell as captain to take the Ashes series by storm. Cricket was making the headlines and when it was proposed that Don should be our man on the tour of India in 1981/82, there were suggestions that a news reporter might be sent alongside him. A counter suggestion was made by the Managing Editor of Radio Sport, Iain Thomas.

Although we had never before sent a producer on a cricket tour, he proposed that Peter Baxter should go to India to produce *Test Match Special* and also do the news reports, leaving Don free to concentrate on commentary.

I was asked what I thought of that and said that I was happy – provided that Don was told the exact nature of my brief. I was reassured on that, but such was Don's irascible reputation, no one ever dared tell him and I always had the impression that he thought I was there to carry his bags. The result was a four-month tour which, while being a fascinating experience for me, was a battle as far as the producer/commentator relations were concerned, coming to an inevitable head at the start of the seventh and final Test of the tour in Colombo, when I was driven to tell him what I thought of him.

He had been contented enough to leave me the job of player interviews – a task he did not care to do at the close of play anyway – with the exception of interviews with Geoff Boycott, whom he reckoned would speak only to him. Although he would then welcome me onto the press bus after a day's play with a bit of a sneer and 'Here he is at last, after interviewing all the gate posts and the groundsman's dog.'

Jullunder in the Punjab was the first place on that tour where the press needed to share rooms in the hotel. Our team leader, Peter Smith of the *Daily Mail*, drew up a list which was presented to us when we arrived at the Skylark Hotel. Don took a look at it and snorted when he saw that, while he had his usual Scrabble partner, Michael Carey of the *Daily Telegraph*, I was down to share with the urbane John Thicknesse of the *Evening Standard*. 'Huh!' he said. 'I see the two public schoolboys have been put together.'

My patience with the chips on his shoulder was wearing a little thin, so I responded that we were not the only two on the tour.

'Who else, then?' he demanded.

I mentioned a photographer and the correspondent of the *Sun*: 'Well, there's Adrian Murrell. He was at Malvern. And then there's Steve Whiting.'

'Where did he go?'

'KCS, Wimbledon,' I told him.

'I don't count that!' he said.

'I'm not sure that I could get away with a remark like that,' I replied.

Funnily enough, there was to be an echo of this almost a decade later, when Jonathan Agnew became the BBC cricket correspondent. Don approached him during one of his earliest Test matches with us to say, 'I want you to know that I don't count you as a public schoolboy.'

Brian Johnston's amused reaction to this, when a slightly bewildered Aggers told us about it, was, 'Oh, the Alderman doesn't rate Uppingham!'

In Jullunder we were covering a one-day international for which the plan had been to use the *Daily Telegraph* correspondent, Michael Carey, to commentate alongside Don. However we arrived to find a telex telling us that the *Telegraph* had refused permission for him to do this. Don's reaction was, 'I shall just have to do the whole day myself.'

I suggested that I could help him out with the odd ten- or fifteen-minute spell to give him a break. 'Not an option,' he declared and in the absence of any backing from London, that is how it was. Don was very pleased with himself at the end of what must have been a gruelling day for him – and the listener – and did not start complaining about how put upon he had been until two days after the event.

We gave each other a match off during the tour. Mine came in early January, when the team went to play in Jamshedpur and I went with my wife for a few days to Kathmandu. Unfortunately that coincided with Geoffrey Boycott and the rest of the touring team settling on a parting of the ways while Don and the rest of the press were not exactly in the communications centre of India.

Later Don took a break at a resort near Madras, while I went to Indore with the team and saw a brutal forty-eight ball century from Ian Botham, on which I reported from the local All India Radio station. This was situated in a rambling bungalow on the edge of town and, when I arrived, all the station's staff who could be spared were lined up for my inspection. I went down the line like royalty on a state visit and was then shown to their best studio.

'It is our music studio,' said the station director, proudly. I entered a large, heavily carpeted room with not a stick of furniture in it, save a microphone in the middle of the floor on an eighteen-inch high stand. I was invited to sit at this cross-legged, in the manner of a sitar player, except with notebook rather than instrument on my lap, and deliver my reports, having first made contact with London from the station's control room, because there was no facility for headphones in the studio itself.

Early in the tour I acquired a nickname that stuck with me among the press party and players long after its origins had been forgotten. I was standing in the foyer of the Taj Mahal Hotel in Bombay, waiting for a local shipping agent who was to help me import a pair of microphones (an epic performance which is worth a book in itself), when a porter walked past bearing a blackboard on which the legend 'MR BARTEX' was written. Mike Carey, who was standing with me, pointed out as it came past a second time that it was an anagram of my name. I tried the bell captain and indeed the message was for me. Over a quarter of a century later, I am often greeted, and written to, as 'Bartex'.

The Calcutta Test match on that tour gave rise to one small incident when Don said in his commentary, as fruit was being thrown at England's deep fielders by the spectators, that he did not know why they were wasting oranges in a country where there was meant to be a level of starvation. This was picked up by the *Guardian* newspaper back in Britain and caused us a sticky couple of days.

We ended the tour in Sri Lanka, where I was asked by one of their radio stations to do some reports on the warm-up games, which led to a mention in one of the local newspapers, which described me as 'the BBC commentator'. With the inevitable mischief of the press, some of our colleagues drew Don's attention to this over breakfast in the Queen's Hotel, Kandy. They were rewarded, as they had hoped, with a Mosey explosion. 'He is *not* a commentator, nor ever will be!' he thundered to any in earshot, which at that moment included me, just entering the breakfast room with no idea what the furore was about.

The following winter, England were due to tour Australia. A new BBC cricket correspondent had still not been appointed to succeed Christopher Martin-Jenkins, who had gone off to edit *The Cricketer* magazine. I consulted the head of the department, 'Slim' Wilkinson, on what plan he might favour.

'It seemed to work pretty well last year in India,' he said. 'Why don't we do the same again? You and Don go out there and mount your own commentary.'

I said that I would have to give that some thought and agonised over a decision for a few days. Eventually, realising that I was talking myself out of what, for all I knew, might be my only chance to go on a tour of Australia, I told him that I really could not go through another three months on tour with Mosey and he had better get someone else to go. I was sure he would not be short of volunteers.

The next I knew about our winter plans came a week later, when I arrived at Old Trafford on the eve of the Test match there. Don passed me in the car park with a face like thunder and spat out one furious and enigmatic line:

'You and your public school cronies!' And away he went to his car.

It was some hours later that Brian Johnston told me that Don had been told he would not be going to Australia that winter. But that was all I knew. I had a Test match to look after and I waited in vain for some word from Slim Wilkinson, who was heavily involved in the coverage of Wimbledon and therefore rather difficult to get hold of in those days before the universal spread of mobile phones. It was not until I was driving home from a washed out final day of the Test that I finally managed to get him on the phone from a call box at an M6 service station.

'So who is going to Australia?' I asked.

'You are,' he said. 'You can put together a commentary team there.'

In the event, the use of Henry Blofeld, who was joined by Christopher Martin-Jenkins for the first two Tests, presumably fitted the bill as my 'public school cronies', although Alan McGilvray, Michael Carey, Tony Lewis and Jack Bannister might have been a little surprised at the description.

Don Mosey did realise his ambition of becoming the BBC cricket correspondent officially for his last year on the BBC staff, when Patricia Ewing, then the Head of Sport and Outside Broadcasts, took a more sympathetic view than her predecessors, who had, perhaps, not reacted well to the tactics of brow-beating. By that time he had, in any case, covered four England tours, for three of which I had been at the London end of his line.

Amazingly, I do have one memorandum of praise from Don Mosey. In 1976 I was manning the London studio during a Test match at Headingley, when the line went down during the final morning's play. In those days it would be routed from the north of England through the control room at Pebble Mill in Birmingham, which did make it more vulnerable to something going amiss.

As was the practice, I started commentating off the television pictures for what felt like an age. I even had the wicket of Alan Knott to describe. I could see, through the double glass to my left, the technical operator on the phone and then fiddling with the equipment, before at last he spoke into my head-phones. Unfortunately, he had a little bit of a stammer when under pressure and now the pressure was building. However, eventually I got the message that I could hand back to Headingley.

Near silence came from the studio speakers, with just a faint rumble of distant traffic. Then a pigeon cooed alarmingly close to the microphone. I decided that this could be dangerous, because the commentators were clearly unaware we had returned to them. I reopened my microphone and described another over before the voice in my headphones said, 'You c-can h-have an-nother go'.

I tried again and was relieved to hear the reassuring voice of Brian Johnston. 'I gather you lost us. We were awfully good while you were away.'

I went through to the technical cubicle to ask what had happened, to be told that when dialling up the broadcast line from Pebble Mill, it was the live microphone in the Big Ben clock tower that had been selected mistakenly, as its number was only one digit removed. Fortunately I had not handed back on the hour, to be deafened by the chimes.

Don was the producer of the Leeds OB, but had apparently been delayed getting to the ground and had not been there when all this happened. His innate sense of professionalism made this really hurt – not that a producer's presence can prevent such a technical mishap. He wrote me a charming note, full of apology and praising me effusively for 'a thoroughly professional job'.

He had achieved his ambition to join the commentary team in 1974, when his first stint at the microphone coincided with a bomb scare that required the stands – and the commentary box – to be cleared. It was the start of a running *TMS* joke that whenever Don sat down at the microphone there would be rain, or a drinks interval, or the end of an innings, or simply a twenty-minute period of play in which only one leg-bye might be scored.

After the 1975 Headingley Test, when supporters of a convicted criminal called George Davis dug up the pitch overnight before the final day's play, Don came to the conclusion that he would have to let go of production duties at Test matches on which he was commentating, and thereafter I would be invited to handle the matches in the north.

In the 1980s another Head of Sport and Outside Broadcasts, Larry Hodgson, dug out the files on Don, when it appeared he had been recommended for an OBE or MBE. It turned out subsequently that the government office concerned had made a mistake and it was his brother who was under consideration, but by that time Hodgson had looked through a stack of vitriolic memoranda which had found their way into Mosey's bulging file and he came to me with a bemused air to say that people's attitudes to Don were becoming a little clearer to him.

All this aside, Don was, for much of his career, an exceptionally good commentator, with the great virtue of bringing something a little different to the *Test Match Special* table. He was never to know that, for all his opinion of me, it was for that very difference I used to defend his inclusion in the commentary team during the 1980s, when others were suggesting that he should be dropped. His use of the language was a great pride to him, though by the end of the 1980s he was getting a little behind the pace of the game and in my view, having produced him also occasionally as a rugby commentator, he never had the speed for that game.

He liked to adopt the expected dour persona of his native Broad Acres and hardly ever allowed himself to be photographed with a smile. If that ever happened there was usually a story behind it, as when Brian Johnston's wife, Pauline, a professional photographer, tricked him into a beaming grin when she was capturing his image for a *Test Match Special* book. I remember particularly his lugubrious report from a Yorkshire county championship match at the start of a Saturday's *Sport on 2* programme: 'It is high summer in Bradford. The rain is falling incessantly from leaden skies.'

And at a Test match in Trinidad: 'If there happens to be a mass murderer handy in the crowd, with nothing particular to do, would he like to tackle these people who are blowing whistles, because it's roughly the equivalent for me of being in an association football crowd in England. And that is a fate worse than death.'

He would pour scorn unfairly on those who preferred to write their reports. It was a point of pride that he did not, although he came from an era when reports were generally well over a minute in duration and therefore neither the time available, nor the necessity for writing, were there. Given the time – and a dead ball situation – any reporter would prefer to write, to get it all in, though the skill is then to make the reading leave the page and sound natural. That art is as much in the writing as in the performance. But equally any sports reporter has to be capable of reporting unscripted from his or her notes and, with live play progressing, that becomes essential.

In Don's case his ability to work without a script was never better exemplified than when I decided to revive the close-of-play summary on *TMS* towards the end of his commentary career. He would sit quietly on his own for five or ten minutes beforehand and the product would be no more than four or five headlines on a notepad, but the resultant summing-up of the day was touched with genius.

One topic of discussion at the annual cricket meeting, every year it seemed, was the future of another commentator who could display touches of genius – Alan Gibson.

Gibson was a brilliant writer and broadcaster, perhaps not as well remembered in broadcasting as he should be. However, there must be many like me who listened in 1963 as he described the closing stages of the Lord's Test: 'There are two balls to go. England, needing 234 to win, are 228 for nine, with Cowdrey, his left forearm in plaster, coming out to join Allen.'

Gibson guided us through the tension of the last over of the match from Wes Hall, in which Derek Shackleton was run out, but David Allen kept out those last two balls to ensure that Colin Cowdrey did not have to face the fast bowler with his broken arm.

There was much of the academic about Alan Gibson – and his commentary. Like Mosey he relished the English language. He would consider the appropriate word at length. I can remember him saying, 'Oh, no, Brian, I wouldn't say you have a large nose. You're just a trifle proboscal.'

With the academic came the rebel. An instruction was to be defied. He said once during a commentary that he would give the complete scorecard at the end of the over. Hastily I passed him a card suggesting that he might wait another minute until the World Service joined the commentary – for neatness.

His response was, 'My producer thinks I should wait until the World Service joins us, but I don't think we want to wait, do we, dear listener?' And he read it anyway. World Service joined the commentary in mid-read, so he had to start again. All because of a cussed nature.

About the time that I took over the production, John Arlott managed to negotiate a change in his workload. To ease the burden of his writing for the *Guardian*, he would only work on radio for the first half of a Test match day. This provided a bit more work for the likes of Neil Durden-Smith, the newly recruited Henry Blofeld, and Alan Gibson, each of whom had the opportunity to take over for the second half of the day. Eventually I argued successfully that it was unreasonable to ask a commentator to feel part of the team when he was coming in to join them after the 'Lord Mayor's show' of Arlott had left for the day, and from then on we used four commentators for the first half and just three thereafter.

For Alan Gibson the main problem of not reporting for duty until after three in the afternoon was staying out of the bar. It was not a temptation he was very prone to resisting. Don Mosey, while producing a commentary which included Gibson at Headingley, issued an edict: 'No more pints of bitter in the commentary box.'

'Are you being pompous, dear boy?' was Alan's reaction.

Don repeated the order and was therefore infuriated to find, within the hour, Alan arriving back in the box for his next commentary stint, armed with a pint mug of brown liquid. 'I said no more pints of bitter!' he thundered.

'It is not a pint of bitter,' said Gibson.

Don seized the glass and sniffed it. It was a pint of neat whisky.

This sort of thing always made Alan's relationships with his producers slightly prickly. My own patience ran out one afternoon in 1975, when I was manning the *Test Match Special* studio, two floors underground in Broadcasting House, during a Test match at Headingley. Phil Edmonds was making his Test debut and his five for 28 in the first innings skittled Australia out for 135. As things panned out, Alan was the commentator for all five wickets, but the description was becoming less detailed for each one and I suspected that there was a little alcoholic influence involved.

At the end of that second day of the match I discussed the situation with Don Mosey on the phone. He said that he had it in hand, but on the fourth afternoon there was more obvious slurring. I talked to Cliff Morgan, who was then Head of Sport. 'Don't do anything, boyo,' was his order, 'until I've had a listen.' Gibson's commentary spell ended within five minutes and he was not due back on that day.

In fact he never commentated on BBC radio again. George Davis' supporters dug up the pitch and poured oil on it overnight and the match was abandoned.

Alan was not due to work at the one remaining Test of the summer and at the start of the following year, it was decided at the annual regional cricket meeting that it was too risky to use him live. A sad way for a potentially brilliant career to end. I talked to Tony Smith, our West Region producer, about it and his advice was that I should not write to tell Alan that we would not be using him. 'He'll know in his heart of hearts,' he said. 'But while you haven't actually sacked him, he'll still think there's a chance.' I am still not sure that was the right thing to have done, but I went along with it.

I did suggest his name to one or two other producers subsequently to record scripts which were just right for him and which I knew would suit his fine broadcasting voice, which frequently appeared on several natural history television programmes, but my next encounter with him was to face a torrent of drunken abuse on a train leaving Cardiff after a rugby international. There were a few other, happier, but probably just as liquid, meetings outside the bar at Taunton from which he used to keep an eye on the progress of county games. His reports in *The Times* became required reading for their delightful eccentricity, which covered the whole experience of going to a county match – travel and all – but sometimes not over-much of the action. Accounts which told you, perhaps, that, 'During the afternoon, Sussex were bowled out for double figures, but I did not see much of this, because I met an old friend behind the pavilion. John Snagge and I agreed that the BBC is not what it was.' On some things, I could agree with him.

If there was the annual apprehension amongst the London contingent, before my first full regional cricket meeting in 1973, at the presence of the 'Cock o' the North' – as Don Mosey sometimes styled himself – the one presence from outside England always attracted an indulgent good humour from his colleagues. The Outside Broadcasts section in Wales was run by the remarkable Alun Williams.

I had really got to know Alun while working on the *Treble Chance* and *Forces Chance* quiz programmes, which he chaired. I used to sit alongside him to do the scoring and provide the link with the producer in the control room behind the scenes. After brief trips together with the rest of the team to various universities around England and also to both Edinburgh and Dublin, I was asked to do the *Forces Chance* Far East trip in April 1969.

In three weeks we were scheduled to record twelve programmes – two on the island of Gan, in the southernmost atoll of the Maldives, which was an RAF station, nine in Singapore, and one in Malacca in Malaysia, where the Commonwealth Brigade was stationed. We were transported by RAF Air Transport Command from Brize Norton to Gan.

The island of Gan is roughly two miles by one mile and the runway was the whole of that two mile length, so that coming in to land – particularly as the seats in the VC10 faced backwards – you could not be sure that there was any land at all. The lights at each end of the runway were set on the coral in the sea. The station's purpose was as a staging post to and from the Far East. An air-sea rescue crew, with a Shackleton search aircraft, was also based there.

With no other purpose in life than turning aircraft round, refuelling and provisioning them for the onward flight, the various groundstaff crews took great and competitive pride in their speed and efficiency in doing this, and it was the usual topic of conversation in the various messes to which we were invited.

The BBC team was led by the cricket producer, Michael Tuke-Hastings. We had an engineer, Ken Keen, and the performers: Alun Williams, the question-master, and the resident panel, who were Neil Durden-Smith; Ted Moult, the Derbyshire farmer who had made his name on such quiz shows; and Pamela Donald, a Scottish actress, who provided the glamour and was something of a sensation in an RAF station where the only other female was the (fairly senior) nursing sister. This panel would compete against a team of four from whatever unit was hosting the show.

Despite having only two half-hour programmes to record, we were on the island for a week, waiting for the next available RAF transport flight on to Singapore. It was not really too much of a hardship, with coral beaches and snorkelling available.

We were a strange assortment on that trip. When we got to Singapore, Michael would hold court at the hotel, shuffling his question cards, having set them all himself, whilst Neil had a great many ex-naval friends to catch up with and I, too, had quite a few contacts made during my father's military career. Ted Moult became a good dining companion, always inquisitive to try new things and see different places. He became a great friend and when I started the *Test Match Special* feature, 'A View From the Boundary', I turned to him to be the first guest at Trent Bridge. I was devastated when, in 1986, I heard that a bout of depression had led Ted to commit suicide. He had seemed the last person to be forced to such a desperate act.

Neil Durden-Smith acted as the team captain and in my early days as cricket producer he was one of the *Test Match Special* commentators. I had first come across him when he was organising coverage of the 1966 football World Cup. That gives a hint as to his very varied career. Having been an accomplished hockey player, he was also used as a television commentator for that sport.

He had come to the BBC after a career in the Royal Navy, which had led to his being aide-de-camp to the Governor-General of New Zealand. In later years he was an energetic chairman of the Lord's Taverners charity and, while running his own agency, put forward a detailed suggestion for a rugby union

World Cup. It was not immediately adopted, but his proposal may well have been the spark that persuaded the International Rugby Board to give the idea serious consideration.

For all that personal achievement, Neil is probably best known for being the husband of the broadcaster Judith Chalmers and increasingly – as is the fate of all proud fathers eventually – as Mark Durden-Smith's dad.

On that trip I furthered my rudimentary technical knowledge, which I suppose was to help me in later years in the coverage of cricket tours, by lending Ken Keen, our engineer, a hand with the rigging and de-rigging of each show. These would be in camp theatres or sports halls and fortunately we always had a detachment of soldiers, sailors or airmen to help with the lifting of any heavy equipment. This frequently involved getting a piano onto the stage. And the need for this piano brings me – by a tortuous path – back to the remarkable Alun Williams.

It was Alun's job to do the 'warm-up'. This involved him doing his little one-man show before he introduced the teams onto the stage. So, for twelve nights, the rest of us listened to the same patter until we were word perfect and for years afterwards we could swap lines from the routine when we saw each other: 'I like blondes ... they get dirty quicker,' or, as he settled at the piano, 'If you've got the right key, you can play in any flat,' or recounting a meeting in the street, 'Ah, Mr Williams, I've seen you on the wireless often,' and many more one-liners before his finale of four different styles of rendition of 'Come into the Garden, Maude'.

It was somehow no surprise that he was to die in harness while performing on another stage.

I was to work with him a lot in his role as a commentator, principally during my eight years as rugby producer. At that time the new editorial regime had hit sports coverage and Alun was not too keen to adapt. He went merrily on his individual way, knowing everything about the Welsh team, but having done scant research on their opposition. Fortunately at the time Wales were on the crest of their wave of success, which may have led to one celebrated faux pas during a Lions Test in New Zealand: 'J. J. Williams scores for Wales ... I mean, for the British Lions!'

He claimed to have done his first broadcasting covering a county champion-ship cricket match in Cardiff. At the close of play he had to get back to the studios quickly and, while he was waiting to go on the air, the announcer could see he was nervous about his debut. 'The trick,' he said, 'is to memorise your first line and then once you've got past that, it's all downhill.'

So Alun paced up and down the passage muttering to himself, 'I've just come back from Cardiff Arms Park, where Glamorgan are playing Hampshire,' over and over again.

At last he was summoned to the microphone, the red light went on and the friendly announcer said, 'Now cricket and here's Alun Williams, who's just come back from Cardiff Arms Park where Glamorgan are playing Hampshire.' Lamely, Alun repeated his memorised first line.

He was a splendid member of the teams covering both the Commonwealth Games and Olympics that I was involved with, mainly commentating on the swimming, but versatile enough to turn his hand to other events. In Edinburgh, in 1970, he had made some mistake in the commentary on a freestyle swimming heat which was being recorded for later use. 'Never mind,' he said. 'Run a tape over the next race and I'll do that previous one again.' So he did, commentating more accurately on the first race, while a completely different one was unfolding under his gaze.

At the Munich Olympics he also specialised on the swimming, but when Britain started to have some success in judo, a commentator was needed. Alun was selected, although he knew next to nothing about the sport. Fortunately, David Vine, on the television team at the games, had come armed with a 'Know the Game' book for every conceivable Olympic event. Alun mugged up with the appropriate volume overnight and next day his commentary included the line: 'He's got him in a koshi-wasa … as we say in judo!'

Alun's jovial presence at that first cricket meeting of mine in 1973 was all the more important, as the first one-day international of the season – and only the fourth ever to be played in Britain – was to be in Swansea in mid-July. Our discussions at the meeting led us to select a commentary team with an appropriately Welsh flavour: Alun himself, who did cover quite a bit of county cricket in Glamorgan, but had never done any international games; the Swansea-born football commentator, Peter Jones, who was a cricket fan, but had never done any commentary on the game; and the young hopeful, Christopher Martin-Jenkins. Our summarisers were Trevor Bailey and the former Glamorgan and England player, Peter Walker.

Although I had been in charge for the three Tests against New Zealand which preceded this, it was the first time that I had travelled further from

Broadcasting House than Lord's or the Oval to produce the commentary and, of course, I did so only at Alun Williams' invitation. He prefaced the occasion by sending everyone involved a welcoming letter, in itself quite a customary thing for any producer to do in those days. It was in Welsh, with (happily) a translation below, and it welcomed us to 'the first Test match in Wales'. One-day internationals were a novel enough form of the game then that they were frequently referred to as 'One-day Tests'.

The letter was discreetly underlining the point that this was *his* outside broadcast and the new young cricket producer was only being invited on to his patch because he was to have a big day commentating. I put him on first, as seemed only right. In studio B9 in Broadcasting House the introductions were done by Nigel Starmer-Smith, 'So let's go to St Helen's in Swansea and say good morning to Alan Williams.'

There was enough of a silence for me to look anxiously at my first commentator. Had he heard the cue? Then, 'It's "Al-in" to rhyme with "sin" and "gin" actually. And since we've got our first Test match in Wales, I really think you ought to get it right. Good morning and welcome to Swansea.'

Our commentary position for this historic game was situated on the roof of the pavilion, with a superb view out into the Bristol Channel, with the steel works of Port Talbot smoking away down the coast to our left. Its principal drawback was that it was between two enormous loudspeakers, which were in frequent use by the enthusiastic public address announcer.

As things turned out, we did not have to suffer this situation for too long because, with the tide in, the ball moved around prodigiously for John Snow and Geoff Arnold. New Zealand were bundled out for 158, in reply Dennis Amiss made a hundred, England won with seven wickets and fifteen overs to spare and we were on our way home in mid-afternoon.

That was the only match that season for which I ventured outside the south-east of England. Three Tests and two one-day internationals with New Zealand were followed by the same mix involving the West Indies. At Lord's, in late August, the West Indies clinched the series in a Test match remembered principally (except presumably by the West Indians, who celebrated a victory) for a bomb scare which had players and spectators in the middle of the ground, being entertained by the umpire, Dickie Bird, while the police checked the stands. Through it all, Brian Johnston continued to describe the scene from the commentary box in the pavilion, berating MCC members who were reluctant to leave their seats, little realising that we ourselves were failing to obey the evacuation order.

Thus was my career as cricket producer launched. I did, of course, have two great assets. I had obviously had no hand in selecting them for the two Test series of this momentous season for me, but what producer could ever have had two such jewels gifted to him, as he embarked on his career, as Brian Johnston and John Arlott?

ARLOTT AND JOHNSTON

Very early in my time in the BBC, I got to know Brian Johnston. His was a great presence, as he breezed his way down the corridors of Broadcasting House, making his trumpeting noise and treating everyone from the lowest tea boy to the mightiest in the Corporation with the same easy familiarity. He was the greatest possible contrast with the other outstanding cricket broadcaster of his generation, John Arlott. Together they made *Test Match Special*'s reputation.

Within a week of my being appointed cricket producer, John Arlott invited me to lunch at the National Liberal Club. This was one of the important rites of passage. I remember him seizing the wine list and suggesting bottles and half bottles from its treasures as we sat in a window overlooking the Victoria Embankment and the Thames. After that, my memory became unavoidably hazy, though I do recall that, as we left in the late afternoon to pour ourselves into a couple of taxis, he gave me his delightfully mischievous grin and said, 'You think *you're* in trouble; I've got to make a speech this evening.' I never heard how it went.

By this time, of course, I had seen quite a bit of Arlott in my occasional appearances helping with the production at Test matches and Saturday county matches. I felt I must have passed some sort of test on one of the latter occasions, when he produced from his large, battered leather briefcase a bottle of claret and one stainless steel goblet and said, 'Get yourself a glass, lad.' The clinking sound it made was always a feature of this favourite old briefcase. It was at much the same time that he passed on to me what he considered the basic requirement of any producer's briefcase – a corkscrew. Mine has always been so equipped ever since.

Both Johnston and Arlott are prime examples of the changes in broadcasting – and life. It is impossible to imagine anyone getting to the positions that they did today following either of their career paths.

Despite a brilliant mind, his rebellious nature led John to leave school at sixteen with no academic qualifications to speak of. He worked in the Basingstoke town planning office and at the local mental hospital as a diet clerk, before joining the police force in the mid-1930s, which took him into the Second World War. Once, after his retirement to the Channel Islands, I met him at Southampton Airport to drive him to the BBC Radio Solent studios where we were to record a programme. He indicated an old factory. 'I had three cold nights in a row on duty in that doorway during air raids,' he said.

Always a keen games player, his choice of service in Southampton was heavily influenced by the opportunities to play and watch cricket there and he became hugely devoted to the Hampshire team of the time. From his school-days he had always been a voracious reader and, while still a serving policeman, he wrote poetry. Some of this he sent to John Betjeman for his comments.

As a result of this correspondence, Betjeman brought the curiosity of a poetic policeman to the BBC's attention and, in the closing stages of the war, John made his first broadcast – on Hambledon Cricket Club, the cradle of the game in the eighteenth century. The BBC then asked him to make a broadcast address to the King on behalf of the police, as part of the victory celebrations. He came through the inevitable ruffling of a few police feathers that it caused and this further contact with the BBC led him to a successful interview for the job of literary producer in the Overseas Service.

In 1946 an Indian touring team came to England to resume Test cricket in the post-war era. The BBC's Eastern Service felt they ought to cover the tour. Young Arlott professed to know something about the game and his first broadcast had been on a cricketing theme, so he was told to do the first few games of the tour, with the proviso that his regular programmes must not suffer. The reaction from India, relayed to the Head of the Eastern Service by the BBC's man in Delhi, was very favourable, so John was told to continue for the rest of the tour. He said later that he ended up 'so broke it wasn't true', but he loved it all.

His efforts brought him to the attention of the domestic service and the Head of Outside Broadcasts, Seymour de Lotbinière, who ventured the opinion to Arlott that he had a vulgar voice, but an interesting mind. The poet Dylan Thomas, a friend frequently involved in poetry programmes for John, wrote to him that he was 'Not only the best cricket commentator – far and away that – but the best sports commentator I've heard.'

The 'vulgar' voice was what has been referred to frequently as a Hampshire burr, but was nothing like any other accent that I have come across. It was to make him instantly recognisable on the radio.

For the last Test of 1947 John Arlott joined the main domestic commentary team – to become *Test Match Special* in 1957 – and he never left it until his retirement at the end of the 1980 season.

At the time I took over the production of *Test Match Special*, John's contract was changed so that he only did the first half of the day to give him more time to write his column for the *Guardian*. Many have suggested unkindly that it was in order for him to enjoy a more liquid lunch. Not that a bottle at lunch-time ever seemed to dim the quality of his commentary – quite the reverse. One of his most celebrated descriptions was of the first streaker to be seen at Lord's in 1975.

John had had a very good lunch with his publisher and was mellow. We were also having a visit from the Managing Director of BBC Radio, later to become Director General, Ian Trethowan. So John, as he could, was showing off. Memorably, as the naked form invaded the field of play from the area of the Tavern, Arlott said, 'We've got a freaker.' He went on to add, 'Not very shapely ... and it's masculine ... and it's seen the last of its cricket for the day!'

In fact, by the time he retired, it would be his first session of commentary of the day that would be the one most likely to be below par. He would have arrived out of breath and in desperate need of his first cup of cooled black coffee. (Shortly after his retirement we had a spoof award amongst us – 'The Arlott Award' – for the commentator arriving in the box in the morning in the worst condition. It was a favourite of Don Mosey's.)

The question often asked was whether John thought up any of his 'bon mots' before he went on the air. I think in some cases a line or a simile must have occurred to him but in many cases I believe it was just the way he saw things.

'The stroke of a man knocking a thistle top off with a walking stick', his description of Clive Lloyd batting in the 1975 World Cup final, is a classic. I suppose he might have seen a stroke like that on another occasion and pondered on what it brought to mind before getting this golden opportunity to use it. He could not have known that David Gower would pull his first ball in Test cricket for four: 'Oh, what a princely entry!' But I suppose a couple of his lines on Dennis Lillee might have been prepared mentally beforehand.

At the Centenary Test in Melbourne in 1977 he had 'the seagulls standing in line ... like vultures for Lillee.' And in England, when Lillee was bowling with his voluminous shirt unbuttoned halfway down his chest, and in the tightest of trousers: 'Lillee comes in ... his shirt big enough for two men ... if they could get into the trousers!'

In his commentary a great love of the men who played the game was evident. He would say of cricketers that he had known only two bad men in his lifetime in the game. Pressed to reveal the names concerned, he would give that knowing, mischievous grin and say no more. The love of the players was an echo of the writings of his much admired predecessor as cricket correspondent of the *Guardian*, Neville Cardus.

John claimed that in a conversation with Cardus he had once suggested that his combination of subjects on which to write – cricket and wine – was better than Cardus' cricket and music. Cardus' response was, 'Oh, I think I'd rather sleep with a soprano than a wine waiter.'

When John embraced any subject, he did it with all his heart and soul. When he discovered the delights of wine, he forsook beer and spirits and made himself an expert on the subject. He was a great collector of books and glass. This latter collection meant that those who were guests in his house were served their wine generously in glasses the size of buckets, which the host was prone to top up when the unwary guest was distracted. This could be dangerous territory, even if one had made the pragmatic decision not to attempt to keep up with Arlott.

For the years up to his retirement he lived in a former pub in the Hampshire town of Alresford, where he would work from the large former public bar, now splendidly lined with books – an old portable typewriter on a table in the centre. Below this usually cool room (John felt the heat sorely) was an extensive cellar, plentifully stocked with wines which, by their sale at auction, ensured that the cellar for his retirement in Alderney could likewise be handsomely installed.

John's dinner table was always an interesting place, though the conversation would tend to be dominated by the great man. This was on occasions an irritant for some of his colleagues on the cricket circuit. Those who were experiencing an evening with Arlott for the first time were usually surprised that other senior broadcasters and writers might be fighting shy of his company at the table. Quite apart from any monopoly of the conversation, there would be the question of the wine bill. The more modest selections of his comrades in arms would be overshadowed by John's more expensive tastes, so that when the suggestion was growled, 'Let's share the bill,' anxieties would grow about getting the expenses past the sports editor.

There were no such worries when John hosted his own table at home, though. I experienced a few of those evenings, both in Alresford and in Alderney, where John had renamed the largest private house on the island, to which he moved, 'The Vines'. A trip to Alderney would entail the morning flight in the 'Yellow Joey' aircraft from Southampton airport with a sometimes alarming landing over the cliffs, to be met in the small terminal building, scarcely bigger than a bus shelter, by the familiar old Arlott briefcase, which would be opened to produce a bottle of Pouilly Fumé and two steel goblets. It was wise to accept this fortification for the experience which would follow.

A tour of the island would be offered in his Renault 5. This could be alarming on the narrow roads and on my first trip culminated in careering through the frighteningly narrow gateway in front of his house and coming to rest with a firm shunt against a large wooden flower tub, which was shifted by three feet. John's lack of concern about this method of stopping suggested that it was normal practice and I speculated about whether it was the gardener's duty to reset the tub every day.

Friends would be invited in for a convivial lunch and even more for a convivial dinner, so that if work had taken one to the island to see him, it was quite difficult to fit that part in, though John was always sharp and to the point when the work had to be done. I did one programme on sport and verse with him for Radio 2. He made his selections swiftly, accepting a couple of my suggestions on the balance, suggested Robin Holmes as the main reader, and agreed with my list of celebrity readers: John Snagge for a rowing poem, Lord

Oaksey for one on steeple chasing, Penelope Keith for Betjeman's 'Hunter Trials' and Roger McGough with his own poem, 'Big Arth from Penarth'. Then we could get the second bottle open.

When we came to record that programme, we compromised between my wish to do it in London and his to do it in Alderney and used a BBC Radio Solent studio in Southampton. 'Right,' I said, when I picked him up at the airport, 'we can rehearse in the morning and record in the afternoon.'

'No,' he said, 'let's rehearse and record in the morning and then we can have a bloody good lunch.' Which we did – and made a pretty good programme.

On another visit I felt that I really ought to go and see my predecessor, Michael Tuke-Hastings, who lived a ten minute walk down the road. John was reluctant ever to forgive and he had felt that Michael had never really appreciated him or his ability. He refused point blank the suggestion that it might be time to bury the hatchet and invite his former producer in for a drink. I did pay my call and ironically it was Michael who met me at the airport on my next visit to the island – for John's funeral.

In 1988, when England's tour of India was called off because of the appointment of Graham Gooch as captain, I suddenly found myself with a bit of time on my hands and set about compiling a 'Best of John Arlott' tape for BBC Enterprises. It was a labour of love in which I was able to include lengthy extracts from his commentaries on the exciting finishes on the 1948/49 tour of South Africa, Bradman's final innings, a great description of Wes Hall bowling to Ted Dexter at Lord's in 1963, and a lot more. I wondered if the old voice would still be capable of linking the extracts and, telling him only that I wanted to let him see what I had selected, I suggested going over to see him early in 1989.

He was not to be fooled. He took the tape I gave him and looked at the list approvingly. Then he fixed me with rheumy eyes. The voice had lost most of its old power. 'You were going to ask me to present it, weren't you? And I can't.' There was no need for me to answer.

John Arlott died at the end of the following year. At his funeral in the large former garrison church on Alderney, amongst the tributes, we sang a hymn that he had written himself and which he used to claim – with a twinkle in the eye – made him more money than anything else he wrote: 'God's Farm is All Creation'.

Arlott was a poet and a maverick. Brian Johnston was – on the face of it – much more establishment, but he was the irrepressible character whose influence gave *Test Match Special* the widespread popularity in the 1970s that it never really lost.

Joining the BBC in late September 1965, I did not really come across Brian (known then in the Outside Broadcasts Department as 'BJ' – 'Johnners' came later, a retaliation by cricketers for the ubiquitous '-ers' added to every name) until the spring of 1966, when he had returned from covering the Ashes series in Australia. Everyone would become aware of a wonderful jovial personality whenever he entered Broadcasting House, with a greeting for all and a quick deflating of any potential pomposity.

From the most junior filing clerk to the Director General himself, all were hailed with a cheery 'Morning, old man!' I remember coming across a pretty and obviously female young secretary looking slightly puzzled. 'Brian Johnston just called me "old man",' she said. I consoled her that it was a term of endearment. Everyone was always glad to see him.

Although he was there at the first Test match I worked on, at the Oval in 1966, he was emerging from the next-door television commentary hut. He had done one Test for radio that year, and was to do a handful more before the decade was out, but it was in 1970 that he was switched full-time to radio for Test cricket. He remained very unhappy about the way this was done, finding out about it only when Robert Hudson said to him what good news it was he was making the move, rather than receiving any word from his television masters. From *Test Match Special*'s point of view it was the best thing that could have happened and I have always believed that, different as they were, it was very good for the wider recognition of the brilliance of John Arlott that the more broadly popular Johnston came to what was surely his natural medium.

Brian was instantly recognisable to a cricket public and far beyond because of the amount of television work he had done, although it did surprise me how long that remained the case, long after his television work had largely ceased. However, I still have a memory of him standing before a queue of young boys waiting for his autograph, muttering, 'Who is he? Who is he?' in the belief that they had only been sent over by their parents to get the great man's signature.

If it was remarkable that John Arlott should have come to the BBC with no academic qualifications and straight from the police force, it would be difficult today to imagine someone doing as BJ did and turning up because a commentator he had met thought it might be a good idea, and declaring his background to be Eton, Oxford and the Guards. His spell in the family coffee business might not have been a help either. Happily, today's narrow interpretations of suitability for broadcasting did not apply in those immediate post-war years.

Brian had served in the Guards Armoured Division in the war, remarkably, to those who remember him trying to get his head round the most basic of broadcasting equipment, becoming Technical Adjutant of his battalion. His reconnaissance scout car was christened FUJIAR, the acronym for the old military adage, 'F*** you, Jack, I'm all right'. Not that this is by any means the earliest example of Johnstonian irreverence.

Despite his claim that, when a senior officer asked him what steps he would take if he were to see German infantry advancing on his position, he answered, 'Very large ones, sir, in the opposite direction,' he won a Military Cross, with the citation suggesting that it was as much for his beneficial effect on the soldiers' morale as any other action. In the *Test Match Special* commentary box, I think we could identify with that.

Given a free choice in life, he would probably have opted for a career as a stand-up comedian, although he was able to try out his comedy talent in the organisation of entertainments for the troops towards the end of the war. As a great fan of the Crazy Gang and the patter of comics of that ilk, he wrote and delivered a music hall style script along the lines of the old, 'I say, I say, I say. It's in all the papers tonight.'

'What is?'

'Fish and chips.'

'I don't wish to know that. Kindly leave the stage!'

That gives a glimpse of the level of humour his colleagues in the commentary box and the office had to put up with over the years that followed. I also still have many of the saucy seaside postcards on which he used to do most of his correspondence.

It was probably Brian's involvement in the troop entertainments that inspired a fellow officer to tip him off when a celebrated pair of BBC voices came to stay in their mess just before D-Day. They were Stewart MacPherson and Wynford Vaughan-Thomas and meeting them was the catalyst for Brian's post-war career. Newly demobbed and looking for some sort of work in the entertainment industry, he ran into them again and they introduced him to the BBC and a vacancy in the OB Department.

There was a bit of the music hall in his early days in the Corporation. These were times when outside broadcasting was an exciting business. In fact his first broadcast was the description of an unexploded bomb being dealt with in St James's Park, which he covered from a ladies' lavatory ('I emerged looking a little flushed'). Brian was involved in broadcasts from West End theatres and then an item in the popular *In Town Tonight* programme, called 'Let's Go Somewhere'. This latter had him engaged in all sorts of escapades, such as riding bareback on a circus horse, lying between the rails as the Golden Arrow train left Victoria Station, concealed inside a postbox at Christmas, or, his favourite, accompanying Bud Flanagan singing 'Underneath the Arches' outside the stage door of the Victoria Palace theatre. For all these he would be live on the air, stopwatch in hand.

There seemed to be no chance of cricket commentary on the radio. Rex Alston, John Arlott and E. W. Swanton were the men in possession. Then a call came through from an old friend, Ian Orr-Ewing, asking Brian if he would like to try his hand at the television cricket coverage that was starting up after the war. That was the start of a broadcasting relationship which lasted twenty-four years, although in that time he was also doing county cricket on radio and in 1963 he was appointed the BBC's first cricket correspondent, which he remained until his retirement from the BBC staff at the age of sixty at the end of the 1972 season.

From John Arlott we remember the words; from Brian we remember the good cheer and sense of enjoyment. He would look for the best in everyone, following the philosophy of Charles Kingsley's creation, Mrs Doasyouwouldbedoneby, from *The Water Babies*. Kindness was his watchword, even kindness in his criticism of a poor shot, taking the view that the batsman did not mean to play it. Not that poor play was not capable of irritating – or more accurately, upsetting – him. I can remember Nick Cook, bowling slow left-arm in a Test match at Trent Bridge and switching to the negative over-the-wicket line. Even at the back of the commentary box, Brian was practically wailing, 'Oh, this is dreadful.'

For some of the Tests in the winter of 1974/75, when England were facing the full fury of Messrs Lillee and Thomson in Australia, Brian would come into the studio early in the morning as my *Test Match Special* presenter. For all but the Perth Test, we were taking only the last two hours of the day's play – from 5 a.m. to 7 a.m. So I would be in the office from the start of play at midnight, contacting Christopher Martin-Jenkins for updates every hour. Then at about 4.30 a.m. the irrepressible Johnners would appear with, 'Oh dear, what news, what news? I can hardly bear to hear it.' And from England's point of view, it was indeed usually bad news.

When he came in on Boxing Day morning, we settled into our usual Studio 4B and as 5 a.m. approached, Brian enquired, 'Shouldn't we have a studio manager by now?' We should have, but I knew who it was meant to be – one of the most reliable in the business, but also one of the most laid-back – a man called Tony Earnshaw.

'Don't worry,' I said, 'it's Tony and he'll cut it fine, just to worry me.'

The control room had alerted me that the line from Melbourne was available and my limited knowledge enabled me to select the right fader and open it. I even laced up the old tape on the machine for the signature tune with which we were starting. Brian remained relaxed, with only a last minute, 'Are we going to be all right, old man?'

I had rung the studio managers' common room, but at 4.45 on Boxing Day morning it is not over-staffed with people wondering what to do with themselves. So at the appointed time I pressed all the right buttons and somehow we got on the air. A spare studio manager arrived within minutes, full of apologies, but hugely amused by the fact that it had been the staunch Earnshaw, of all people, who had failed to appear. We agreed that, in his way, he would be rushing to the studio, but would actually come through the door as laid-back as ever. That is exactly what happened.

For the end of the series, Brian made it down under to the country he always loved to visit. And in that enjoyment of touring, too, he differed from Arlott, relishing the camaraderie of the tour with old friends from the press like John Woodcock of *The Times* and Michael Melford of the *Daily Telegraph*.

Brian was always helpful, self-effacing, but well aware of his fame, and willing to help, with the interests of the programme very much at heart. After his death, one of the things I missed was his unique willingness to discuss aspects of *Test Match Special* other than those that directly involved him. No one else would remind me if we had forgotten to give thought to our selection of the Champagne Moment. Indeed that particular award came about only because of Brian.

He was dining in the Savoy Grill one night (as one does), when the manager came across to put an idea to him for something to celebrate the hotel's centenary. They would present a bottle of their own champagne to a player for a particular feat each Test match. Brian was on to me next morning and we refined the idea of the Champagne Moment, to be awarded for a moment that captured the imagination. It might be a great shot, a great ball, a great catch or maybe an act of outstanding sportsmanship. Whatever it was would be selected by the radio commentary team.

After one – we thought quite successful – season in 1989, the Savoy said that they did not want to continue, as that had just been for their centenary year. Veuve Clicquot heard of this and were quick off the mark to offer themselves as a replacement, though I had to divert them via Cornhill, the sponsors then of Test cricket in England, to deter any accusations of illicit BBC advertising. After Brian's death in 1994, a listener made the happiest suggestion, that we should rename it the Brian Johnston Champagne Moment. Veuve Clicquot did not hesitate to agree and so it has been ever since. It meant that, whenever we had a clash of suggestions for the winner, the question would be asked, 'What would have appealed to Johnners?'

While the 'A View From the Boundary' lunchtime session was not actually Brian's idea, it became his fiefdom and his contacts in show business came in very handy when we were looking for guests. Indeed, to turn it round, the guests were always keen to come on the programme to talk to him. It was an example of his kindness that if he detected a weakness in cricketing knowledge, he would not pursue the subject, although the violinist, Max Jaffa, said to me after his session that he had wanted to talk more about cricket. Brian had held back, not wanting to embarrass him.

It has become standard practice that when it rains at a Test match the team in the commentary box just keep going. These days the discussions are fuelled by emails and Jonathan Agnew, in particular, is quick to promote some subject which might get the electronic correspondence flowing. It was not always so. Prior to 1976, the habit was to return to the studio from whence would come the stream of light classical music. The day that changed that was the Saturday of the Lord's Test in 1976, when, with a full house, a light drizzle started to fall just as the umpires were taking the field. The rain was never so heavy that play would not have started as soon as it stopped. So we started to talk.

There was no play that day and the discussion went on throughout. On the Monday morning after the rest day, Brian came in with a piece of name-dropping that amused him. 'My friends at the Palace [and he had a few] tell me that Prince Philip thought we were awfully good on Saturday!' With such an endorsement, how could we not continue?

Brian's pile of letters always exceeded everyone else's and he felt it was a happy way of answering those who were good enough to write. Otherwise he would spend a Sunday at home in the garden – or in a park during a Test away from London – answering them by postcard. The post was always opened with the constant refrain, 'Aren't people kind?'

Brian's laugh was dangerously infectious. The famous – or infamous – 'leg-over' incident bears testimony to that. It is, I am sure, the main reason why no one can keep a straight face when listening to the moment in 1991 that Jonathan Agnew planted the thought in Johnners' mind that Botham, in being out hit wicket, 'didn't quite get his leg over'. When the laughter came, and the tears rolled down his cheeks, and all he could get out was a high pitched, 'Aggers, do stop it!', there was no help for anyone else either.

Don Mosey found himself unable to continue commentating once when Brian, at the back of the box, had been leafing through the Israeli Cricket Association's handbook and had discovered that their tenth-wicket partnership record was held by Solly Katz and Benni Wadwaker. For some reason this tickled his sense of humour and he started to laugh. Don, at the microphone, describing the action, had no idea what the mirth was about, but picked up the infection of it and soon his shoulders were heaving, too. That only added to Brian's laughter and it was hard to break the vicious circle to restore sanity.

On the occasion of Brian's seventieth birthday, I decided to make a lunchtime feature on him and centre it on an interview. We agreed to record it in the commentary box at Lord's, when I was there for a county match. Every time we started, we would catch each other's eye and 'corpse'. After three or four aborted attempts, we did the interview with both of us staring fixedly at a pillar in the middle of the box.

One can imagine that schoolmasters must have despaired of the apparent buffoonery of the young Johnston and it would be easy to dismiss the grown man as a mere buffoon, but the rapid resort to a pun whenever the situation offered one (the older the joke, the better), was part of the evidence of a very sharp mind. He was keenly interested in politics and always au fait with every-thing that was going on in the news.

As *Sport on 2* on a Saturday afternoon changed its style in the 1970s Brian came gradually to the conclusion that it was scarcely worth his while to be sitting at a county championship match to do perhaps a total of three minutes' reporting in the afternoon. The producer of the programme was rather surprised at this reaction but, despite his disappointment at losing Brian, did nothing to change his approach to cricket coverage.

On Test match mornings it became the practice to have one of the commentary team at the ground at 8.25 a.m. for the sports spot on the *Today* programme, in order to provide a view of the morning's weather and talk to the sports presenter about the prospects for the day. This was not an over-popular shift, particularly as the early start to a long day was often rewarded by being squeezed for time on the programme. Brian would take his turn uncomplainingly, but one morning at Trent Bridge he had the usual detailed briefing from Garry Richardson, who was doing the sport that day.

'I'll start by asking, what's the weather like there this morning, Brian? Then I'll ask you about the England batting and then about the Australian bowling. So three questions and if you can get it all into a minute and a quarter from when you start talking, that would be splendid.' Brian just agreed to the plan.

When the first question came, he replied with an exact minute and a quarter, including all the points that Garry had required. Unfortunately, Garry let himself down by picking up afterwards with, 'Oh, I thought I was going to get a question in there.'

Brian looked at me with an air of innocence. 'Did I get something wrong?'

'Oh no,' I said. He had known exactly what he was doing and Garry had been done by a master. Later in the day it was suggested to me by the sports editor that Brian should be spared that particular duty at his time of life.

When, in 1980, I was asked to take on the production of the radio coverage of the Boat Race, the year after John Snagge retired from doing the main commentary, it was really inevitable that I went straight to Johnners to take over as commentator in the launch, following the crews. By that time he had been a course commentator at almost every other point along the river, latterly always on Chiswick Bridge, below which the race ends.

As with everything else he did, he brought a great sense of fun to proceedings, both at our rehearsal the day before, when we would meet in the

Star and Garter at Putney, and on the race day itself. He did produce a protest from our television colleagues, because, as such a well-known figure, the presidents at the toss would ignore the TV presenter and turn first to Brian to talk about their choice of station on the river. Then at the end of the race, when he had come ashore, he was always a great magnet as we sought out interviews with the members of the crews. Everyone always wanted to talk to Brian.

On a freezing cold and foggy Saturday morning in December 1991, Brian rang me to tell me that he had just had a call saying that John Arlott had died. Could I confirm? I made a few calls and it was confirmed that John had died early that morning.

One morning almost exactly two years later a call from Pauline Johnston alerted me to the fact that Brian had suffered a heart attack while in a taxi taking him to Paddington station and a speaking engagement in Bristol. He was resuscitated at Maida Vale Hospital and taken to St Mary's, Paddington. That was where I saw him for the last time a few days later.

It was a heart-breaking meeting. He was only vaguely aware of who I was, because, with my presence, he seemed to think that he was in the commentary box. He was sitting in his pyjamas beside the bed, on the end of which was an enormous pile of mail from well-wishers. It was bothering him. Ever the conscientious Johnners, he was concerned that he had not answered them and he was daunted by the task. I put them on the window sill, out of his view. On my way out I spoke to the ward manager. 'Will he make a full recovery?'

'Oh yes,' she said, but, with no medical knowledge at my disposal, I had my doubts.

Calls to Pauline kept me abreast of his progress. He was out of hospital for Christmas, over which period Pauline took him for a walk round Lord's to jerk his memory. She pointed out the commentary box, then in the privileged position in the top of the pavilion.

'*Test Match Special*,' he said, to her delight.

On the morning of 5 January 1994 I was sitting in my office in Broadcasting House, working on the planning of the forthcoming England tour of the West Indies. At the other end of the room I was conscious of a discussion going on about a programme that was due to go out that evening called *Chris Cowdrey's Cricket Night*. Chris had had to pull out, however, and the possibilities for an alternative were being chewed over. I was adding a few thoughts from my end of the room, when my phone rang. It was Pauline Johnston and somehow I knew immediately what was coming. Brian's wonderful life had ended early that morning.

I told the *Cricket Night* planners that they might have to change their ideas and within ten minutes they came back to ask me to present an hour and a half's tribute to Brian in its place. Happily, on a day when I seemed to be in great demand for pieces on Brian, written and broadcast, I was given the best possible producer in Rob Nothman, later among his other credits to be an outstanding 'roving reporter' on *TMS*, who guided me brilliantly through a difficult day, so that the full impact of what had happened only sank in over a beer with him after the programme.

So many people had so many happy things to say about Brian that, desperately sad though the evening was, it was the beginning of a celebration of his life and his personality.

A memorial service was obviously needed to follow the private family funeral and only Westminster Abbey could begin to hold the quantity of people who would want to attend. Nonetheless the Dean told us that, while the Abbey held 1800, the congregation on these occasions always levelled out at 1500, no matter how great the life that was being celebrated. Over two thousand crammed into the mother church of the nation that day in May for a very special service. My own part was to read a lesson, before Brian's three sons each gave readings, and there were twin addresses from Lord Colin Cowdrey and the Prime Minister, John Major. The congregation left the Abbey to the signature tune of Brian's favourite television soap opera, *Neighbours*.

Politically, the event served to underline the BBC's position in the fabric of the country at a time when the Corporation's charter was heading for review.

For the millions of listeners who really felt they knew him personally, a friend had been lost. For me, it felt as great a loss as that of my own parents.

THE PILLARS
OF *TMS*

SHAKESPEARE HAD HIS THREE WEIRD SISTERS IN
Macbeth. The trio that took *Test Match Special* to the end of the
twentieth century and into the twenty-first might be slightly
better groomed and have less of a taste for eye of newt, but they
do have their peculiarities. Jonathan Agnew, Henry Blofeld and
Christopher Martin-Jenkins are the three ball-by-ball men around
whom the programme has revolved now for more than half a
generation. And it is on the base of the commentator – the
describer of the scene and the action – that radio commentary
rests. He (or she) is the eyes of the listener.

Robert Hudson, keen to pursue young talent, decided to use the start of
one-day internationals in England in 1972 to blood two aspiring commentators
in Christopher and Henry. In those early years of their careers, there was
something of a competitive edge between the pair of them, though Hudson's
bold decision in 1973, the same year that he had appointed this twenty-six-
year-old cricket producer, to make Christopher the cricket correspondent at the
age of twenty-eight, did cement his place.

Unusually – for both of us – I first met Christopher at a football match. We
were both at Stamford Bridge for an evening game in 1970; I was there as the

producer of the commentary and he was the reporter for Sports News, our roles separated by the inter-departmental politics of the time. I had heard of him before. There had been talk in the Outside Broadcasts Department about this eager, lanky young man, who had joined the Sportsroom after a spell at *The Cricketer* magazine and the word was that E. W. Swanton, no less, reckoned that he was very promising.

On the face of it, Christopher must have been a little bit of a round peg in a square hole in the old Sportsroom. On his arrival, the terse Sports Editor, Angus McKay, looked at the double-barrelled name and declared, 'You'll be known as Chris Jenkins.' But Christopher stuck to his guns and thirty-five years later the name was still taking up two lines in the *Radio Times*.

That relationship with the Sportsroom was to play a part in encouraging him to leave the staff of the BBC in 1980 to become editor of *The Cricketer*. Even as the BBC's cricket correspondent and a *Test Match Special* commentator, he was expected to be in on a winter Saturday, when he was not away on a tour, doing such tasks as the football divisions three and four round-ups for *Sports Report*. Also, even then, the length of those winter cricket tours was becoming a problem, particularly for anyone with a young family.

Partly to allow others the chance to commentate and partly so that the correspondent could be heard on the sports news network – then Radio 2 – Christopher did not necessarily commentate on *Test Match Special* for every Test in those days, the point being made that 'correspondent' did not have to mean 'commentator'. This was a principle that was being applied at the time in football, where Bryon Butler, an excellent and authoritative correspondent was not often let loose as a descriptive commentator, which was not the strongest part of his game. Despite the fact that Christopher was himself a superb cricket correspondent, he would always be irritated whenever he was not on the ball-by-ball team.

The situation was not improved by the fact that the Test match overlapping with Wimbledon was usually the one chosen for him to be on reporting duties, following an editorial view that it would be 'good to be able to talk to our corre-spondent whenever we want to'. In practice, when it seemed that the whole editorial effort of the department had been moved to Wimbledon, no other sporting event ever got a look in. (Some editorial policy does not seem to have changed over the intervening years.)

At the time that Christopher came to the job of cricket correspondent, reporting on sporting events had been a fairly leisurely affair – at least as far as the Outside Broadcasts Department was concerned. The expression 'eye witness account', usually shortened to EWA, was generally one of the instructions on the list of commitments at the end of a game. These might well be in excess of two minutes in duration. The disciplines imposed by Angus McKay in *Sports Report*, however, brought an icy blast to this cosy practice and, with someone like Christopher now working on a regular basis with the more leisurely OB Department, there was a murmur of wonder at his ability to sum up a day's play inside a minute. (A minute would seem like luxury today for those who report on Radio 5 Live, where thirty seconds is the norm and the command, 'Fifteen seconds … and keep it tight!' has been heard.)

Christopher's more recent colleagues might raise an eyebrow that, in those days, he was so adept at the concise report. His relationship – or lack of it – with any clock or stopwatch is a standing *Test Match Special* joke. Once, on a tour of the West Indies, I had a somewhat fraught evening of a Test match in Barbados. It took a long time for the studio, late at night in London, to take in all the close-of-play recordings we were sending them. Replacing the unwieldy shutters in the commentary box took a back-breaking half hour and then I got caught up in the traffic jams of central Bridgetown. All this was making me late for another appointment with Edward Bevan, the Radio Wales reporter, and I had no way of contacting him. The crisis was then deepened by the road having been dug up from my hotel to his, necessitating a tortuous detour.

The next morning I was driving Christopher to the Kensington Oval for the start of play and regaling him with my nightmare. 'It was just like that John Cleese film, *Clockwise*,' I told him.

There was a lengthy pause. Then, rather sadly, he said, 'My whole life's like that.'

The similarity with John Cleese – or more accurately with Basil Fawlty – at least in length of limb, obtusely led to Christopher's press box nickname of 'The Major'. The line from *Fawlty Towers* seems to fit:

'What ho, Fawlty. See Hampshire won again.'

'Did it, Major?'

Christopher had one particularly Fawlty-like evening on our 2006 tour of India, when we decided on an end-of-Test-series *TMS* dinner. He had been recommended a restaurant called the Copper Chimney, which it transpired, when we took taxis to get there, was easily walkable from our hotel. Our evening gathering was graced with the presence of that great cricket enthusiast, Stephen Fry. To nobody's surprise, CMJ was not ready when we were leaving the hotel and he said he would join us when he had sent his last piece to *The Times*. We explained to Stephen that this was quite normal.

As the evening wore on over an excellent meal, the restaurant door opened and Griff Rhys-Jones came in, to be hailed by Stephen Fry and persuaded to join us. Then the text messages started. At first Christopher was merely enquiring, 'Where is the restaurant?' Then more demanding: 'URGENT. What is restaurant address – PLEASE!' They became more frequent and panic stricken. When he staggered in as we were paying the bill, it transpired that his taxi driver had found another Copper Chimney in a distant part of Bombay and there he had been shown into a business dinner in a private room. Subsequent taxi drivers had been unable to locate any other Copper Chimneys.

Mike Selvey took pity on Christopher and stayed with him while he bolted a chicken curry. This turned out to be a huge mistake, as within a few hours he was so stricken with sickness that he had to delay his flight home and took some considerable time to be fit again, even after being restored to the safety of Sussex.

Having been with him when we were meant to be going to a function on a few occasions, I think I have understood the cause of his being dubbed 'the late CMJ'. His life is so busy that he will usually try to cram in one more task just at the moment when he should really be leaving. The notion of arriving anywhere early would, I believe, represent to him an unforgivable waste of time.

After a few years as editor of *The Cricketer*, Christopher returned for a second spell as BBC cricket correspondent at the end of 1984, on a contract to combine the two jobs. These days, thanks to digital telecommunications, BBC correspondents are able to have a broadcast quality line in their homes, saving a great deal of trouble, but making them permanently on call. Most would reckon the benefits far outweigh that loss of privacy. In the 1980s, however, those out and about, or working from home, would usually be dependent on a network of unattended studios. These were often in council offices, or hotels, or somewhere where a key could be held locally for access to a small room with basic broadcasting equipment. (In my early days in the BBC, taking bookings for these was one of my duties.) They also provided a bit of pin money for local stringers who knew the ins and outs of their local studio and so could hold the hand of a reporter who was unfamiliar with one of them.

The nearest unattended studio to Christopher was in Horsham and sports producers would occasionally make the daring decision to take him 'live' into the main evening *Sports Desk* programme. Unfortunately, on the principle of not wanting to waste any time hanging about and knowing exactly the time from his house to the studio, that was precisely the time that Christopher would allow. The fact that this was a record, wind-assisted time, which depended on all traffic lights being green, and parking, access to the studio, and communications being straightforward, never seemed to bother his initial confidence. After a few of these scheduled appearances had been missed, it became most producers' insurance policy to ask me to be on standby in case he failed to make it in time. The most piteous times were those when the line would appear just as we finished the programme and a voice could be heard, pleading with the studio manager, 'But why can't you take this piece now?'

Among Christopher's considerable talents, he is an excellent mimic. Some of his imitations have made it onto the air in end-of-year sports spoofs and they illustrate his repertoire of after-dinner stories and indeed his conversation. I can remember being in a studio with commentators at four different matches as we covered the quarter-finals of one of the county knockout competitions. I put down the appropriate key to talk to John Arlott at Southampton and he seemed to answer perfectly, and it was only when I took my finger off the button that I saw that I had pressed the wrong one and it should have been Christopher Martin-Jenkins at Lord's. The perfection of his imitation had completely fooled me.

He does sometimes seem to court the persona of the absent-minded professor with his increasingly scatty sayings and doings. Among them is his own particular dictionary of curses. In order not to upset those who might overhear, they do not carry the usual sexual or blasphemous references. 'Fishcakes and buttercup pie!', however, can be delivered with every bit as much force as any sailor could manage. An old Indian spinner might be a little surprised to hear that 'Bishen Singh Bedi!' has also become an expletive.

Christopher famously confused Mike Selvey one day in New Zealand with an attempt at the Cockney rhyming slang that Mike enjoys – especially more inventive versions. 'I think I've gone in the Conrad,' he declared.

Mike kept a puzzled silence for two overs of play, not daring to venture a comment. He had tried 'Joseph Conrad' in his mind, but all he kept returning to was 'Conrad Hunte', the former West Indies opener. And that did not seem possible. At long last his curiosity had to be satisfied. 'The Conrad?' he enquired, nervously.

'The Conrad Black. My back's gone,' said an innocent Christopher.

Selve was again on hand for CMJ's spectacular start to the 1998 England tour of the Caribbean. They were on the drive from the opening match in Montego Bay across Jamaica to Kingston and Christopher was trying to get through to his office on the mobile phone without success. As is his wont with things technical, he bashed it on the dashboard and cursed it. Selvey glanced at it. 'You won't get through with that.'

'Why not?'

'It's the TV remote control from the hotel.'

It was only a couple of days later that he was sitting in his hotel room in Kingston, contentedly bringing the newspaper cuttings in his notebook up to date, while listening to music on his Walkman. Suddenly the music stopped. Impact technology was applied to the Walkman with no result. Then the penny dropped. He had cut through the cable to his earpieces. To be fair, none of us would have known about that if he had not owned up, but only two days after that, at Chedwin Park, west of Kingston, while walking round the ground he lowered his head to duck through a gate in the security fence, but did not allow enough room and knocked himself off his feet with the force of the contact with head and lintel. (My own perambulation round that ground, puffing happily on my pipe, was interrupted by a call from a fellow watching the game from the branches of a tree just outside the perimeter wall. 'Hey, man, why don't you come here and let me put sometin' more interestin' in dat pipe!')

My favourite CMJ mishap also befell him in the West Indies. We were in Guyana for a Test match in 1990 and – not unusually for Guyana – it was raining. Nonetheless, *Test Match Special* had to go on the air, although the increasing size of the puddles on the outfield gave us the considerable clue that there was unlikely to be any play. The most direct route to our commentary position on the tight little Bourda ground was across a corner of the field of play.

Fortunately, an experienced tourist like Christopher was not to be deterred by a bit of standing water. His family had given him a pair of galoshes against just such a circumstance and now – with, we onlookers felt, a hint of smugness – he sat on the benches in front of the old wooden pavilion to put these over his suede shoes. Then, very pleased with himself, he stepped out of the pavilion gates – and into eighteen inches of water.

A morning swim has been part of his routine on tours, whenever possible. He can be seen in bathing shorts, with a towel over his shoulder, heading for the hotel pool as others are making for breakfast. Our hotel in 2001 at Weligama, on the south coast of Sri Lanka, had a pool situated on top of the cliffs, overlooking the beach and the Indian Ocean, and Christopher was able to get in several lengths of breaststroke before breakfast. By chance, Jonathan Agnew's room overlooked the pool and he was able to watch not only his predecessor at his constitutional swim, but also the troupe of monkeys returning afterwards to use the pool as they habitually did – as a lavatory.

Arriving at Nagpur in India on the 2006 tour after dark, Christopher asked those of us who had been there a few days if the hotel had a pool. We replied – truthfully – that it did, although we did, to our shame, omit the detail that it was full of builders' rubble. This he discovered early next morning as, in bathing shorts, with the towel over the shoulder, he caught sight of the amenity from the stairs.

Christopher's prime care in his work has been for the game of cricket. He has deplored the steady reduction in the quantity and the quality of the reporting of the county game, especially on the radio. His commentaries have always been meticulous, with perhaps a hint of the would-be coach about them. This latter attribute has led him sometimes to be less than assiduous about giving the score because, when a shot has been played, he is liable to discuss the technique involved, when a more prosaic statement of the score might be welcomed more by some listeners. But if this is a fault, it is the fault of an enthusiast for the game.

Ironically, Henry Blofeld, for all the butterflies, pigeons and buses that vie for space in his commentaries, is a very good giver of the score. In his early days in the job (it seems incredible now) he was inclined to concentrate almost exclusively on the action on the twenty-two yard strip in the middle. This prompted me to encourage him to raise his eyes occasionally and describe the scene. The result has been 'frightfully good-looking lady policemen', 'medium-paced aeroplanes', 'rather attractive litter bins', and a plethora of 'thoughtful pigeons'.

Flights of fancy can get him into trouble. When we took over a new commentary box at Trent Bridge, Henry was commenting on the fact that our change of ends had, of course, given us a completely different view. 'There's a rather nice hill over there behind the pavilion … with a church on it. And look, there's a column of smoke. The vicar must be having a barbecue.'

We were having a visit at that moment from two members of the Nottinghamshire committee, who quickly informed us that Blowers' 'church' was in fact the Wilford Hill Crematorium.

Henry inevitably polarises opinion. The regular correspondent who leads for the prosecution sent me a very kind email of good wishes for my retirement but added the PS 'Please take Henry with you'. In defence comes the barrage of complaint I used to receive for any Test match where he was not on the team. This came to a head for the final and deciding Test match of 2005, when England stood poised to recapture the Ashes at long last. Before the season started and I was allocating Test matches to the commentators, Blowers asked if he could avoid the Oval Test. This was for purely economic reasons, as he gets a great many speaking engagements in the hospitality boxes at the Oval. However the *Daily Mail*, never shy of running a good anti-BBC story, got stuck in without checking its facts, and that prompted a good raft of abusive mail to me. A question was even asked in the House of Commons. Blowers himself was characteristically apologetic.

The great thing that Henry has on radio is his distinctive voice. In these days, when so many broadcast voices are impossible to distinguish from each other, this is a very valuable asset. And, for all that his detractors claim that he sometimes sounds a little confused, he does know what he is talking about. Almost everyone who saw him as a brilliant schoolboy wicket-keeper/batsman when he was at Eton has no doubt at all that he would have gone on to play for England had he not had an unfortunate accident in his final term, when his bicycle encountered a bus.

He suffered some very serious head injuries, but, despite his chagrin at missing the Eton and Harrow match at Lord's, he was back on the field that season. Frustratingly, though, he knew that he was not quite the brilliant player he had been before. Nonetheless he went on to play for Cambridge University and Norfolk and has over 750 first-class runs and a first-class hundred to his name.

Henry was saved for the nation as a cricket journalist, when he was taking the early steps of a City career, by the thoughtful actions of John Woodcock, the long-serving cricket correspondent of *The Times*, who gave him his first chance to report some county matches for that paper. He dines out on the tale of the audition process with the then Assistant Head of Outside Broadcasts, Henry Riddell, but he really cut his teeth when he was in the right place at the right time to get the chance to commentate in the Caribbean on the West Indies' series against New Zealand early in 1972. This encouraged Robert Hudson to give him his first pair of one-day internationals at the end of that English season, which was followed in 1974 by his *Test Match Special* debut.

His is the life less ordinary. Things happen to him. Often he seems to be Bertie Wooster in person. This impression is underlined by his being a great devotee of P. G. Wodehouse and a frequent quoter of many of his best lines. One morning during a Lord's Test, Don Mosey recalled having had a terrible time the previous evening getting into the St John's Wood tube station. There seemed to be some sort of hold-up at the ticket booth and the queue was rapidly growing and extending out onto the pavement. Don peered round to see what the problem was and heard a clearly recognisable voice. 'But, my dear old thing, I really have nothing smaller than a fifty pound note.' At least – surely unlike his model, Wooster – Henry was attempting to take the underground.

Brought up on the family's estate in Norfolk and then educated at Eton and Cambridge, his background may seem a little out of step with today's world. When I stayed with him in his house on the estate in the 1970s, I was briefed before a visit to his parents in the big house. 'They'll offer you a drink, but just ask for sherry. It's all there really is.'

I did as I was told. Then Henry was asked what he'd have.

'I'll have a glass of champagne, thanks,' he said. The work of a master.

When Henry was awarded the OBE in 1996, Simon Mann worked out what it must stand for and at the next opportunity he handed over to Henry as 'Odd But Entertaining'. That opportunity – during Simon's first Test match as a commentator, as it happened – was later that year at Bulawayo, when Blowers added to the legend and the language of the commentary box by 'doing a Bulawayo', as it is now known to all.

England had come back from an indifferent start to their first Test match against Zimbabwe to be left a target of 205 to win from thirty-seven overs. Blowers finished the game with a remarkable hour and a quarter's commentary stint. Commentary spells are normally twenty minutes on radio, but Henry, as he admitted later that evening, 'took a view' and carried on. I was the commentator who was due to follow him, with Simon after me, and, as it turned out because of Zimbabwe's ever slower over-rate, Henry would have returned for the finish –

the only Test match instance of a draw with the scores level – but having been sent out there as the senior commentator, he decided to ignore all suggestions of handing over. Nowadays, if any commentator over-runs his time, particularly if it is Blowers who is the culprit, the cry goes up in the box, 'Bulawayo!'

Henry may have justified that decision in the knowledge that I always rated him as a very good man for the tight finish in a one-day game. In recent years he does emphasise the tenseness of such a situation with frequent exclamations of, 'Gosh, this is exciting'. It makes him an eternal schoolboy perhaps, but it is this very enthusiasm which is so appealing to his considerable band of supporters.

Test Match Special ran two serious risks of losing Blowers. As the 1990s started, he left us to go to BSkyB television. They were not doing Test matches 'live' then, but did cover quite a few domestic games and broadcast evening highlights of international cricket. His departure coincided with the arrival of Jonathan Agnew, so, with Brian Johnston, CMJ and usually a visiting commentator, it was probably not a bad bit of judgement that his *Test Match Special* opportunities might be slightly reduced. Anyway, Sky were offering significantly higher fees than BBC Radio.

With his absence from the commentary team attracting its usual crop of queries and protests, Johnners said to me that he felt we really ought to say something by way of explanation. I said rather stuffily that I did not feel we should be giving Sky a plug.

'Don't worry,' said Brian. 'I'm sure I can get round that.'

What he actually said on the air, to those who were wondering what had happened to Blowers, was fairly cryptic. 'He's gone, shall we say, to a place in the Sky.' Next day we received three black-edged cards commiserating with us for our great loss.

Henry was not a total stranger to work on television. As an archetypal English character, he would appear on Australian screens in Test match intervals, prompting a banner on the Sydney Hill to be unfurled, reading: 'THE BESPECTACLED HENRY BLOWFLY STAND'. Astutely, Blowers converted this fame into other TV ventures beyond the cricket arena in Australia and New Zealand.

As things worked out, his time with Sky was fairly brief. We used to pull faces at him as he did a little pre-play chat 'in vision' with Geoff Boycott at a coffee table on the boundary's edge. By 1993, however, the lucrative little sojourn had ended. He was still doing television work overseas, chiefly in India, where his tendency to mention things he had spotted beyond the boundary, which memorably included ladies' earrings, earned him a reputation which still seems to follow him in that part of the world.

After the death of Brian Johnston at the start of 1994, I looked at the prospective commentary team for the forthcoming season. We had Jonathan Agnew, now firmly established as he was approaching his fourth season with us. Christopher Martin-Jenkins, of course, was there and we would be joined by two very competent overseas commentators. Bryan Waddle would be with the New Zealanders on his second tour as their correspondent, and his trip would be followed by the first series in England for South Africa for twenty-nine years and they would be accompanied by Gerald de Kock.

These were excellent commentary teams in prospect, of course, but in the aftermath of the loss of Brian it was inevitable that we should be missing a bit of a spark. Was it, therefore, a good time to bring back Blowers? A constant press enquiry was, 'Who are you bringing in to replace Johnners?' which made me reluctant to put that pressure onto him just at that point.

I was still having this internal debate when I sat down with the new Head of Sport, Bob Shennan, to pick the commentary teams for the summer. (By this time we had long dispensed with the meeting of all the regional producers to take all day doing what now took half an hour. This was partly because we had also dispensed with the regional OB producers.) Being new to the job, Bob asked his predecessor, Mike Lewis, to come along too, and Mike was adamant that you should never go back and the era of Henry Blofeld on BBC Radio had gone. I was not so sure and I negotiated to pick the teams only for the New Zealand half of the season, which came first.

By the time a decision had to be made for the second half of the summer, I had become convinced that it was time to reintroduce Blowers. Now I got a vote of confidence from Shennan. 'If you think that's the right thing to do, go for it.' So I rang Henry.

'Go a bit easy on the buses and the dear old things.'

'Backers, I won't let you down.'

Blowers was on his best behaviour throughout both the Tests on which he commentated in that series. All commentators get criticism, as well as praise, in the listeners' comments that come in by letter and, these days, much more by email. The loves and hates even out to an extraordinary degree. During the second half of that 1994 season the return of Henry Blofeld received only praise. I had expected a degree of vilification for having brought him back, but it simply did not come. Every correspondent was delighted, it seemed, to have him back.

Early in the spring of 1999 I was up to my elbows in the arrangements for covering the seventh cricket World Cup and it was all the more hectic for this one being in England. A call from Henry one evening gave me a warning that he was going into hospital for a few tests, but no one expected it to be too serious a problem – he had just suffered a little tightness of the chest while walking down the road in Chelsea. He was featuring quite a bit on my large wall chart, which was planning everyone's movements for the tournament. He would ring me the following day just to confirm that all was all right.

His call the next day was not quite so reassuring. He was to have a heart bypass operation and might miss the first week or so of the World Cup. The operation was scheduled for a Friday morning and that evening I rang the Blofeld home to enquire of Bitten, Henry's wife, how things had gone. There was no answer, so I left a message.

It was not until Monday that a very emotional Bitten rang back. 'Oh, Peter, we've had a terrible time.' Henry had come through, but only after revisiting the operating table. Even after I saw him in hospital during the week, when he was adamant in his command not to make him laugh, because that was agonising, he had to be opened up again following an infection. By then he had said that there was no chance of him taking part in our coverage of the World Cup, although all medical predictions were that he would be fit for action for the Test series with New Zealand which would follow.

The other major blow which hit us in the preparation for that World Cup concerned slightly less immediate plans. Mike Lewis, the former Head of Sport, was now the man in charge of rights negotiations, which had become such a huge part of life in sports broadcasting. One morning in Television Centre I found him also in the office, almost with the dawn. I enquired without any real concern if all the rights had been sorted out for the forthcoming England winter tour of South Africa.

'Well, it's a funny thing,' he said. 'I keep ringing Ali Bacher [the former South African player who was now managing director of the United Cricket Board of South Africa]. I leave messages and they promise he'll ring back, but he never does. You know him, why don't you give him a ring and find out what is going on.'

Without delay I rang Johannesburg and was put straight through to Dr

Bacher, who gave me a cheery greeting. I enquired if all was well with our sorting out the rights for the tour and almost immediately I felt I could hear his feet shuffling uncomfortably under his desk.

'We've had an offer from Talk Radio.' He gave me a figure, which was certainly more than we would normally have expected to pay.

'Fair enough,' I said. 'So that's what we've got to better, then.'

'Well, we've sort of accepted it.'

'You have accepted it – or not quite yet? Are we going to get a chance to put in our bid?'

'We sort of didn't think you would be able to bid any more.'

'Of course we will.'

'Well, we've sort of accepted it.'

I found out later that the key to the rather underhand dealings that had gone on was apparently that Talk had made their offer conditional on the BBC being kept in the dark.

This news obviously sent a bit of a shiver through the corridors of Television Centre. We were used to television having rights problems, but this was a new era for radio and it was a particular surprise that cricket had been targeted, as the very length of a playing day would have seemed to make it an unpopular sport for any organisation without a number of wavelengths to juggle. Strangely, within the BBC politics that had dogged *Test Match Special* for much of my time with the programme – the question of where to put it in the schedules at times had seemed to threaten its very existence – our star was now in the ascendant. No one could really believe that we were not actually going to be mounting commentary on a Test series and, within and without the Corporation, people rallied to support us.

Meanwhile, Talk's managing director, Kelvin McKenzie, was approaching a few of the *TMS* team to try to recruit them, which, following his claim that Talk's commentary team would be younger and more lively than *TMS*, was perhaps surprising. Jonathan Agnew and Christopher Martin-Jenkins certainly had calls – Jonathan several of them. It is a fair assumption, then, that some effort must have been made to get hold of Blowers, who was under the surgeon's knife at just about the time that this news was bursting on us.

Reflecting on that later, I was surprised that in those circumstances news of Henry's heart surgery had not got into the papers. At his request, we said nothing until he was safely at home recuperating, and listeners were beginning to comment on his absence from our extensive World Cup coverage. Eventually we did have him on the phone for a live lunchtime interview and it was good to hear him back on the air sounding perky.

Over the next two winters, with the England tour of South Africa followed in 2000/01 by trips to Pakistan and Sri Lanka, *Test Match Special* found itself pushed out by Talk, which rebranded itself 'TalkSport'. In this comparatively short space of time you could sometimes hear people saying that, of course, the BBC does not do commentaries from overseas. Meanwhile other listeners would write angrily demanding to know why the BBC was not making sure of these contracts or why they had 'decided not to cover the tour.' That was all very galling.

When this unfortunate run was broken in 2001 for the tour to India, we pushed the boat out. It seemed now that even the BBC accountants were regarding us as an institution worth defending. So we had an engineer with *TMS* for the first time on a tour, Angus Fraser was sent as a summariser – the first time we had done that, having always picked up our experts already in situ – and to prove that *Test Match Special* was really back in business, we had Henry Blofeld there to complement Messrs Agnew and Martin-Jenkins.

Henry had a splendid tour. Aggers appointed himself as his minder, which became a risky business on a bumpy flight from Madras to Lucknow, when, having secured adjacent seats, he discovered that the airline was serving soup. Blowers may have relished it, but Aggers found himself in a noisy and dangerous area. Henry's delight at discovering that the open-sided gents' lavatory at the KSCA Stadium in Bangalore afforded a view of a statue of Queen Victoria ('She looked rather disapproving!') was touching, but he did have recurring disappointments with the sparse nature of Indian wine lists and a complete puzzlement with the refusal of internal flights to serve anything stronger than Pepsi Cola, even though he kept on asking.

A prodigious author of books, his definitive autobiography was titled *A Thirst for Life*, encapsulating the enjoyment of the experience and the various narrow squeaks on operating tables. That enthusiasm is reflected in the one-man shows with which he tours, entertaining his audiences with an array of only slightly tickled-up reminiscences.

Like Arlott and Johnston before them, Blowers and CMJ have provided for thirty-five years the sort of splendid contrast that is so important to *Test Match Special*.

AGGERS
AND THE NEW BOYS

LATE IN THE 1990 CRICKET SEASON I BECAME AWARE
– although he did not tell me – that Christopher Martin-Jenkins
was in negotiation with the *Daily Telegraph* with a view to
becoming their cricket correspondent. This was not a huge
surprise to me, as I could well imagine that E. W. Swanton, with
his ongoing influence at the paper, would be recommending him.
It was more of a disappointment that it was not until mid-
October, shortly before England were to depart on tour to
Australia, that Christopher did ring to tell me that he was going
to the *Telegraph* straight after the tour.

With only one of the five Test matches due to be played before Christmas,
we had agreed to split the tour. I would cover the first half with one Test and
several one-day internationals, with CMJ arriving on Christmas Day, ready
for the Boxing Day Test in Melbourne.

I had already started giving the task of filling the post of BBC cricket
correspondent a great deal of thought. Brian Johnston had suggested to me
that I should give it a go myself, while Don Mosey, still a member of the *TMS*
team since his retirement from the BBC staff, was pushing the claims of Pat
Murphy, the Birmingham-based producer/reporter.

Flying out to Perth at the same time as the team, I gathered in the departure lounge at Heathrow one October evening with the rest of the press corps. Amongst them was a cheery soul on his first tour as a journalist but known to all of us. He had played his last first class match the previous month and now Jonathan Agnew was the correspondent of the *Today* newspaper.

It was in India that I had first met Jonathan Agnew. He was flown out to Calcutta a couple of days before Christmas in 1984 as a replacement for the injured Paul Allott. In that most approachable of all the England cricket teams with which I have toured – thanks to the tone set by the captain, David Gower – he fitted in well with the atmosphere of what was a very successful tour. (He will, however, talk wryly of the way it fell apart when they moved on to Australia to take part in an international one-day tournament to launch the floodlights at the Melbourne Cricket Ground.) Since then I had used him on occasions as a neutral expert summariser for county quarter-finals and semi-finals when we were doing commentaries.

In 1987 the general election campaign included a Saturday morning spot on Radio 4's *Today* programme with three MPs discussing how things were going, with a refreshing lack of partisanship and enormous good humour. By a strange chain of thought, which is probably how all producers get what little inspiration might come their way, I imagined how a similar spot might work for cricket with three county players in conversation. Agnew was the first name I wrote down. When I spoke to him I tried the name of Graeme Fowler on him and I asked them both for a suggested third. They both, independently and unhesitatingly, came up with Vic Marks. Little did Julian Critchley, Austin Mitchell and Charles Kennedy know what they had inspired.

So Agnew, Fowler and Marks started off on 'County Talk' during the first day tea intervals of Test matches. We had to record the session at the close of play in their matches on the eve of Tests, with none of them currently in the England team. This entailed each of them being issued with a small set of broadcasting equipment and having to find the radio point on the ground at which they were playing. Amazingly, it mostly seemed to work, and we did not often have to resort to the telephone. However, it was quickly clear that Aggers was the most adept at the technical side, thanks, no doubt, to his winters spent working at BBC Radio Leicester.

Early in 1988 I came into Broadcasting House one evening to man the *TMS* studio for the overnight broadcast of a day's Test cricket from New Zealand. There on the sports news wires was the information that the Leicestershire fast bowler, Jonathan Agnew, had announced that he would make the coming season his last. I rang him up with the idea of recording a telephone interview which would help to fill the lunch interval at about midnight. He offered to go into Radio Leicester to use their studios and lines which would have the effect that, with better quality, we could run the interview longer. A publisher was driving home late that night, heard the interview, and conceived the idea for a book which would be the Agnew diary of his last season as a cricketer.

In the event, Aggers changed his mind mid-season and played on for another couple of years, but now at Heathrow I felt I could suggest to him that he might like to throw his hat in the ring to be BBC cricket correspondent.

'No,' he said, 'I've got far too good a deal with *Today*.'

As it transpired, in the next few days I was approached by another former Leicestershire player who was interested in the job. At a practice game in a leafy and affluent suburb of Perth, I was joined on my ramble round the ground by David Gower, a somewhat disaffected player on the tour on which he was to exhaust the management's patience with a flight in a Tiger Moth. He enquired about the position in the sort of jocular fashion that would give him a get-out if necessary, but afterwards I came to the conclusion that he was serious. Later in the tour he was to confirm that when, on one of those fierce Perth days when you keep to the air-conditioning of your hotel, we murdered a decent bottle of sauvignon together, while discussing the possibilities.

By that time, however, I had received another application.

Having just retired from the first class game, Aggers had packed his bowling boots and offered his services as a net bowler if the England team needed him. It had been made clear all round that if he picked up some team tittle-tattle as a result of being on the other side of the fence, he would not use it in his newspaper and even *Today* seemed happy with that. While he was bowling in the Perth nets he did become aware of some minor altercation, but adhered to his promise. Unfortunately it appeared in the *Daily Star* and the *Today* sports desk picked up the story and used it, unforgivably giving it the Jonathan Agnew by-line. Aggers was furious and, as we walked back together from the WACA (Western Australia Cricket Association) ground through Queen's Gardens to the hotel, he said, 'So you can put my name in the hat for BBC correspondent.'

The match immediately before Christmas was a low-key three-day game at Ballarat, in Victoria, and for the purely selfish purpose of getting myself home for Christmas Day, I asked Aggers to cover it with reports. I had a telephone ordered for this and I armed him with other gadgets to see him through. Having checked that all was in order at the ground, I drove back to Melbourne for my flight home. Aggers was still a little self-conscious, however, and had the phone moved from the press box to the relative intimacy of the groundsman's hut next door. It was only relatively intimate because the groundsman kept in the hut, alongside his mowers, a rather large Alsatian.

Discussing the possibilities on my return, Aggers was my recommendation, and ultimately became the correspondent in time for the start of the 1991 season. His first match reports were on the season's traditional chilly opener between MCC and the champion county at Lord's in April. As the time for his first live update approached, he rather diffidently asked me to leave the commentary box, as he was still very self-conscious about doing these reports. I must have anticipated something of the sort – probably following the tales of Ballarat – so I had a small radio in my pocket and was able to keep an ear on these early efforts.

By coincidence, as I was leaving the ground quite some time after the close of play on the first day of that game, thanks to interviews and follow-up pieces and a bit of a debrief with Aggers, I ran into the new cricket correspondent of the *Daily Telegraph*. CMJ had had a bit of a baptism of fire, too, I discovered, with a lengthy and weighty piece being required of him. It had evidently been a landmark day in the cricket media.

On the county circuit Jonathan had usually been known as 'Aggie' or 'Spiro' – the latter showing that American politics must be a hot topic in county dressing rooms, following Richard Nixon's vice-president, Spiro Agnew. A matter of minutes working alongside Brian Johnston made sure that he was 'Aggers' for ever more.

For his first season as BBC cricket correspondent, I thought it sensible to ease him in as an expert summariser, supporting the commentators and getting the feel of the box for the five-Test series with the West Indies. He was able to cut his teeth on commentary on the county quarter- and semi-finals in the two cup competitions. Then he made the switch to the ball-by-ball description for the last Test of the 1991 summer, a one-off match with Sri Lanka at Lord's.

It was, I suppose, something of a poisoned chalice for a commentary debut, when one looks at the list of names on the scorecard. Our knowledge of Sri Lankan cricketers was a lot sparser than it is now, though Aggers did have the advantage of having played a Test against them in 1984 and had toured there with an England 'A' team. Nonetheless, for that match we were kindly lent by the Sri Lankan dressing room a member of the playing squad who acted as a race-reader, pointing at the fielders' names on the scorecard. Unfortunately, while that was a great help for most of our team on the first morning of the match, Don Mosey had left his reading glasses at his hotel and all the names were a blur, a situation which reduced him to a fit of giggles to the mystification of our helper – one Marvan Atapattu.

Before that Test Match, Brian Johnston and I had accepted an invitation from the Sri Lankan High Commission to a reception for the cricket team. Brian reckoned it would be an excellent chance to identify some of them. One charming young man came up to us to introduce himself, slightly mischievously. 'I am Wijegunawardene,' he said. But seeing Brian's look of horror at the apparent tongue-twister, he laughed and said, 'In Australia the commentators called me "Alphabet".'

Brian found the name on the crib sheet he was clutching. 'I shall call you Weejers,' he announced. 'He won't play, will he?' he muttered to me afterwards. But he did and, far from calling him Weejers, Brian made him sound like a Wagnerian operatic hero – 'Veejay Goona Vaardinner'.

For all the problems that identifying and pronouncing Sri Lankan names might have caused him, Aggers sailed through and by that time I was not surprised. It was quite clear he was a natural and had been relaxed enough by the Fifth Test with the West Indies to have been the catalyst for one of the most celebrated, or perhaps notorious, moments in sports broadcasting. It is now just known as 'the leg-over'.

At the close of play, in those days, we used to have a commentator and one of the summarisers going through the scorecard together in detail. On the second day at the Oval, that lot fell to Messrs Johnston and Agnew. During the day's play, Ian Botham had been out hit wicket when, in trying to hook a short ball from Curtly Ambrose, he had lost his balance and had tried unsuccessfully to vault the stumps as he did so. He had brushed off a bail with his thigh as he went.

Shortly after this, Aggers, as he does, had paid a visit to the press box and there the correspondent of the *Sun* had planted the idea that Botham 'couldn't get his leg over'. The die was cast. As the close-of-play summary went along, Brian and Jonathan got to the incident of the Botham wicket. In fact, they were almost done with the subject when Aggers casually threw in the line, 'Yeah, he just couldn't quite get his leg over.'

At this crucial point Brian always claimed subsequently to have been more professional than at any other time in his career – for all of thirty seconds. True, he gave a little sort of hiccup, but then he carried on manfully.

I had seen the potential for catastrophe and after a momentary thought, *Did he really say that?* I had made sure that nobody caught his eye to cause him to falter. To his right, Bill Frindall was still working away on his various sheets and appeared not to have fully heard the remark, but I made him lean back in his chair, and Aggers too, on Brian's left. The other man on the commentary desk, busily writing his reports for the *Nation* newspaper in Barbados, was Tony Cozier, who was keeping his head down.

By this time Brian's professional thirty seconds had run its course and he had apparently rerun the 'leg-over' remark in his head. It started with a little half chuckle. He became aware of Aggers laughing silently beside him. His 'Do stop it, Aggers' was probably an attempt to keep himself going, but he was now completely and hopelessly lost. The descent into incomprehensible, wheezing laughter was inevitable and rapid. Aggers had long since caught the infection of the giggle and was a lost cause, so my helpless behind the scenes appeal, 'Somebody say something!', might not have been all that well advised.

'Yes, Lawrence played extremely well ...' was all Aggers could chuckle before the whole thing disintegrated, but still Johnners tried to keep going and amazingly, he came through eventually with 'I've stopped laughing now', but it had felt like an age.

That whole incident has passed into folklore. It seems that there is no one in Britain who has not heard it. I have played it to cricket societies up and down the land and, though they all know what is coming, none can keep a straight face. Brian's laugh has that effect. Incredibly, Radio 5 Live listeners voted the incident the greatest sporting commentary of all time, even though it was not a commentary. Nonetheless, Brian and I left the Oval that Friday evening with the feeling of disaster weighing us down. Jonathan wondered if maybe he had taken the old boy a bit too far.

Next morning we heard it had been replayed on Radio 2 and was the talk of the airwaves. Someone even suggested putting it up for a Sony Radio

Award, which in the light of the preparation behind most of the entries might have been a step too far.

The taste for initiating the odd 'wind-up' was certainly not diminished in Aggers by this hiatus in an evening's broadcast. His next 'corpse' with Johnners was perhaps more accidental. Doing a similar summary together in 1992 Brian suggested that Javed Miandad had 'opened his legs like a croquet hoop'. They caught each other's eye and were lost in soundless and incapacitating mirth. After that I decreed that they must not be trusted on the air together.

The following year *Test Match Special* was going through one of its many crisis periods where planners were finding it awkward to place. In the aftermath of the Thatcher-inspired Peacock Report, the BBC had been required to give up two of its AM frequencies, and one of these had been the home of *TMS*. Now we were to be divided between Radio 5 in the mornings and Radio 3 – but only on FM – for the last two sessions of play.

Radio 5 required a more up-beat opening than we had been accustomed to. There was a signature tune (chosen by someone else) with a seven-second headline woven into an appropriate pause in the music. Aggers used to record this before we went on the air and then open the programme. With the confidence of relative youth, he reckoned that he was the only member of the commentary team who could do it. 'Wouldn't it be funny,' he put it to me, 'to tell Johnners he has to do it one day.'

I ventured that Brian, being such a consummate old pro, would probably be fine with it, even though it was not really his style of broadcasting, but I went along with it. On Sunday mornings, because of a tighter schedule, we did not have to use the signature tune, but we guessed that Brian might not have spotted this. So the plot was hatched. The idea was that Aggers, having gone home from Leeds to Leicester overnight, had been delayed on the motorway, so Johnners would have to stand in and record the opening headline into the music. It went something along the lines of, '420 runs behind, with only three wickets in hand. Can England force a draw?' As I had suspected, Brian was pretty well spot on, though we had fun with his declarations of, 'I'm a one-take man!' I kept him at it, telling him it was half a second too short or too long, but when I had to agree it was perfect, the wily old bird said, 'It's a leg-pull, isn't it?'

Aggers was very pleased with the way it had gone, but behind his back another, even more intricate plot was forming.

The excellent BBC television floor manager, Steve Pierson, had been aware of what had been going on and came up to Johnners and me with a suggestion. Why didn't they do a TV interview with Jonathan, making him believe he was live on the air when he was not, and ask him really awkward questions?

I liked the idea, but thought we might just turn it around. 'Why not have him handling some really awkward interviewees? He's keen to do some television, so he'll jump at the chance to do it and if he's in the chair he'll have to keep going.'

The trap was set for a Saturday tea interval at Edgbaston. The subject had been decided as the desperate need to find a new generation of England fast bowlers. Aggers would interview Jack Bannister and Fred Trueman, believing himself to be live on *Grandstand*. To my surprise, the television producer, Keith Mackenzie, who had never been any sort of friend to his radio colleagues, joined in the spirit of the thing.

Aggers was placed on the scaffolding gantry above the commentary boxes beside his two guests. I asked Steve if he had a make-up bag. 'Good idea,' he said and at the last minute affected to take a message in his earpiece. 'Too shiny? OK.' With that he buried Aggers' face in a powder puff.

Fred Trueman was asked first about the fast bowling problem and he responded with a long-winded and completely incomprehensible answer. So Aggers turned to the always sensible Jack Bannister. 'I agree with Fred,' was all he offered. Now Aggers knew he was in trouble. So the twelve-minute interview continued as Aggers' panic rose. Fred's cigar smoke drifted in front of him and, as he struggled on, it did occur to him that some trick might be being played, but he dismissed that thought when he looked up at the number of people involved. At the end, he was about to throw down the uncomfortable earpiece through which Keith Mackenzie had been badgering him to make the pair answer his questions, when he heard Brian's voice from the TV control truck.

'Has the big-nosed commentator got his revenge?'

'Bastard! Bastard!' was all the BBC cricket correspondent could offer. He still recalls the horror of the experience.

By that time I had been away on the first of more than twenty overseas tours that I was to share with Aggers.

It was to the World Cup early in 1992 in Australia and New Zealand. When I met him in Sydney, he had already covered England's successful tour of New Zealand, sharing commentary with the local team. We had had a few lengthy middle-of-the-night live conversations on the air in rain breaks, in which we discovered our potential to talk endlessly about practically nothing at all.

That 1992 World Cup was certainly the best since the competition lost its innocence after the first three tournaments in England. It even survived the Australian marketing men's efforts. For a start it was a round-robin, with everyone playing everyone else up to the semi-final stage. There was only one non-Test-playing country involved – Zimbabwe – and they had their big moment when they beat England at their first attempt. To cap it all, it was the big return to the fold for South Africa, after the years of isolation over the apartheid regime. There was an awful rule to settle rain-affected games, but despite its high profile appearance in the semi-final between England and South Africa, it had little influence on the outcome.

I had asked for an extra man to help us cover the spread of the tournament, but that had been declined, so Aggers and I travelled hither and thither, not always with each other, putting together commentary teams wherever we needed to, or joining local ones. The vast area meant that on the first day I called New Zealand home for their win against Australia in Auckland and then passed to Aggers in Perth only two overs into England's floodlit game against India.

On the final day of the round-robin, Pakistan could go through only by breaking New Zealand's one hundred per cent record and then hoping that Australia, who had had a wretched time, beat the West Indies. Both those results came to pass and we had an extraordinary day's cricket coverage, started by Blowers in Christchurch, then Aggers and CMJ with the commentary on England's debacle against Zimbabwe in Aldbury-Wodonga, and finally I reported from a floodlit Melbourne Cricket Ground on Australia putting the West Indies out of – and Pakistan into – the semi-final.

Time difference then made it possible for me to commentate on both semi-finals and the final. I remember the close-of-play interview with a shocked Martin Crowe in Auckland after his New Zealand side had seemed home and dry, only to run into a youngster called Inzamam-ul-Haq; then, late the next night, squatting on the floor in the Sydney pavilion to get the explanation of the chaos at the end of the second semi-final, when South Africa had needed 22 runs off one ball after the rain break; and finally Imran Khan, in his celebrated tiger T-shirt, explaining calmly how his team had come from no-hopers to take the World Cup.

A year later we were in India, where I can still remember the warmth of the welcome I received from a relieved Agnew, after he had covered the opening two matches on his own in the trying circumstances of a pilot's strike and religious unrest. The latter led to the first one-day international being cancelled and the former made for some interesting journeys in the first half of the tour before it was resolved.

The Board of Control for Cricket in India largely washed their hands of England's travel arrangements, apparently unconcerned about how, or indeed whether, they could make it from their three-day game in Cuttack to Calcutta for the First Test. But the England tour manager, Bob Bennett, showed determination and enterprise in having an extra carriage attached to the back of the Puri to Howrah night express train for the combined use of the team and the travelling press. Thus I found myself reclining on the next shelf to Aggers while a game of cards and a frightened field mouse held sway below. I was a little surprised to hear our correspondent describe the diminutive animal as 'a plague of giant rats' on the radio a little later, but it was no more of an exaggeration than calling that most ponderous of trains an 'express'.

Even after the strike was resolved we had some extraordinary travels on that trip. Between one-day internationals in Bangalore and Jamshedpur, we first had an afternoon flight to Calcutta with an apparently mad pilot, who invited us to look out of the right hand side during the flight up the coast, 'to see the shadow of my beautiful aeroplane'. This was followed shortly by a very bumpy landing in Calcutta, during which the cockpit door flew open and we could see panicky wrestling with the controls, while a cry of 'Aieee!' was broadcast inadvertently on the intercom. Aggers and I speculated about whether it was a shout of joy at having landed, or one of sheer terror.

We knew that our troubles were not over that day, as we had a bus ride to the hinterland of West Bengal for which advance estimates varied between eight and twelve hours. (In the end it split the difference at ten, but only because the driver missed Jamshedpur in the dark and drove for half an hour past it.) Aggers decided to go for the back seat of the bus and stretch out for a sleep, which judging from the oath at every bump – and there are a few between Calcutta and Jamshedpur – may have been a mistake.

Somewhere in the wilds we came to an abrupt halt. Bandits, known there as 'dacoits', had laid a log across the road to hold us up. We had with us a courier by the name of Raju, who had not always found dealing with the contrasting demands of the British press all that easy. He claimed noble blood as a descendant of the Rajput princes of Rajasthan and so, at the outrage of this proposed highway robbery, he bravely and nobly descended the steps of the bus. We could hear a lot of agitated chatter and after about ten minutes he appeared again, the door shut, the tree trunk was moved, and on we went.

We were intrigued and those who had been dozing uncomfortably were now fully awake. 'What did you say, Raju? How did you get rid of them?'

The little man drew himself up to his full four foot three. 'I told them to fuck off!' he declared. His time with the British press had not been wasted after all.

For all these tours, any battle to get *Test Match Special* on the air was more likely to be with programme planners than with cricket boards. All that changed when TalkSport (then still known as Talk Radio) did their secret deal with the United Cricket Board of South Africa in 1999. My proposal was a close-of-play programme to be called *TMS Report*, to contain a few highlights recorded from the local SABC commentary, player interviews and expert guest opinion, all held together by Aggers. We were to do this for two tours of South Africa, and one each of Pakistan, Sri Lanka and West Indies.

Jonathan may have done it brilliantly – and it was not easy under the pressure of time that we set ourselves in order to make it up to date – but he is very much a commentary animal. Indeed, after that first season in the expert summariser's chair, he has always resisted any move to repeat it, even when circumstances would have made it handy to have done so for a short period. So to be covering a Test match with only reports left him very frustrated and sometimes quite grumpy.

In Sri Lanka in 2001, when TalkSport had the rights, we were assiduously following our allocation of two minutes' reporting every hour and then doing *TMS Report* back at the hotel each evening. However, on the second morning of the First Test at Galle, we were met at the gates of the ground by a security guard refusing us entry. The two media managers of the Sri Lankan Board, who had previously been quite friendly, were lurking in the background, but refused to come and explain what the problem was. As it became apparent that this might be a lengthy stand-off, I asked Aggers to go round to the southern end of the ground where the walls of the old Dutch fort overlook the playing area and always attract a smattering of non-paying spectators. I suggested that he should not try to exceed our legal two minutes an hour, even when we would be operating outside the ground.

Off he went with Simmonds, our trusty driver, and set up his station depending on battery power and our portable satellite dish, a device which has revolutionised all our reporting around the world. Simmonds held an umbrella over him to provide shade, while photographers had a field day snapping the scene. Meanwhile, in the dust outside the locked gates, with a busy bus station at my back, I attempted to make some contact with Sri Lankan officials. Rumour had it that they had decided, although they had not allowed us to bid for the rights to broadcast the series, they would quite like to take some money off us now. But they seemed reluctant to discuss the issue. I talked by mobile phone to the television company who held all the broadcasting rights and established that they were perfectly happy for us to continue as before, so the problem seemed to be only with the board.

Eventually, it was the arrival of the chief executive of the England and Wales Cricket Board, Tim Lamb, that broke the stalemate. After a chat with me he suggested to his opposite number that this scene did little for the reputation of the game of cricket. I was admitted to the ground and those who had been refusing to speak to me now became all sweetness and light again. Such are the ways of the mysterious Orient.

In the VIP box Tim's wife, Denise, delighted in pointing out to me Aggers and his entourage on the fort walls at the far end. So I rang him and invited him to return. Bizarrely, the security guard who had first refused me entry reckoned subsequently he had become my greatest friend and when he was also on duty for the Third Test of the series in Colombo, greeted me most warmly.

At the time that I left *Test Match Special* I was in no doubt that its future depended in no small part on Jonathan Agnew. He is only too well aware of this burden of responsibility, but his hands are safe ones. In time he is bound to lose the company of Christopher and Henry. Already part of the team is Simon Mann, who made his debut as long ago as 1996 in Bulawayo.

Simon has himself been a good travelling companion on various overseas tours. Before he joined us in Zimbabwe on that tour, he had covered several England 'A' tours, which made him friends among players and press men who, like him, graduated to the senior tours. He is a very useful club cricketer, who keeps himself fit. His loudly expressed disappointment when a perfectly legitimate goal in a rain-soaked press football match in Trinidad was disallowed was testimony to his competitive spirit.

I enjoyed a very relaxed fortnight in Sri Lanka in 2002 with him and Jonny Saunders, covering the ICC Champions' Trophy. It might not have been quite so relaxed for Simon, who had just left the BBC staff to go freelance and thus only earned his full fee on days when he worked. So the rest days between commentary matches were busy for him as he volunteered for any interviews that might be needed.

Part of the easy-going nature of that trip was brought about by England's early exit, which meant that, although we were committed to commentaries on the semi-finals and final, there was little demand for us to do much else. However, we did enjoy the moment when that most amiable of characters, Jonny Saunders, was paged by the hotel front desk as 'Mr Surrenders'. For some of us that has remained his nickname.

England's first tour of Bangladesh in 2003 was another that Simon and I shared. The original proposal for England's two short pre-Christmas tours that year was that we would not mount a *Test Match Special* from either Bangladesh or Sri Lanka, which seemed to me to be a dangerous piece of value judgement by programme planners. If the ICC deems it to be a Test match, who are the BBC to say it is not really up to scratch. My argument held sway for the three Tests in Sri Lanka, but I failed to persuade them over the two in Bangladesh that preceded them.

Simon had his fortieth birthday on that tour, celebrated in Chittagong, where we occupied the Hotel Harbour View – a misnomer on both counts. It is the depressing return every morning to the same food stain on the breakfast table cloth, in a windowless and dingy dining room, that makes one wonder if this is quite the romantic way of life some suppose it to be. But on this occasion I discovered the unlikely combination of a Hallmark card shop (quite what the locals made of some of the messages, I could not guess) and a cake shop and, with a card from his infant daughter, Isobel, produced by Vic Marks, that lightened up the great day. We celebrated at a joint players and press quiz night – the sort of occasion which now occurs only in such beleaguered situations.

Our communications from Bangladesh for our regular reports were rudimentary, but everyone there bent over backwards to be helpful. In Dhaka the authorities provided us with a runner to attend to our every need. This sad-faced youth had an accreditation card round his neck proclaiming him to be 'BBC BOY', but since we shared no word of common language his presence was fairly pointless. He hung around mournfully, occupying precious space in our tiny commentary box, but nonetheless felt that he had earned his tip at the end of the series.

Simon's finest hour was probably on the extraordinary evening when Pakistan forfeited the Test match at the Oval in 2006. No information was being offered by the authorities as to what was going on, when Inzamam refused to bring his team out after tea on the fourth day to resume the match, following the penalty of five runs being imposed by the umpires for ball tampering. While Jonathan Agnew held the fort in the commentary box, I despatched Simon, with our production assistant, Shilpa Patel, to the far end of the ground where the dressing rooms were situated, to report by radio microphone on any developments.

In the commentary box we were sustained by a flood of emailed opinion from our listeners, sadly and irrationally dividing mostly on purely nationalistic grounds. As the time ticked away, two of our summarisers, Mike Selvey and Angus Fraser, found themselves up against newspaper deadlines and Geoffrey Boycott felt he had said what he wanted to on the subject, so, gallantly, CMJ sat beside Aggers, writing his report for *The Times*, while providing Aggers with a sounding board on the air. Meanwhile Simon interviewed anyone who could shed any light on proceedings at the Pavilion End (and a few who could not).

On that evening, radio certainly won the information battle with television hands down. Simon was a crucial part of that and so, of course, was Shilpa, who has been assisting the production of *Test Match Special* for well over a decade. That evening she did what she does best, persuading the key people to come and talk to the programme. Set the challenge of getting a guest for *TMS*, principally for the 'A View From the Boundary' spot, she will move heaven and earth to accomplish it. I have always maintained that if I had said that I heard the Pope was rather keen on cricket, he would be walking through the commentary box door within the hour.

The production assistant's job has grown over the years, since Michael Tuke-Hastings' secretary, Brenda, used to help me with the cricket paperwork. Three of her successors stand out. Kate Hempsall, a Yorkshire lass, who went on from *TMS* to be a very popular media relations officer for Surrey and then to become involved in public relations in the commercial world; Louise Jones, for balance a supporter of the red rose, who was the first in the job actually to come to the Test matches on site and whose meticulous efficiency meant that I could safely forget most of the administrative drudgery; and Shilpa Patel, Kenyan-born, but a passionate Middlesex supporter, whose ability to charm the birds off the trees was a delightful contrast to the withering greeting that commentators who were careless about notifying her of changes in their arrangements might receive. These have all been crucial *Test Match Special* team members.

For the long-term commentary future of *TMS*, Simon Mann should be a sound stalwart alongside Aggers. Other commentators will be needed. Mark Saggers is among the new generation, a brilliant schoolboy wicket-keeper/batsman who went on to play Minor Counties cricket for Cambridgeshire, he first came to *Test Match Special* as a production assistant in the 1980s, but then left for higher things in Sky News. His return to the BBC fold has been principally as presenter of the evening *Five Live Sport* programmes, but for his own benefit and for *TMS*, an accommodation should be worked on between what are sometimes conflicting interests. Another programme presenter who made a *TMS* debut in 2008 is Mark Pougatch, who was certainly confident and promising enough, but for whom *TMS* is unlikely ever to be the main interest.

The big problem in determining the heirs of the pillars of *Test Match Special* commentary has been the paucity of quality training slopes. *TMS* itself really needs only about three top-notch commentators to call on at any time. BBC managers' preference seems to be to look no further than their own offices. This policy has given us Jonny Saunders, Arlo White, Mark Pougatch and – regrettably briefly – John Murray, but *TMS* should be special and use only the best possible commentators, and cast its net wider. The successor of Martin-Jenkins or Blofeld, or eventually of Agnew, might well be now among the ranks of county cricketers, in a press box somewhere or perhaps, like John Arlott, even pounding the beat in a police uniform.

THE EXPERTS

IF THE BALL-BY-BALL COMMENTATOR IS THE CAMERA, he has alongside him the expert to interpret the detail of the picture. We tend to refer to this expert – for Test matches, this would be a former Test player – as the summariser, and it does not, of course, suggest that the commentator is inexpert. This is a different system from television, where two expert summarisers discuss what the cameras are showing.

When I first walked through the commentary box door at the Oval, the regular incumbent summarisers were two former England captains, Freddie Brown and Norman Yardley. Freddie gave the impression of the bucolic country squire, with tweed suit and pipe. Memorably, when he bowled England to victory in the final Test of the 1950/51 tour of Australia, they were selling cabbages in the markets with 'hearts as big as Freddie Brown's'. His bluff manner could be a little daunting, but I did have one point of contact when I first encountered him, having been at school with his son, Christopher, himself a talented cricketer.

Norman was the most charming and welcoming of men. It was he, on the same Oval ground where I first met him, who had called his England team to give three cheers when Donald Bradman came in to play his last Test innings in 1948. Distressingly, when I was appointed cricket producer, one of the earliest duties I was charged with was to ring him and tell him that we were dispensing with his services. Characteristically, he made it as easy as possible for the embarrassed young man and whenever we met subsequently he was always very friendly. The last time I saw him was at his home in a leafy part of Sheffield, when I sat him down to record his memories of Sonny Ramadhin bowling West Indies to victory in 1950.

One of the features of *Test Match Special* when I took it over was the close-of-play summary by E. W. Swanton. He had started with the BBC as a commentator, going to South Africa to cover the tour there in 1938/39 and having the opportunity to commentate live on a Test match hat-trick. Listening to the archive recordings of his commentaries from 1948, I formed the opinion that ball-by-ball description did not come as naturally to him as his close-of-play essays. He started those in the 1950s and in them he really achieved his broadcasting pinnacle on radio and on television.

It was always a sign that the end of a day's play must be approaching when Swanton (always 'Jim', never his given name of Ernest) would enter the box. Alan Gibson, the last commentator of the day, once announced this arrival with, 'The close of play must be near, as the Angel of Death has arrived.' Swanton was not amused.

As the young producer, I would be clearing the place for him to sit. A stop-watch set at midday to give him the precise time would be put in front of him, with a card on which would be written the time to finish. The time on the card was all he would need and definitely not someone sticking up a finger in front of him to indicate one minute to go. For my first year he would give me the sonorous command every time: 'No signals!'

Those were the days of the 6.30 p.m. close of play, rather than today's need to complete ninety overs in the day. Nonetheless, Jim's nominal ten-minute summary could well be halved if a fast bowler were to start the final over half a minute before 6.30. So his preparations had to be for anything from five to ten minutes. He controlled the timing by always insisting on giving the final read of the scorecard himself. (Again, the mischievous Gibson, who knew this well, was always tempted to read it anyway in the last over.)

The summary was delivered with the authority of his experience and care for the game, from only the barest notes. It would be a masterful, unscripted essay and was probably a run-through of the final version of his *Daily Telegraph* report on the day. The great Jack Hobbs, seen leaving Lord's early on a Test match day, assured a friend that it was all right, because Swanton would tell him all he needed to know about the day.

Lord Runcie, the former Archbishop of Canterbury, in giving the address at his funeral in 2000, said that Jim 'was not a man plagued by self-doubt'. Brian Johnston always enjoyed poking fun at his legendary pomposity, usually with the old gag that he was too important to travel in the same car as his chauffeur. On one occasion, as he was about to deliver the close-of-play summary and had hung his jacket over the back of his chair, Brian pulled back Swanton's braces as if to let them snap into his back. There was no reaction from Jim as he started talking and Brian eased them back gently. Afterwards Jim said, just like a weary schoolmaster, 'Oh, Johnston. Always fourth form.'

That may be a mild example of the courage that had seen him through his harsh wartime incarceration in a Japanese prisoner of war camp. Here he kept up morale with mocked-up commentaries on imaginary Test matches, fuelled by his most precious possession – his 1939 *Wisden Almanack*. I know of former comrades who served under him in the Bedfordshire Yeomanry who held him always in the highest possible regard and he always kept in touch with them.

After he finished his *TMS* close-of-play pieces in the mid-1970s, Jim recorded a series of advance obituaries on cricketers, to sit on the shelf until they were needed, shrewdly insisting on being paid for them at the time of recording, rather than waiting until they were used. One day when he was coming into the studio to record four or five of these, he told me that he had been staying the night with Sir George 'Gubby' Allen. Swanton had told him over breakfast what he had been going into the BBC to do. 'But I didn't have the heart to tell him that his was one of the ones I was doing.'

There is one other person who was there in the corner of the *TMS* box on my first acquaintance with it. Amazingly, he was still there when I retired from it. (I think he had moved a little in the interim.) Bill Frindall had started scoring for *Test Match Special* at the beginning of that 1966 season. In the intervening forty-two years his beard became a little greyer, but his attention to detail remained as insistent and the concentration he owes to RAF training as intense, even if his patience with commentators asking him for obscure records had worn somewhat thinner.

We were all shattered by the news of his death after a short illness early in 2009. Bill had just been one of those ever-present features of the programme – as much for the listeners as for us – and it was impossible to imagine him not being there.

We all owe a great deal to being in the right place at the right time and in the wake of a spate of deaths among the scoring fraternity, starting with the father of broadcast scoring, Arthur Wrigley, Bill was ready, willing, and able to step in. The crucial skill, of course, once you have found yourself in that well-timed right place, is not to blow the opportunity and Bill made sure of that. John Arlott took him under his wing, recognising his use, not only as a supplier of statistics, but also as a chauffeur. Bill always quoted Arlott's welcome to him: 'I hear you like driving. Well, I like drinking. We're going to get on well.'

Then, when Brian Johnston moved over to radio, he created Bill's role as his straight man, christening him 'The Bearded Wonder', inevitably shortened to 'Bearders'. Bill shared with Brian the complete inability to let any opportunity for a pun go by, but his humour was infinitely drier and became more laconic as the years passed. He was certainly in the front rank of the commentary box chucklers, a fact I was only too well aware of as the 'leg-over' incident unfolded.

New commentators – and even their seniors – trod carefully, wary of a swift put-down if they overstepped the mark, and woe betide any careless broadcaster who spilt anything on the precious and pristine scoresheets. But it was a sign of his skill that his colleagues in the box took a childish delight if he made a rare mistake. His wife, Debbie, was frequently on hand, to telephone his copy to the newspaper in pre-broadband days and to provide a more palatable alternative to the boxed lunch that might be on offer.

Bill would play the game whenever he got the chance, bringing a whole new meaning to the term 'hairy fast bowler'. He ran his own wandering team, the Maltamaniacs, but much of his cricket would be played in support of charity. He was President of British Blind Sport and his premature death followed a trip to Dubai with the Lord's Taverners. Such involvement, as well as being the longest serving member of the programme, helped to make him a proud MBE in 2004.

By the time Norman Yardley and Freddie Brown finished on *Test Match Special*, Trevor Bailey had already been part of the team for six years and in 1974 Fred Trueman appeared in the box. A new summarising partnership had been born that was to last a quarter of a century.

Trevor and Fred were a wonderful double act. Unspoken, their relationship was like the amateur captain and his senior professional. My memory of meeting Fred for the first time was in the commentary box in the pavilion at Lord's. He surveyed the wonderful sight of the sunlit 'Home of Cricket' filling up in anticipation of the day's play and pronounced, 'It makes you feel like a bloody amateur.' Trevor would have given a remark like that a wry smile, but they had enormous respect for each other.

A good long grumble from Fred, usually ending with 'I just don't know what's going off out there,' was something to be savoured, though on his most grumpy days he might make life quite hard for the commentator beside him. John Arlott once reacted with, 'But, Fred, you're paid to know what's going off out there,' while the Australian commentator, Neville Oliver, once finding Fred silently opening his mail at the end of an over, gave him a prompt.

'Fred.'

'Yes?'

'You're supposed to say something now.'

'Oh, I can't watch this rubbish.'

It took a very special player to command Fred's respect, having been a great player himself, the first to three hundred Test wickets, and having played with some of the best.

Trevor once asked me if I thought he was too critical and certainly he could be quite scathing, but his criticisms were always reasoned and he was just as likely to come out with one of his trademark comments, 'Nice little player … like him in my side.' Such clipped remarks encouraged Brian Johnston to nickname him after the Dickens character from *The Pickwick Papers*, 'Mr. Jingle'.

It was Trevor who first suggested the idea of a *Test Match Special* phone-in. He envisaged a technical coaching session by telephone. We started this as 'Cricket Clinic', which proved rather a mouthful to announce. It was suggested by Don Mosey that 'Cricket Surgery' might have been easier. Trevor's idea was that club or schoolboy cricketers might ring in to talk through technical problems with their game, but these were soon swamped by more general enquiries and opinions on the game, so the lunchtime session opened out and eventually became known as 'Call the Commentators'.

Trevor had, of course, been an all-rounder in the classic sense, worth his place in a side as either batsman or bowler. Indeed on occasions he opened both the batting and the bowling in Tests. But I always felt that in the expert summariser's chair he thought like a bowler and I have an instinctive theory that it is bowlers who generally make the best summarisers. Maybe it is the thought that every bowler has to give to the plotting of a batsman's downfall. Many batsmen are closer to relying on instinct.

Trevor's nickname, 'The Boil', came from his Cambridge days, when he was playing football abroad, alongside Doug Insole. The ground public address announced the Cambridge forwards as 'Eynsole and Boiley'. 'Boil' stuck.

During the Oval Test match of 1988, a massive banner appeared on the gasholder: 'GAS BRINGS TEA TO THE BOIL (AND FRED)'. It was part of an extravagant British Gas advertising plan which changed each day. The previous day we had been honoured with: 'FIVE DAYS OF NON-STOP GAS. TEST MATCH SPECIAL WE SALUTE YOU' and the next day it was: 'MAKE HIS DAY. BAKE JOHNNERS A CHOCOLATE CAKE'. Unfortunately, the match finished in four days, which prevented us getting to the last one they had prepared: 'GAS MAKES YOU COZIER'.

With that stalwart pair's departure from *TMS* we lost the huge fund of Fred's stories and memories. A rain session in the box could be transformed by Fred drawing not only on his own time in the game, but on his knowledge of much that had gone before. I can remember a wet day at Headingley when Aggers was joined by Mike Hendrick, and those two England bowlers of later generations started off, with tongues in cheeks, mischievously asking Fred about how he would have bowled in times past. An hour or so later they were still spellbound by the great man.

I think it was Fred who suggested to me that Colin Milburn, the former swashbuckling and Falstaffian Northamptonshire and England batsman, would make a good addition to the commentary team. To join us, Colin always had to get leave of absence from his job at Butlin's Holiday Camp, and would bring all the jovial good humour which presumably he had been bestowing on the holidaymakers there. His cricketing career had been cut short, just when it appeared to be at its zenith, by a car crash that cost him the sight of one eye and damaged the other, but there was not a hint of bitterness at this cruel hand of fate. He was there to enjoy life.

Unfortunately he had the capability to enjoy it overmuch on occasion. One Headingley Test went into the weekend rest day with a very wet Saturday, during which Colin – known to all as 'Ollie', after the similarly rotund Oliver Hardy – fell in with two England players who were not involved in the match, Messrs Lamb and Botham. When he returned to the box to join in the current discussion, it quickly became apparent that he had lost some conciseness of reason to the grape or the grain. I hauled him away from the microphone and he was contrite. He assured me that I could still rely on him to be at the ground as scheduled at 8.25 a.m. on Monday to report on conditions for Radio 4's *Today* programme. This was important, because I was going home for Sunday and would probably not be back at the ground by then.

On Monday morning, as I approached Leeds, I was listening to Radio 4 in the car. I heard Garry Richardson say that we would now get the latest from Colin Milburn in Leeds. (I wondered, Why did he not say 'at Headingley'?)

'What's the weather like there, Colin?'

I heard the telephone line. What had gone wrong? I knew the engineers were meant to be there to get Ollie on the air.

'I'll just go and draw the curtains and have a look, Garry,' came the familiar Geordie voice. He had still been in bed after the Saturday afternoon bender had continued on Sunday. I had to fight to keep his place for the final Test at the Oval, but there he did not let me down again, mortified as he was by what had happened.

From 1974 to 1999 Fred Trueman and Trevor Bailey were at the heart of *Test Match Special*. Fred in particular, however, polarised opinions. *TMS* without him was unthinkable to some. To others, it was unlistenable with him. Opinions were expressed that their view of the game was too rooted in the past, and an expert summariser's worth is in what he can tell you about what it is like to be actually out there, in the middle at this moment. The ECB were making it known, with an air of menace, that they felt the pair were a little too negative about the modern game. I would never want to bow to that sort of pressure, but the signs were there that it might be time to move on.

In the event, after the 1999 season, probably knowing how difficult I would find it to dispense with the services of two old friends, the then Head of Sport, Bob Shennan, took the bull by the horns and rang each of them to tell them that this was the end. Then he told me how hard it had been. Unfortunately, both of them held it against me. On reflection, it was the right thing to do, even though we subsequently missed both of them at times. The new 'Trevor and Fred' became Vic Marks and Mike Selvey.

The best England tour that I went on did not have the most promising of beginnings. For a start, I was not too keen to go on it. I had previously toured India with Don Mosey, and then Australia, where the enjoyment of that country had been slightly dampened by an antagonistic sports editor at the

London end. Now I would miss my daughter's first birthday and her first Christmas, for three months in India. Don Mosey had retired and Christopher Martin-Jenkins was returning for his second spell as BBC cricket correspondent in the New Year.

In October 1984, I was on the England team flight that landed in Delhi. Five hours later, the Indian Prime Minister, Indira Gandhi, was assassinated.

Under curfew together for a week in our Delhi hotel, the team and, at that stage, the relatively small press corps were thrown together in a way that has probably not happened since and a great esprit de corps developed. After the state funeral, we left India for a week's breathing space in Sri Lanka, returning to a rearranged schedule, which took us through Jaipur, Ahmedabad and Rajkot to the First Test in Delhi. Over this early period, I came to know Graeme Fowler, who made his mark during the course of the second match with the classic heart-felt remark, 'It's Friday night; what the hell am I doing in Ahmedabad?' and in Rajkot with a timely pre-Test century. He became a regular breakfast companion, something that would be unthinkable on tours nowadays, when players enjoy their own section of an hotel dining room. He would go on to contribute to the winning of the Fourth Test, and the series, with a double hundred in Madras. His time as a *TMS* summariser lay ahead of him.

Twenty-four hours before the First Test in Bombay, another murder put the tour in jeopardy for the second time. This time it was the British Deputy High Commissioner in the city, Percy Norris, who was the victim, on the morning after he had hosted a very enjoyable drinks party for the players and press. The Test went ahead, not without some expressed misgivings, and in these unpromising circumstances, Mike Selvey made his *Test Match Special* debut.

Mike had just retired at the end of the summer after two years captaining Glamorgan, preceded by ten successful years at Middlesex, and had offered his services for the first two Tests of the series, as he would be there to try his hand at some freelance journalism. He took great pleasure from seeing his former Middlesex colleague, Mike Gatting, reach a Test century at last. Even in what was a losing cause, it seemed the significant moment that it turned out to be. Selve was witnessing the rough end of *TMS* at Bombay's disgraceful Wankhede Stadium. Our commentary position was a trestle table, situated deafeningly amongst the seats at the back of the stand, and certainly not far enough away from the Indian spectators' victory fireworks, which caused some alarm in the circumstances of the violent build-up to the match.

Although we were not doing ball-by-ball commentary on the one-day international which followed the Test, Mike joined me at the broadcasting point in Pune to give the expert view. There we had been given a table on the pavilion roof, where we attracted a small crowd of onlookers, not least when we explored our grease-stained lunch cartons. A very self-important pair pushed their way to the front of the throng and one announced himself.

'Hello, I am brain surgeon and this is my friend, chartered accountant,' he said.

'Did we order a brain surgeon and a chartered accountant?' I asked Mike.

The match was otherwise memorable for another Gatting hundred and the emergence of an England side that might have been in danger of being written off, at last achieving a victory. It took us on to the crucial Second Test in Delhi.

The commentary team was Tony Lewis, Michael Carey and Ashis Ray. As an ex-captain of Glamorgan and England, Tony had started with the programme as a summariser, but with the need for extra commentators to cover the 1979 World Cup he had made the transition to ball-by-ball description. He was to move on from that role to become the front man for the BBC television cricket coverage, in succession to Peter West. A brilliant piece he had done for an end-of-year sports programme had led to his becoming the first presenter of the Saturday morning Radio 4 programme, *Sport on 4*, later taken on by Cliff Morgan.

On this occasion he was in India for only the first two Tests but, apart from his commentary, he contributed several other items, for which we had to repair to the studios of the Indian Overseas Communications Service in downtown Bombay and Delhi. If he had time to kill before one of these sessions, he would amaze me with his ability to put his feet up on a sofa and snatch a cat-nap.

In Delhi, he stayed with an old friend, the former Indian Test cricketer, Abbas Ali Baig, who also joined us in the commentary box for that Second Test as a summariser. I enjoyed a delightful evening in the Baig household for dinner with Tony, plus family, and the *Daily Telegraph* cricket writer, Dickie Rutnagur. The Baig children had already christened him 'Dickie Uncle', so Tony's daughters quickly decided that I would be 'Peter Uncle' – and to them, I still am.

The Delhi Test match seemed to be heading for a draw at the start of the final day, but it was still a slight problem that the previous evening Abbas had left me with the news that he could not come for the fifth day, as he had a business meeting in Bombay. The crisis deepened during the morning session, when Selve gave the pained look that travellers to those parts know all too well. 'Sorry, Bartex, got to go.' And with that he headed for the fastest auto-rickshaw he could find back to the hotel.

Reinforcements were required. I headed for the England dressing room and the tour manager, Tony Brown. He looked around and decided on a player who could be spared for BBC duties – Vic Marks. That afternoon, as Kapil Dev decided, rather earlier than his captain would have liked, that India were safe and holed out going for a big shot, setting up a run chase, radio listeners were treated for the first time to the chuckle that comes up from Victor's boots. England won with a bit to spare and we went to Calcutta for Christmas and the Third Test with the series all square. In the bar of the Grand Hotel, I told Victor that I reckoned he had a future on *Test Match Special*. His wife, Anna, looking forward to seeing a bit more of him in retirement, groaned and Victor chuckled.

Before he took the regular summariser's spot, he had the technical challenges of 'County Talk' to tackle. The fact that he managed to get through from a grassy bank by the pavilion in Bath, says a great deal about his determination. I had already been using Victor as a summariser for county knockout matches while he was still playing at Somerset. In fact the negotiations for his joining the *Observer* as their cricket correspondent in 1990 were carried out at the foot of the steps up to the commentary box at Southampton during a NatWest Trophy semi-final.

For the tour of the West Indies in 1994, I used Vic as a ball-by-ball commentator. I thought he did a good job, but it was not something we repeated. He seemed more at ease in the other seat, although it was fun to see and hear him commentating alongside his former Somerset team-mate, Viv Richards. When Brian Lara was approaching what was then Gary Sobers' record Test score, I am afraid I did little to ease the pressure by telling Victor that the moment was likely to fall in his commentary spell and it would be in the archives for ever. As it happened, I think he was relieved that it fell to CMJ to describe it.

Both Vic and Mike eventually joined *TMS* at home while Brian Johnston was still the driving force of the programme and, in different ways, they both

I
The end. Michael Vaughan and Jonathan Agnew say goodbye.

2 ABOVE
Checking the commentary rota at
Lord's, while Johnners commentates.
(*BBC Publicity*)

3 OPPOSITE
John Arlott in the box at Lord's on his
final day with TMS in 1980, with Bill
Frindall in support. (*Eagar*)

4 ABOVE

The TMS team at Edgbaston in 1993: *Standing*: PB, Neville Oliver, Jonathan Agnew, Bill Frindall, David Lloyd *Sitting*: Fred Trueman, Brian Johnston, Trevor Bailey (CMJ missed it). (*Eagar*)

5 OPPOSITE ABOVE

A trio of wit and wisdom: Brian Johnston, Fred Trueman and David Lloyd at Old Trafford. (*Eagar*)

6 OPPOSITE BELOW

The Oval 1991. It's the end of the season and Brian Johnston is about to present Graham Gooch with that case of Veuve Clicquot champagne for the best century of the series against the West Indies. (*Eagar*)

7 OPPOSITE ABOVE
The three pillars of Test Match Special –
Henry Blofeld, Christopher Martin-
Jenkins and Jonathan Agnew at
Edgbaston. (*BBC Publicity*)

8 OPPOSITE BELOW
Principal commentators for thirty-five
years – CMJ and Blowers at Edgbaston.

9 ABOVE
The producer supported by the pillars of
his programme at Old Trafford, 1995:
Christopher Martin-Jenkins, Jonathan
Agnew, Henry Blofeld, Bill Frindall.
(*Eagar*)

10 OPPOSITE ABOVE
Shilpa Patel – a power behind the scenes
for over a decade.

11 OPPOSITE BELOW
Trueman at the controls. Fred helps the
engineers (Andy Leslie, Brian Mack and
Nigel Edwards) at Lord's.

12 ABOVE
1984/5 England team and press contingent
in India. (*Graham Morris*)
Back row: Graeme Fowler, Richard
Streeton (*The Times*), Vic Marks, Paul
Downton, Martyn Moxon, Richard
Ellison, Neil Foster, Norman Cowans,
Chris Cowdrey, Tim Robinson, Bruce
French, Geoffrey Saulez (scorer), John
Thicknesse (*Evening Standard*)
Middle row: Bernard Thomas
(physiotherapist), Allan Lamb, Pat Pocock,

Mike Gatting, David Gower, Tony Brown
(manager), Phil Edmonds, Paul Allott,
Norman Gifford (coach)
Front row: Charlie Pinto (travel courier),
Graham Morris (photographer), Colin
Bateman (*Daily Express*), Matthew Engel
(*Guardian*), Chris Lander (*Daily Mirror*),
Michael Carey (*Daily Telegraph*), Peter
Smith (*Daily Mail*), Peter Baxter (BBC),
Ted Corbett (*Daily Star*), Paul Weaver
(*News of the World*), Graham Otway (PA)

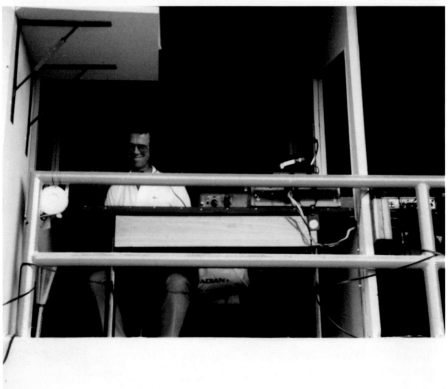

13 OPPOSITE ABOVE
Pakistan 1987 – 'The Sahiwal Seven':
Qamar Ahmed, Graham Morris, John
Thicknesse, John Woodcock, PB, David
Lloyd, Michael Austin.

14 OPPOSITE BELOW
Christopher Martin-Jenkins in the
Calcutta commentary box prepares for the
1987 World Cup final.

15 ABOVE
This piece for *The Times* obviously requires
some thought from their correspondent,
CMJ. (*Eagar*)

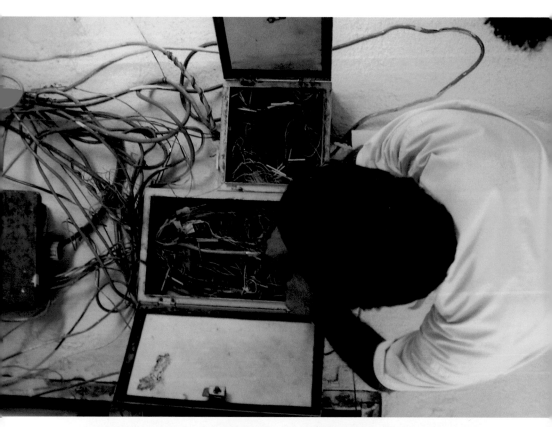

16 OPPOSITE ABOVE
It really will work. Telecom engineer
connecting TMS in Bombay in 2006.
And it did work – eventually.

17 OPPOSITE BELOW
Pakistan 2005. A cold commentary
position in Lahore. Scorer Jo King with
Aggers and Vic Marks.

18 ABOVE
Pakistan 2005. Another makeshift studio
for Aggers amongst the laundry on the
roof of the Shiza Inn, Multan.

19 ABOVE TOP
Pakistan 2005. A blank canvas – the
commentary box at Multan the day before ...

20 ABOVE
... and after. In full swing with TMS and
Radio 5. With carpets and furniture
purloined.

21 ABOVE TOP
Close of play interview. Simon Mann hears from Andrew Flintoff whose team have just beaten India in Bombay in 2006.

22 ABOVE
India 2006. The view that told CMJ he was unlikely to get a morning swim in Nagpur.

23
England have just beaten Bangladesh at
Chittagong. Time to interview the England
captain, Nasser Hussain.

found that a little difficult. Brian was used to the summariser beside him being more of his own generation and, while I would have expected Victor, at least, to be very much in tune with Johnners, he felt by his own admission slightly overawed by the presence of such a famous broadcaster. In Mike's case the two were completely at odds in their approach to the game and almost everything else in life. None of this was at all obvious on the air, but it probably meant that the two of them blossomed most in the post-Johnston era.

One man who certainly was in tune with BJ was David Lloyd. He came to *Test Match Special* in 1990 after having been mentioned to me by a number of people because of his entertaining after-dinner speaking. Those who heard him always insisted to me that he would be a great asset to *TMS*. So in 1989 I gave him a go in the commentaries we were doing on the Refuge Cup semi-finals – the brief play-off tournament at the end of the Sunday League, which is probably better remembered in cricket circles for its experimental use of orange balls than for the launch of the broadcasting career of 'Bumble'.

Nonetheless, it was a significant moment when I had David as my summariser at Old Trafford – particularly as we watched his son, Graham, come out to bat for Lancashire. 'I'm sure I left him in bed this morning,' was his comment. He had slipped into the world of radio easily and next year was quickly involved in all the jolly japes of the *TMS* box, winding up Johnners with spoof faxes, which set a mould for dummy information about our guests on 'A View from the Boundary' becoming a regular feature. David's own debut as a 'View' interviewer came to grief when Andy Goram, the Scottish goalkeeper, failed to turn up. That was a blow for Bumble, who had been up since dawn going through his notes.

David's direct involvement with cricket was not finished, though. When he went back to Lancashire as the county coach he was able to negotiate some Test matches for which he could join us, but his appointment as England coach inevitably ended his *TMS* career. In Australia, during the 1998/99 tour, I took him out to dinner one night when I felt his time coaching the national side might be approaching its end. He hinted that, delighted though he was to be encouraged to return to radio, there might be something more lucrative in the offing. So it turned out. After England's disappointing World Cup performance in 1999, Bumble was off to Sky. Not that that made us immune from the spoof emails and irrepressible humour. Temperamentally he has remained a *TMS* man.

By the nature of things, there is more of a turnover of summarisers than of commentators. *Test Match Special* likes to welcome people to join the familiar voices, and is conscious of keeping the fresh contact with the game as it is being played. Graeme Fowler was on the *TMS* radar because of his contributions to 'County Talk' and, with the departure of David Lloyd to his coaching duties, the tradition of Accringtonian humour was in safe hands with another very successful after-dinner speaker.

There is about 'Foxy' Fowler an apparently carefree lightness of touch which also characterised his batting. It is not all like that under the surface when the serious streak comes out and his success coaching at Durham University, and for the British Universities side, bears that out. That coaching role – the 'day job' – has curtailed his availability for broadcasting duties for BBC radio and for Sky television in the first half of the season, which is a pity for us, but good news for his student charges.

Another of the players from that 1984/85 tour, Chris Cowdrey, seemed destined for a long spell on *TMS* when he joined the programme in 1995. When he was playing his first Test in Bombay, the story came back to us that his father, Colin Cowdrey, had been out in his car, with *TMS* on the radio. He heard that Chris had come on to bowl his first ever spell in Test cricket and, in his excitement, turned the wrong way into a one-way street. A policeman quickly stopped him and, while he was trying to explain the unlikely circumstances, they both heard Chris take a wicket – Kapil Dev, no less – in his first over. This time it was the policeman who was excited enough to let off the proud father.

Chris asked for a meeting with me in September of 1998 to discuss how much work he might get from the BBC for the 1999 World Cup in England. I felt I was fairly generous, well in advance of most of the detailed planning, but before the tournament started he had jumped ship for TalkSport, who gave him a central role in their overseas coverage.

After Fred and Trevor left *Test Match Special* I had a feeling that, while we would have some excellent summarisers who had been good – even very good – players, we seemed to be lacking any former player who could truly be said to have been 'great'. Sky's box was packed with former England captains and while in our case the ability to broadcast was paramount, it would be good to have that flash of cricketing genius in our midst occasionally. So we turned to Graham Gooch and Mike Gatting. Both have many other irons in the fire, but have added to the programme considerably just from the experience of their past achievements.

The need for some big names in our line-up was spurred on by the negotiations for our rights agreement with the England and Wales Cricket Board at the start of 2000. The threat from TalkSport was very real at that time and the eyes of several of the ECB marketing committee had come alight at the almost unlimited money they were apparently offering. Happily there were some sane heads involved as well.

Central to the TalkSport bid was Geoffrey Boycott. Indeed, Geoffrey had been central to the start of TalkSport's involvement in cricket commentary, which appeared to have been partly fuelled by anti-BBC resentment on more than one front. In Geoffrey's case this seemed to have arisen from the court cases in France in which he was convicted of assaulting his then girlfriend, Margaret Moore. After the first conviction – at a trial which Geoffrey declined to attend – an appeal was being arranged as we were heading for the 1998 England tour of the West Indies. Geoff was due to join us on *TMS*, but as I was preparing to leave, I looked at the lurid newspaper headlines and my concerns grew. I consulted BBC management and was advised that they would get back to me.

In the fortnight before they did so, the matter was referred to lofty levels within the Corporation. Then, on the very eve of the First Test in Jamaica, I received a call. 'You can't use him.'

Geoff was out on the golf course and I had to wait for his return to give him the bad news, which stunned him. It caused some consternation, too, in the ranks of Sky, for whom he was also working. Sky were using the output of Trans World International, but clearly had considerable influence on the commentary team. The presence of Boycott had been something of a bone of contention for them. The Sky producer was at best lukewarm about it, but the American TWI boss was very keen. My dropping of the news that we would not be using him was a pebble that created considerable waves and eventually they followed our lead.

The appeal was lost and Geoffrey was as far as he could be from joining any BBC commentary team. But in that mood, and with his contacts, he was just what TalkSport needed to secure the rights in South Africa and then in Pakistan and then to be at the centre of their commentaries.

In 1995 he had been part of the *TMS* team that covered the first official

England tour of South Africa for thirty-one years. For that series we shared commentary with the South African Broadcasting Corporation. They would divide their time between the English language commentary and the Afrikaans version. While SABC listeners were hearing Afrikaans, the English commentary would continue for the BBC. However, there was a twenty-five minute period on weekday mornings when *TMS* gave way for Radio 4's *Yesterday in Parliament*. If this coincided with SABC's time for Afrikaans, we were broadcasting to nobody. The possibilities for a scam were not lost on Aggers.

At the Wanderers ground in Johannesburg he found himself in that position as he was joined by Boycott. He did not let on that their audience consisted only of engineers and their recording machines.

Mike Atherton was setting out on his heroic match-saving innings, giving Aggers his starting point.

'Mind you, you were pretty stodgy, Geoffrey.'

Geoff defended the role of a good defence, but between sparse commentary Aggers turned the knife, referring to crowds leaving the ground or falling asleep when Boycott was batting. 'God, you were boring,' was the line that had Geoff looking quizzically at such a gratuitous insult. Eventually, Radio 4 rejoined and as Aggers welcomed them back and revealed to them that, while he had not been on the air for some time, Geoff had thought they were, the familiar Boycott lopsided grin reappeared with some relief.

I suppose there is something about the meticulous way that Geoffrey organises his life that sets him up for irreverent souls to enjoy pulling his leg. A simple, but utterly certain, prediction that there would be no rain in Nagpur in 2006, preceded an overnight storm that flooded the commentary hut. Next day, Geoff was persuaded to say, 'OK, I were wrong.' His sense of humour was severely tested when he heard it being played back a few times.

During the Boxing Day Test match in Melbourne in 2006, Andrew Symonds came in to bat at 84 for five in Australia's first innings. Playing and missing early on, Geoffrey offered the view that, 'If he's a batsman, I'll eat my hat.' When Symonds passed 150, we were searching for the Boycott autographed panama.

The negotiations for the Boycott return to BBC colours were conducted at a higher level than is normal. The plan was devised to have him in the team, with his talents rationed between Radio 5 Live and *Test Match Special*, for the 2006 season. A new contract with the ECB, uncontested by the new owners of TalkSport, was the catalyst for this move.

Like Fred Trueman, Geoff Boycott manages to polarise opinions as much, if not more, than in his playing days. He has certainly worked out that a trenchant, and if necessary controversial, view is very marketable.

More understated is the broadcasting of Angus Fraser. After a splendid career of fast medium bowling for Middlesex and England, Gus joined us as a summariser for a few one-day internationals and then on the 2001/02 tours of India and New Zealand. That was part of our announcement that we were back, after two winters losing out to TalkSport on rights. Shortly after that tour he was appointed cricket correspondent of the *Independent*. While I am sure that there were days when, about to run in and bowl for the umpteenth time in the day, he would have looked wearily up at the press box with some envy, there must have been times, as the close of play approached and a blank laptop screen stared back at him, when he looked enviously down at the players on the field.

The former lugubrious presence on the field has been replaced by a splendidly down-to-earth, common sense approach in the commentary box and an impish sense of humour that fits in well. As a member of the ICC Cricket Committee, Gus used to receive a great deal of leg-pulling about meetings in Dubai, along the lines of having spent three days on the beach drinking piña colada, before coming up with substitutes for one-day internationals or the opinion that a certain latitude in the straightening of a bowler's arm might be allowed. That was probably not very fair, but it was an easy target. Gus has now left the *Independent* to return to Middlesex as managing director of cricket.

In the weeks after I left *Test Match Special*, a number of summarisers were used – nine of them during the Lord's Test of 2007, for instance – so it is reasonable to assume that this is the area where the biggest changes can be expected.

FAR PAVILIONS

IT WAS 31 OCTOBER 1984 AND IN MY DARKENED HOTEL
room in Delhi the phone was ringing urgently. Having flown in
from London overnight, I had not seen my bed until 4.30 a.m.
and had that alarmed feeling of disorientation as I groped for the
receiver.

'Peter Baxter? It's the Newsroom in London. It's about this Gandhi business.'

'What Gandhi business?'

'Aren't you in Delhi?'

'Yes.'

'Well, you must have heard. She's been shot.'

For anyone who has been on cricket tours, the best travellers' tales seem to
come out of India. But this was the biggest. While the England team and the
accompanying press had been sleeping off the flight, the Indian Prime
Minister, Indira Gandhi, had been shot by Sikh members of her own
bodyguard.

The BBC radio newsroom's first concern was that Mark Tully, the BBC's
legendary India correspondent was out of town, following Princess Anne's visit
to the country. Would I get down to the BBC office, where Tully's number
two, Satish Jacob, was keeping things going for the early morning news
programmes.

What I found there was a harassed Satish, handling ringing phones and a
chattering telex machine, while churning out telephone reports. I assessed the

situation as I saw it and stationed myself at a battered portable typewriter on a ping-pong table to start writing his scripts from the incoming information. At last came a call from a friend of his, working at the hospital to which the Prime Minister had been taken, with the news we had rather been expecting, that she was dead.

I was mindful of the BBC policy that two independent sources were needed before we could announce a death and this seemed to be about as sensitive a death to announce as could be imagined. As I was putting this to Satish, the telex machine coughed up the same information.

'Are these two sources both reliable?'

'Absolutely,' he assured me.

I rang the Foreign Duty Editor (FDE) in London and put it to him. He was surprisingly relaxed. 'Well, if you're satisfied, go for it,' he said.

I took a deep breath and for Satish's next report I wrote that Indira Gandhi had died.

Back in Britain the *Today* programme finished. That gave us a bit of breathing space. The days of rolling news had not quite reached us then. The FDE rang to say, 'Right, one of you stay by the phone to cover any further reports and one of you go out and try to interview some Indian politicians. I don't mind who does which.'

Satish looked a bit apprehensive. 'I think I'd better stay by the phone,' he said.

'OK,' I said, 'but the number of Indian politicians I knew by sight has just taken a bit of a dent.'

Nonetheless, off I went to grab one of the taxis which seemed to wait permanently in front of the house. We tried the roads round the Prime Minister's residence, where the shooting had happened, but inevitably they were all cordoned off. So I asked the driver if we could go to the hospital where she had been taken. En route I could hear the news on his radio. The Prime Minister, it said, was fighting for her life. Not on the BBC, I thought. God, I hope we were right.

The taxi dropped me at what turned out to be a quiet back entrance to the very smart hospital. I waved a BBC staff pass and a cassette tape recorder at the security guard and walked in. Inside I was assured that a top team of doctors was working hard to treat the Prime Minister's injuries. She was definitely still fighting for life, I was told.

The front of the hospital presented a very different picture from the back. Television camera crews, photographers and reporters were several rows deep with thousands of onlookers pressing behind them. I latched onto some Indian journalists and we watched large cars bringing celebrity well-wishers to the hospital.

'Can you let me know who some of these people are, please?' I asked.

'Well, you knew the man in that last car, didn't you?'

'No.'

'Don't you get Hindi films in England?'

'Yes, but somehow I don't go to them as often as I should.'

The local press had a feeling that any announcement about Mrs Gandhi was being held back until the Indian President could return from the Yemen, where he was on a state visit. They were not so naïve as to believe the legend that she was still alive.

I had been bidden to be at the Overseas Communications Services studios in time for the Radio 4 one o'clock news, with whatever I had. So, late in the Delhi afternoon, I eventually made my way there, noticing an eerie calm on the streets, and that was the theme on which I reported for the news. Back in his office, Mark Tully had arrived, understandably harassed and annoyed that he had been away for the biggest possible event. I felt it best, having reported in, to return to the team hotel. After all, we now had a big question mark over what would happen to the tour.

By now my Sikh taxi driver was very cautious about the route he took, as the news was out that Mrs Gandhi was dead and violence was breaking out in some areas. It was the start of a week under curfew in our hotel, although the team were escorted daily to the British High Commissioner's residence, where his extensive gardens gave room for some form of training. At the hotel we speculated about the fate of the tour and the waiters pointed out the plumes of black smoke. 'That's a Sikh-owned petrol station; that's a Sikh school,' and so on.

We stayed until the day after the state funeral. As with the terrorist attacks of 2008, the Indian Cricket Board were reluctant to let the team leave India, for fear that they might not return, but Sri Lanka offered a week's retreat and some cricket, and the Sri Lankan President offered space to the players on his plane when he returned from the funeral. We, the media, might have more of a problem getting to Colombo.

Our situation was resolved by a film crew, who had been similarly incarcerated in the hotel during this period. They were making a TV mini-series, *Lord Mountbatten: The Last Viceroy*, and had to go to Sri Lanka to shoot scenes of railway massacres. By chance, Mrs Gandhi had been due to meet the stars, including Nicol Williamson, who played Mountbatten, on the day she was killed.

Their large aeroplane had plenty of room for a small party of journalists, though we did have to cough up a few hundred US dollars each to get on it. Snapshots of the journey stick in my memory. Ian Richardson, who was playing Nehru, waiting in the hotel foyer in white linen suit and panama and Sam Dastor, who had had to change his appearance greatly to play Gandhi, being held up at Indian immigration, because his passport picture did not now resemble the man. (When he told the immigration officers the reason, however, he was treated like royalty and served tea in the superintendent's office.) The American lady director wanted to meet these English journalists she was helping out and so we were lined up at the airport each to express our thanks as she reviewed us like a military inspection.

A first-class game for the practice and a one-day international to pay for it all was the programme for our visit, although the one-day international was spectacularly rained off at the halfway stage and when I visited the dressing room for an interview with the captain, David Gower, I found it flooded, with the players sitting on tables. Gower and I set a precedent, which we followed for most of the rest of the tour, of doing the interview in the bathroom, which on this occasion provided the only dry ground.

Back in India, the itinerary had been completely rejigged. Three first-class games in Jaipur, Ahmedabad and Rajkot led up to the First Test. In the first of these an Indian off-spinner had such a dubious action that we were all preparing to report as much until an emissary from the England dressing room begged us not to. 'We think they're going to pick him for the Test team … and he's not very good.' But he failed to make the team.

In Bombay, now known to some as Mumbai, on the eve of the First Test came the murder of the British Deputy High Commissioner, Percy Norris, and a few days later we had the news of the terrible chemical spill at the Union Carbide factory in Bhopal.

Both those pieces of news reached me in the Taj Mahal Hotel, one of the great hotels of the world, sitting majestically on the Bombay waterfront by the Gateway of India. The hotel has been a comfortable home base for many cricket tours and has a place of affection in the hearts of players, officials and journalists on those tours. That feeling heightened the horror of the terrorist attack on the hotel in November 2008. The other Bombay hotel involved, the Oberoi, is also well-known to cricket tourists. It is only a gentle stroll from there along Marine Drive to both the main cricket grounds, the Brabourne Stadium and the less welcoming Wankhede.

The understandable apprehension of an England team in India at the same time as that attack in 2008 cannot have been helped by images of the huge bomb that devastated the Islamabad Marriott, another hotel with which we are all very familiar, two months before. New Zealand teams have twice, in recent years, been actually in hotels in Colombo and Karachi when terrorist attacks, neither of them aimed at them, have taken place.

The 1984/85 tour seemed at its outset to be ill-starred. But from England's purely cricketing point of view, the resurgence after the loss of the First Test to take the series two-one made it a great success.

Despite the catalogue of disaster, the Christmas celebrations in Calcutta after the series had been levelled were among the cheeriest I can remember on tour. The *Daily Telegraph*'s Mike Carey and I put together some songs which the press performed at the pre-lunch drinks party and poked a little fun at the team, which would surely not have gone down as well on some subsequent tours. Our 'Old Man Robbo' celebrated Tim Robinson, whose painstaking century had set up the win in Delhi.

'He's not like Gower, he's not like Gatting; for some strange reason he keeps on batting,' we sang. And to keep a seasonal flavour, we introduced India's new leg-spinner with, 'I'm dreaming of Sivaramakrishnan.'

On Boxing Day we flew to Bhubaneswar for a one-day international on the following day at Cuttack. Arriving in the hotel, I desperately needed to get a telephone call through to London to report for *Sport on 2*. I went straight to the hotel operator. 'Can you get me a line to London, please? As soon as possible.'

'Acha. Oh yes.'

He made no move, so I said gently, 'London?'

'Yes.'

'Now?'

'Acha. Why you want Laundry?'

I did not speak to London that day.

Back in Calcutta for the New Year, I made my *TMS* commentary debut.

I have always enjoyed doing some commentary myself, though inevitably it has been much easier to do it on the rare occasions when someone else has been looking after the production and that has really only happened when I have been working on the local broadcasts in Australia, New Zealand or South Africa. It may explain why the *TMS* regulars never seem very keen on the producer commentating. In fact, while people more removed from the programme – within the BBC and without – have generally been very kind about my commentaries, those closest to it seem almost to have pretended it has not happened. Good or bad, I am certain it has helped me to understand the way a commentator goes about his job and the problems he faces.

The match I picked for my debut was not very thrilling. Kapil Dev had been made the scapegoat for the Indian defeat in Delhi and had been left out, so there were going to be no more grand gestures. The weather contributed, as did the prolonging of the Indian innings, batting first, until the fourth afternoon. Only two things, therefore, stick out from my first Test match commentary. One was the huge crowd waiting for Shastri to complete his hundred towards the end of the third day and then all moving towards the exits, giving the impression of some giant stick having been thrust into an ant hill. The other was the substantial pillar situated in front of our commentary box, which was at the back of the top deck of the pavilion stand. Behind this pillar three fielders could be hidden from the commentator's view. Our technique to combat this problem was for commentator and summariser to sit well apart, thus covering the entire field between them. At one stage, when I was commentating, a ball was played firmly into the invisible ground behind the pillar. I ventured the suggestion that it must have been fielded. Jack Bannister was my summariser. 'Actually,' he said, 'I'm afraid it was dropped.'

Having gone on my first England tour with Don Mosey in 1981, the following year had seen me landing in Bombay en route for my first visit to Australia. As we stretched our legs in the transit lounge there, I had a strange sense of disappointment that I was not renewing my acquaintance with the great subcontinent. India does that to you. Inevitably, I have always been glad to leave it at the end of a long tour. But one does hanker to return.

Many years later I was sitting next to Paul Collingwood as we flew to Jaipur. He looked out at a parched landscape as we approached. 'Looks a little dry,' he said.

'The Rajasthan desert,' I offered.

'Have you been here before, then?'

'This is my eighth tour here.' He was incredulous.

My third visit was in 1987 for the fourth cricket World Cup, shared between India and Pakistan. A hardy knot of journalists started in Delhi for the opening ceremony in September, when the summer heat had not yet left the city. The ceremony itself was the first one attempted for the tournament, the first to be held outside England. It was not too lavish an affair – the main event being a curtain-raiser game between India and Pakistan, not part of the tournament. But a feature of the ceremony preceding the game was the dramatic release of a host of balloons, as the World Cup was declared open. Unfortunately, these balloons proved to be considerably heavier than air and lurked around the outfield of the Nehru Stadium until they could be corralled by some pyjama-clad stewards, so that the game could begin.

We moved on from there to Pakistan, about which I had some appre-hension, following so many scare stories in the past. In fact, for the World Cup, people could not have been more helpful. The first match was England v the West Indies at Gujranwala, about an hour's drive out of Lahore. A couple of days before the game Micky Stewart, the England coach, and I both needed to do some reconnaissance of the ground, so we agreed to share a car. The dual carriageway that took us to Gujranwala was better than any road I had seen on my two trips to India, although the basic rules of such a road seemed to have passed some of the local farmers by, as when we realised that the tractor and cart we were bearing down on at speed in the outside lane was in fact coming towards us.

After checking the facilities at the stadium that we were each interested in, we were invited for refreshments at the local organiser's house. Protocol demanded an acceptance, though Micky muttered that he was not a great fan of spicy food. Therefore, when a trolley of snacks was brought in, he selected an innocuous-looking sandwich. As his teeth were making their first impression on the bread, our host said to him, 'I hope you are liking green chillies.' Though his eyes were out on stalks, Micky took his medicine manfully.

On the day of the match, fearful of traffic problems and large crowds, a convoy assembled before dawn at the Lahore Hilton with a bus each for the England team, the West Indies team and the press, accompanied by lorry-loads of armed police fore and aft and several motorcycle outriders. It was the start of what was to become a long, hot and sticky day. In addition to the ball-by-ball commentary, we had to provide reports for Radio 2 and Radio 4 from a telephone in the telex office, two floors below the commentary box. This was my responsibility, once I had ensured that everything was working in the box, and it had me running up stairs to meet the various calls and back to check that all was well with the commentary.

As the day heated up, this was becoming quite challenging and in the middle of it all, CMJ turned from his microphone with a snap of his fingers to attract my attention. 'When you've got a moment, a cup of tea would be nice.' He would never know how close he came to being shoved over the precipitous drop below the low window sill.

An indication of the heat and humidity came from Allan Lamb, whose heroic innings gave England a remarkable victory. The effort required meant that he had to be helped back out onto the field to receive the man-of-the-match award. When I asked for an interview I was told, 'All right, if it's only you', and I talked to the match winner as he slumped in a basket chair in a corner of the dressing room.

The 1987 World Cup provided the unique experience of having BBC television on an overseas cricket tour. Less used to 'mucking in' in these circumstances, they succeeded in antagonising the rest of the press corps. From the radio point of view, we had agreed beforehand to share a few members of their team. Tony Lewis and Jack Bannister were key elements for both, but towards the end of the group stage, one morning in Karachi, Tony was in full flow of radio commentary when Keith Mackenzie, the television producer, burst into our box, pushed between CMJ and myself at the back, and tapped Tony on the arm urgently in mid-sentence. 'You're wanted,' he said and again there was no word to us as he left.

Christopher took over the commentary, but I never had a word of explanation or apology from Mackenzie. His assistant did come to explain, as did Tony, but their message was that their masters in London had forbidden any more sharing of commentators with radio. We still had two England group matches to go and were reduced to just Christopher to do the commentary. I would have to be one replacement, but I had to think who else might join us.

Going round as part of the press party, just for the adventure, was Tim Rice. At the time he had been doing a programme on Radio 2 and he was a current regular radio broadcaster, so I decided that he was someone who could step into the breach and, as one of the most successful lyricists of all time, he should have the words.

My call to his hotel room caught him still abed, but a couple of hours later he emerged into the hotel foyer enquiring, 'Backers, did I just dream that?' He certainly had no hesitation in accepting and he made his commentary debut in Jaipur, for the second England v West Indies match. It was a good game, too, with England again prevailing after a Viv Richards onslaught, and Tim did not let us down.

His next game was in Pune against Sri Lanka. This was more problematic, with line problems keeping us off the air for a long period, thanks mainly to the radio link between Pune and Bombay. There were several sections in the link with London and at each one there was a man at the controls, starting with Pune Coaxial and ending with Broadcasting House control room. For some time Pune, Bombay and London were all complaining that our output was too quiet, but at last we started getting acknowledgement that it was broadcastable. Then, just as Alastair Hignell, who had been manfully holding the fort in the studio, was about to hand back, a voice came into my headphones. 'This is Pune Coaxial. Please raise your level.'

It had been a difficult morning and I had had enough of it. 'London are happy and Bombay are happy, so sod off, Pune Coaxial.'

It enabled Tim Rice to taste the joys of his first commentary on Sri Lanka in the field. With so many splendid names to choose from, it was noticeable that 'the burly John' was heard doing a great deal of the fielding – often at third man and long on in the same over.

That game saw England into a semi-final meeting with India in Bombay, while Pakistan were at home to Australia. In both cases the visitors misread the script and the final between India and Pakistan that had been widely anticipated for Calcutta became the old firm of England and Australia.

On that chaotic day the match seemed to be decided by two critical moments in the England innings as they chased 254 to win. Bill Athey was run out when he looked well set. Then Allan Border brought himself on to bowl and to his first ball Mike Gatting fell to a reverse sweep. The commentary on that latter wicket was done by Peter Roebuck. He was summarising, but the commentary box was so tight that when commentators changed, it could take some time, and Henry Blofeld had not quite got into place before the ball was bowled.

The Australian Broadcasting Corporation had not sent anyone to cover the tournament and so they were taking our commentary on the final, a fact that Henry was very well aware of as he reached the middle of the final over, with England just mathematically out of contention. 'Now you really can charge those glasses in Australia. I give you my final, final permission.'

From the razzmatazz of the final, a hard core of us moved to Pakistan for the three-Test series that became known for the 'Gatting/Shakoor Rana affair'. The key to that affair lay in the fact that England had won each of the three one-day internationals that preceded the Tests. As I made my way back to the hotel from the ground in Peshawar, where the third match had just finished, I saw the Pakistan team heading off down the road to Islamabad, where, I heard later, they and their bosses were told firmly by the president, General Zia himself, no less, that they must be sure to win the Test series to avoid national disgrace.

The result was a severely under-prepared pitch for the First Test in Lahore, on which Abdul Qadir performed brilliantly with the considerable assistance of the umpires. That latter fact produced an extraordinary visit to the press hotel on the third evening of the match by the England manager and coach. We assembled on a wide, gloomy landing to be told by Peter Lush and Micky Stewart about the impossibilities of playing against Pakistan in their own country. However true that may have been, there were several of us there that night who felt that this was not the way to deal with the problem.

Pakistan duly won the match and when I interviewed the captain, Javed Miandad, he affected to be astonished that there was any talk of controversy.

After everything had worked so well for the World Cup, it was proving slightly more uphill going on our return. For the first hour of the Lahore Test our commentary had to be on the telex office phone, as the local telecommunications had booked circuits via Islamabad, but British Telecom had gone via Karachi.

Between the First and Second Tests there was a three-day game at Sahiwal. Rumours abounded before we were due to leave for our four-hour bus ride from Lahore. There was virtually no accommodation. There were absolutely no communications. The journey could take ten hours. It was the usual touring fare. In the end we were trimmed down to a hardy seven in the press party: John Woodcock of *The Times*; John Thicknesse of the *Evening Standard*; Michael Austin of the *Daily Telegraph*; David Lloyd of the Press Association;

Graham Morris, the photographer; Qamar Ahmed, a London-based Pakistani who was covering for Reuters; and me. The rest of the press stayed in Lahore and, as we settled into the Government Rest House in Sahiwal, we christened ourselves 'the Sahiwal Seven'.

The Rest House was not fancy, but functional, though it had no restaurant and we had to find somewhere else to eat in Sahiwal, which was a little bit of a challenge. We were fortunate to have Qamar Ahmed with us, as one of the half-dozen or so languages he speaks is Punjabi, which was the only way of communicating with our attendant. This morose character would cook up breakfast for the seven of us in the morning and deliver all of it to the room that Graham Morris and I were sharing, which was a sociable, if abrupt way of starting the day.

We appeared to have done better than the players, who were housed in the Montgomery Biscuit Factory and, when we visited their digs on the first evening, they were not looking best pleased.

At the ground itself there were two telephones, but they were not able to manage overseas calls. I tried sending a telex to London with the phone numbers, but that seemed not to get through. I made enquiries. There must be a Central Telegraph Office somewhere in a town the size of Sahiwal. An address was written for me, in Punjabi, on a scrap of paper and proved enough for the rickshaw driver I hailed at the close of play. He took me to a busy crossroads down town, where on one corner there was a queue of people lined up to wait their turn at a ragged hole in a wall. A European being a rarity in central Sahiwal, the owner of the face which peered out through that hole gestured me to go round to the back entrance of his office.

I picked my way through a crowd of chickens and off-duty rickshaw drivers relaxing on their charpoys and entered what seemed like a Victorian coal hole. I could just make out, against the light coming through the hole in the wall onto the street, that the clerk who had invited me in was perched on a tall stool with a large ledger on his desk. A quill pen would have completed the illusion of his being Pakistan's answer to Bob Cratchit.

With no confidence at all I asked if I could have a telephone call to London. I wrote down the number. He invited me to sit on a nearby bench and I settled down for a long wait. To my astonishment, within a minute I was talking to the studio in London on a relatively clear line. To the clerk with the ledger it seemed to be all routine to have someone broadcasting from his office and he did not even turn a hair when I dismantled his old bakelite telephone to attach the necessary leads, in order to send over the taped interview I had recorded. Sahiwal had been like the dark side of the moon for the BBC, but suddenly we were on the radar.

On the cricketing front, in an otherwise unremarkable game, we had our first sight of a seventeen-year-old leg-spinner called Mushtaq Ahmed, who tied England in knots. While we had a feeling we would see more of him, I doubt if any of us would have predicted his being instrumental in bringing successive county championship titles to Sussex two decades later.

Our next stop was the Second Test in Faisalabad. *Wisden* describes it as 'one of the most acrimonious Test matches in history'. The incident that made it so came on the second evening. I was commentating at the time and in fading light we were unclear as to what was going on. To make matters less easy, after some criticism of the umpiring the previous day, all the television monitors had been removed from our box and the press box. We were aware of an altercation between the England captain, Mike Gatting, and the square-leg umpire, Shakoor Rana, but could not work out its cause.

There had been an earlier incident, when Ijaz Ahmed had appeared to be perfectly well caught at short-leg but had been given not out and the captain's ire had clearly risen, but this time things had gone a little further and fingers had been wagged in both directions. This much we could tell. We were also aware that England, having got themselves into an excellent position with a painstaking hundred from Chris Broad, were now pushing at the end of the day to get another over in. The umpire's intervention had delayed matters enough to make that impossible.

Jack Bannister returned from the press box below us to offer a view that the altercation might have arisen because of too many fielders being behind square on the leg side, but that did not seem right.

The two television news reporters – BBC and ITN – had not been able to operate from Faisalabad for lack of any means of sending their pictures back and so were in editing suites in Lahore. It was when their close-ups reached London that we, now returned to the hotel, all started to get calls back from our respective offices, asking for follow-up pieces on the row.

The incident was gradually explained. Gatting had made a late move of a fielder after the batsman, Salim Malik, had settled into his stance, but had told Salim what he had done. Shakoor Rana had then started shouting at Gatting to the effect that this was sharp practice. It was one straw too many for a captain who felt his opposition was not just confined to the eleven men he was playing against, and a great deal of high volume, very plain speaking followed. If the aim was to prevent the extra over being bowled, it was certainly successful.

The next day, as the starting time approached, we noticed that the roller was still parked in the middle, attended only by ground staff taking their ease. In our commentary team was Ralph Dellor, who had made his *TMS* debut in Madras two and a half years before. That Test match was eventful on the field. This one was to give him a great deal of work, up and down the stairs, to and from the officials three floors below, to gather information and interviews. It was some time later we gathered that, when all seemed to have been resolved shortly before play, Javed Miandad had insisted that Shakoor Rana must not allow himself to be so insulted. A cynic might think that, had Pakistan been in a better position in the match, play would have started on time.

For all that third day there was no play, and throughout the day and the scheduled rest day that followed, rumour and counter-rumour abounded. I interviewed the England team manager, Peter Lush, as he was setting off for Lahore and a meeting with the president of the Pakistan Cricket Board. That worthy managed to delay meeting him until the following day, claiming a dinner engagement on the evening that Lush arrived.

The two teams and the press were all housed in the same Serena Hotel, which was built on the lines of a sultan's palace, with nooks and crannies and courtyards, where whispered intrigue seemed only too appropriate.

On the fourth morning, a terse and misspelt apology from Mike Gatting to the umpire proved enough to get the action moving. Ralph Dellor again came up trumps with a scoop of an interview with Shakoor Rana. Could the time be made up, we wondered. There were spare days between this and the Third Test for that to happen, but the Pakistan Board were unsure. Eventually, on the fifth day (with Pakistan still not in a good position in the game), their team manager, Hasib Ahsan, told the press that it would be impossible to play another day because seven of his team were getting married between matches. A word of congratulation to the dressing room seemed to take them by surprise. The final Test – almost predictably – was a low-key draw.

After such an introduction, I was naturally apprehensive about a return to Pakistan in 1996 for the sixth World Cup. But this time everyone went out of their way to be helpful. There were inevitably some of the frustrations and amusements which always accompany each other, in equal measure, on the subcontinent. On one arrival at what was then the fairly dilapidated Lahore airport, I was champing at the bit to get my luggage, as I had to be at the Gadaffi Stadium to report on a game. For a long time there was no activity on what passed for a baggage carousel. The porters leaned on their trolleys waiting patiently. The BBC man was less patient. 'This lot couldn't organise a piss-up in a brewery,' I muttered.

A helpful porter overheard. 'You want toilet?' he asked.

The tournament was shared this time not just with India, but also with Sri Lanka, which had recently suffered a few terrorist bomb blasts. The Australians were in the Sri Lankan group and so were the West Indies and neither team was keen to go to that island.

After a few days' acclimatisation in Lahore, we went to Calcutta for the opening ceremony, but the build-up was entirely dominated by the Sri Lanka question. The tournament organising committee was chaired by the combative former president of the Indian board, Jagmohan Dalmiya, who was trying everything to get the Australians to change their minds. He seemed largely to ignore the fact that West Indies were in the same position.

Much behind-the-scenes arm-twisting culminated in a large press conference by the International Cricket Council in the Taj Bengal Hotel. I set out a microphone to record the proceedings and enquired of an ICC official who would be speaking. 'Only the ICC chairman, Clyde Walcott,' he said. So his was the seat that I covered with my microphone.

Walcott made a few introductory remarks, but the rest of the conference degenerated into a hysterical rant from Mr Dalmiya, frequently fuelled, rather than questioned, by Indian journalists. Fortunately, so loud was he that I had no need to move the microphone. Walcott looked slightly bemused beside him, as it was confirmed that Australia and West Indies would not go to Sri Lanka and their scheduled matches there would be considered as victories for the home side. In the event, both teams got through their preliminary round, and as far as the semi-finals, even without those points.

England were not a great one-day side at that stage and it was apparent that the captain, Mike Atherton, and the coach, Ray Illingworth, were not exactly on the same wavelength. 'Why does no one in this team play bridge?' was one frustration I heard from Ray.

Thanks to wins over Holland and the United Arab Emirates, England did reach the quarter-finals, but that was as far as it went – they were eliminated, on their first return to Faisalabad after more than eight years, by Sri Lanka.

We were still committed to mounting commentaries from the two semi-finals and the final and had had to work out where England might go if they qualified, because of the always tortuous travel arrangements. Jonathan Agnew and Simon Mann would go to Calcutta for what eventually became India v Sri Lanka and I would go to Chandigarh for what turned out to be Australia v the West Indies. First I had to report from Karachi, on the quarter-final between West Indies and South Africa, and at 4 a.m. next day I set out for Chandigarh in India.

I knew as I started that there was one impossible link in the proposed chain of my journey, but John Snow, our travel agent – safely in Sussex – had airily said, 'Well, the chaps on the ground there think it will work.'

'Not a chance,' I said.

First I had to catch a PIA flight to Bombay. Because Indian internal tickets could only be issued in India, I then had to be met by a travel agent, who drove me to his office in the centre of Bombay, an hour in heavy traffic, where they took another hour before they found my ticket to Delhi. Then an hour back to the airport and a wait for the afternoon flight.

We landed in Delhi only about ten minutes late – something of a triumph, I thought – but I knew that this was the impossible connection. There was only half an hour between the scheduled flight arrival and the departure of my train to Chandigarh from the centre of Delhi. The local agent greeted me accusingly. 'You are late.'

It seemed that I was still the only person who had spotted the inevitable flaw in the plan. I was driven to the travel firm's office in the city, which, just to add more enjoyment, was being rebuilt and was therefore full of piles of rubble and thick with noise and dust. There I waited for three hours for a driver to be found who might take me to Chandigarh – about a six hour drive.

We set off as dusk was starting to fall over Delhi to drive up the Grand Trunk Road, which is a terrifying experience, as one usually spends more time in the opposition's half than in one's own. And the opposition consists of a great many heavily laden and uncompromising lorries.

I had not been relishing the prospect of the establishment to which I was bound – the Hotel Aroma – but at 2 a.m., I was quite relieved when we pulled up outside it. However, joy, such as it was, was short lived. The man behind the desk said he had never heard of me or any booking in my name. Unfortunately for his case, my name was on a list pinned to the wall behind him.

'Yes,' he said without apology, when I pointed this out, 'you have been moved to the Hotel Metro 35.'

I do not know if the Metro 35 was an upgrade from the Aroma. It was horrible. I put in a call to my office to announce my arrival and contact details. After more than twenty-two hours on the road, even on a bed as hard as a marble slab, I was prepared to sleep, but there was an urgent knocking on my door and a demand for money for the phone call.

'Can't this wait till I check out?'

'Oh no. Must be paid now.'

The following evening, the Australian commentator, Jim Maxwell, and I watched on television the riot that ended the first semi-final in Calcutta, when defeat for India was certain. Our semi-final on the evening after that was also dramatic, but only in a cricketing sense, as the West Indies appeared to throw away a certain match-winning position.

Securing a flight back to Lahore for the final was now the priority and the authorities had been reluctant to guarantee anybody a seat on the two shuttles being run by the one charter aircraft. An anxious day was spent arguing, bargaining and parting with vast quantities of rupees, in what appeared to be inducements to be issued with a ticket for a flight that had been paid for some time before. Before going in a spirit of uncertainty to the airport, I bade a none-too-sorry farewell to the Hotel Metro 35.

My bill must be paid for in cash. I had travellers' cheques or credit cards.

'We cannot change travellers' cheques here. You must go to the bank.'

'It is Sunday. Will it be open?' I asked.

'No.'

Eventually, faced with no other option, he agreed to take a credit card. I signed the slip. Then, checking the signature against the one on the card, he took out a ruler and measured the two. 'Is not the same,' he said.

'It's not the same length,' I said. 'Of course it's not. Have you ever tried signing that little strip on the back of a card?'

He was not convinced, but after an animated discussion between three of them, he must have felt I had an honest face.

The airport entrance was jammed. The great and the good of Indian cricket had made sure they were on the first journey of the charter plane, so these were the crowned heads of the rest of world cricket, together with a few Australian journalists and me.

We had no idea if any of us would get on this flight until a man stood on a box in the entrance hall and called out names to hand out the tickets. To see the childish excitement and relief of the chairmen of national cricket boards as they won their tickets, in what seemed like a lottery, was entertaining – once I had secured my own, of course.

Chandigarh is not an international airport, but, having been elevated to that status just for this evening, the local officials were determined to make the most of it. There were more passport, boarding card, and customs checks than you would normally get in an entire tour. At last, we were all crammed into the spartan departure hall. The aeroplane was a hundred yards from us across the tarmac. The doors were opened by a policeman. We all surged forward and then he held up a hand. 'We have to wait for a VIP to board first,' he said.

'What did he say?' asked the chairman of the Australian Cricket Board, just behind me.

'They're waiting for someone important,' I told him.

When we were eventually allowed up the steps onto the aircraft, sitting in seat 1A, with a huge smile on his face, was Sunil Gavaskar. 'Fair enough,' I said to him. 'There aren't too many more important than you.'

Now for the next worry of the trip. During the two months of the tournament and its warm-up phase, I had stayed in the Pearl Continental Hotel in Lahore on seven different occasions and had observed the progress of their building a new wing, which would more than double the size of the hotel. From talking to the hotel staff, I had found that this wing would be a crucial part of the accommodation plans for the World Cup final. Two things became clear to me. First, it would not be ready in time and second, it was fully booked. Therefore the hotel would be short of rooms and I could well imagine that a foreign broadcaster on the second flight coming from the second semi-final was a prime candidate to be kicked out.

I had tried to pre-empt this when I was last there by making sure that my booking was set in stone but more importantly, unknown to me, Aggers, who had arrived there the previous day, had explained to them that should they not have a room for me, they would experience an explosion that would make Pakistan's nuclear deterrent seem like a pop-gun. Thus, when I came into the utter chaos of a foyer full of VIPs clamouring for rooms, I was hailed by the man at the desk and a key was passed to me over a host of jealous heads.

Forty-eight hours later, several of those VIPs were to find that, when they went for interval refreshments between the innings of the final, their seats were taken by others with seemingly perfectly valid tickets. My last impression of the final was of hundreds of people crowded onto the presentation stand, so that Benazir Bhutto, then prime minister of Pakistan, could hardly be made out in the throng as she handed the World Cup to Sri Lanka's Arjuna Ranatunga.

DOWN UNDER
AND BEYOND

My first experience of Australia came in 1982, the year after my first trip to India. I soon discovered how very different two tours can be. If broadcasting from the subcontinent has its little problems, on the whole, travel and technical facilities work down under.

I started in Perth and on my first night was dined in the wonderful old colonial Weld Club by Henry Blofeld and *The Times* correspondent, John Woodcock. It was a splendid but untypical introduction to the wide brown land. The WACA ground in Perth was then still more like an English county ground than the other large Australian Test grounds. The ABC commentary box was a hut on scaffolding at the unbuilt-up Swan River End of the ground and from there I enticed the veteran Australian commentator, Alan McGilvray, to visit us periodically at the opposite end for a session of commentary.

In Sydney for the game against New South Wales I was able for the only time to sit on the famous 'Hill' which led up to the splendid old scoreboard. By my next visit the Hill had gone and a stand had been erected right in front of the scoreboard. That was a listed building, so could not be demolished, thus a different sort of vandalism had been required.

Fond as I am of the Sydney Cricket Ground, its radio facilities have never been ideal. For my first series there, the BBC position was at a long desk below the press box windows, where we were looked after by an American engineer who became fascinated with the game for the first time – a triumph for *TMS*. By that stage of the tour our commentary team had been bolstered by the arrival of Messrs Trueman, Bailey and Johnston, whose first grandchild was born during the course of the Test match.

The day before the Sydney Test, Johnners had turned up at my hotel in a borrowed Mini, wearing shorts and a floral shirt, and announced that one simply had to go to Bondi Beach on New Year's Day. So he took my wife and me there, hurling himself into the surf with gay abandon, and being thrown up on the beach like a torpedo when he got it right or spitting out seawater and declaring that he had been 'dumped out the back' when he did not.

On first setting foot in the old SCG pavilion, I met Harold Larwood, the diminutive Nottinghamshire bowler who had been the scourge of Australia on the 1932 'Bodyline' tour. Knowing that *Sport on 2* was starting a 'Where are they now?' spot, I arranged to go to interview the great man at his home in the Sydney suburbs. When I told Alan McGilvray about this and the purpose of the interview, he offered another possible victim, the swimmer, Dawn Fraser. By sheer coincidence, I had recently seen a film based on her life, with the gold medals won at three successive Olympic Games and her run-ins with authority, culminating in her ban, for swimming the moat of the Imperial Palace in Tokyo to claim a flag.

On the same memorable evening, therefore, I went to interview two sporting legends. First the diffident Harold Larwood, still resolutely a Nottinghamshire man, while his children and grandchildren, who popped in and out, were inescapably Australian. There on the mantelpiece was a ball presented to him by 'Mr Jardine' for bowling out Australia.

Then on to Balmain to meet Dawn Fraser in the pub she was running. It was an unsophisticated, white-tiled establishment in the old Australian style and we conducted the interview across the bar. We were interrupted occasionally by her need to serve another customer and at one stage a sorry-looking individual appeared in the doorway. In mid-sentence, she just pointed at him and said, 'You, out!'

'Aw, Dawnie,' he whined.

'I've told you before … out!' And as he staggered back into the night she turned back to me. 'Now, where were we?'

I finished by asking about the flag. 'It's on my bed upstairs,' she said with a twinkle.

We did cause the ABC some consternation on that 1982 tour by our desire to mount our own commentary, rather than taking their version with our own commentator added, but it was the way things were going in the BBC, with a greater desire for editorial control. In Brisbane we were given a perch on the camera scaffolding above the press box. When the inevitable evening storm would blow in, we would be almost swept off, but an ingenious ABC engineer rigged a tarpaulin at our backs, which worked until wind forces increased to the point where it acted as a sail and made the structure move. We kept that same position for all our visits until the Gabba was redeveloped as a football stadium at the turn of this century, a move which sadly cost the ground all its unique character. (I had affection for the old place for having met my third wife there, too.)

The Melbourne Test match in 1982 had one of the most thrilling finishes of all time. After some fine bowling by Norman Cowans, the last Australian pair, Border and Thomson, came together on the fourth evening needing 70 for an improbable win. Allan Border was out of form and Jeff Thomson had few batting pretensions. The England tactic was to allow Border the single in order to bowl at Thomson. By the close of the day, however, they were still there.

Our commentary point there was a small cordoned-off area amongst the members' seating at the top of the pavilion. On the bench in front of the commentary desk I had a telephone on which to do my regular Radio 2 reports. The problem was that it was situated immediately under a public address loud-speaker and that, combined with crowd noise echoing under the roof, made it impossible to hear the handover from London. So I was lent a large leather equipment box into which I could thrust my head to hear the cue, emerging to see the scoreboard and my notebook. On my splintered bench there I also squirmed as Border and Thomson inched Australia towards victory.

At the end it all seemed to me to happen in slow motion. With four needed to win, Botham bowled to Thomson who edged it fast, I thought, through the slips. But Chris Tavaré at first slip had got a hand on it and knocked it up. The ball seemed to hang there as Geoff Miller, from second slip, ran behind Tavaré to hold onto it. Incredibly, the match had been won by England by three runs. The next time I saw that commentary position was in 2002, when we were offered it for Pat Murphy to use for his Radio 5 reports.

That win just kept Bob Willis' side in with a chance of retaining the Ashes that Mike Brearley had won. The previous Test in Adelaide had been an abject defeat after Australia had been put in, in ideal batting conditions, and had won by an innings. After the match had been done and dusted on the final day, my wife, Sue, and I had strolled along the Torrens River to Adelaide Zoo. After a pleasant and peaceful couple of hours strolling around, we found out why it was so peaceful. The zoo had been closed for the last half hour and we were locked in. It explained why the animals were studying us with such curiosity. Happily, we were hailed from the cassowary cage – thankfully by a human voice – and released.

In Adelaide, too, I suffered some mistaken identity. It happens on the fringes of a touring team. In India the previous winter I had been asked to sign autographs as Mike Brearley. Early on in this tour a man had enquired if I was Bob Taylor. (A grey-haired theme was emerging.) One day I stepped out of the team hotel in Adelaide to find a man with an autograph book in hot pursuit.

'Look,' I said, 'I'm not Mike Brearley.'

'No, I know that.'

'And I'm not Bob Taylor.'

'No, mate,' he said, apparently unconvinced by my accent, 'you're Vladimir Ashkenazy, aren't you?'

The relative sophistication of Australia means that there is not such a rich vein of stories of unusual events as there are from the Indian subcontinent, but there can be quite a sharp contrast with the big cities when you get out into the country areas.

Just before Christmas 1982 England played Tasmania in a one-day match at Launceston. It was a cosy little ground with a cosy little press box. In the centre of that was an unattended set of broadcasting equipment. During the early exchanges of the game this crackled into life. 'Hello, Bruce, are you there?' The question was repeated loudly, to the irritation of the assembled travelling cricket writers.

'Bartex, can you deal with that? You're the radio man,' said one.

I found the appropriate switch on the unfamiliar gear and responded. 'Can you give us a score, mate?' said the voice. I did so. Twenty minutes later he was back for another score. Then he wondered if I could do a live report on the radio for him. I was well in with Radio Launceston, it seemed.

Some time after the interval, Bruce appeared. 'Sorry, I'm late, mate,' he told his studio. 'Me car went crook.'

'That's OK, mate,' came the answer. 'Some kind old gentleman's been helping us out.' That was greeted with a shout of joy from my colleagues.

I made a slightly more planned appearance on an Australian commercial station on a subsequent tour. I had been joining KYFM Bendigo for periods of commentary on Victoria's game against England and was invited to come on the Sunday evening chat show. Soon after dark, my fellow commentator, who had invited me, came to pick me up from my motel, suggesting that I follow him as he would not be able to get away straight after the programme.

We drove in convoy into the outskirts of Bendigo, ending up to my surprise in a dark railway yard. He led the way onto platform one of the small station and at last I could see one light on in the booking office. 'This is quite an improvement,' said my host. 'We used to be on platform two.' He gestured to what was little more than a bus shelter, which I could just about see on the other side of the track.

In the building there was a large lever set in the floor. 'What would happen if I moved this?' I asked.

'Change the points, I guess.' He did not seem too concerned. I soon found out that while the station might be decommissioned, the line was still active, as the express from Melbourne thundered through.

Off the hallway was the station master's office and a sign saying 'LADIES' WAITING ROOM' and peering through the window I could see a little old lady – waiting.

It turned out she was waiting for her husband, a man in a dog-collar, who was presenting the *Religious Hour* programme. Actually the 'hour' was now well over an hour and a quarter, because my friend was late, but the reverend gentleman was prepared to play another recorded hymn, while we equipped ourselves with cups of coffee.

Still I had seen no live souls other than the vicar and his wife and the two of us. This 'chat show' was likely to be a little thin, I felt. While the kettle was boiling, however, I was offered the chance to see the KYFM control room. At last, I thought, some more human life. That hope was soon dashed, as he opened a cupboard full of blinking lights and meters. 'What if you have a technical problem?' I asked.

'Aw, the engineer can get here in half an hour or so. We're not usually off the air for more than an hour or two.'

So we settled in to our programme. For more than an hour he played a few songs and we talked about cricket and England. I like to think I even did my bit for the British tourist board, before I left him on his own in the small building on platform one, to pick my way back through the darkened back streets into the centre of Bendigo.

My sequence of tours of Australia was broken in 1986/87, when we reverted to sending only Christopher Martin-Jenkins to join the ABC commentary team for the Tests, so I was back on the graveyard shift in the studio. The practice in those days was not to take full commentary on the one-day internationals. However, England got themselves into a position where, having won the Test series to retain the Ashes and taken the one-day series held in Perth as an adjunct to the America's Cup yacht race, they were poised to take the triangular one-day series as well. So we made a late decision to take the ABC commentary on the decisive floodlit match in Melbourne.

At 2 a.m. on a filthy February morning I drove in to Broadcasting House. The rain was coming down in sheets as I arrived. With our late change of plan, we had been allocated a drama studio right under the sloping slate roof of the old part of the building. Being a large area used for radio plays, the studio manager arranged some screens around my desk and microphone to create a more appropriate atmosphere. It left dim and distant dark areas, with curtains hanging in random fashion, and stairs and doors going nowhere to make the right sound effects for the various plays.

The first problem presented itself before we went on the air. Our late line bookings did not seem to have impressed themselves on the necessary telecommunications authorities and we had no broadcast contact. In Melbourne, however, CMJ found a telephone to use while this was being sorted out. Unfortunately, this not being our usual sports studio, the phone was barred for international calls. I had to plead with a BBC switchboard supervisor to be allowed to call Australia, backed with a note of my staff number to bear the charges if it turned out that I was trying it on.

So we went on the air with Christopher commentating. After about twenty minutes he was relieved by Neville Oliver. Then as he was just getting into his stride, we got a crossed line. The voice of someone in a hospitality box appeared, and hearing Neville talking, enquired who he was.

'I'm doing commentary, mate.'

'Nah! Who for?'

'The BBC.'

'Strewth, mate! Hey, guys! The joker on this phone says he's commentating for the BBC!'

At this point the studio manager spotted my urgent gestures to close the line and I started commentating off the television set in the studio, while they wrestled with the communication problem. This is something that does happen occasionally and it is not as easy as it might seem. For a start, you are operating in total silence. Then you are completely dependent on the pictures you have in front of you and action replays can cause you problems. A shot may be played, the director cuts to the fielder, and you are then trying to work out from the shot where that fielder is stationed.

While I was getting round those sorts of pitfalls and glancing frequently at the studio window to observe people on telephones trying to sort out the problems, I heard the ominous sound of another one. The rain had found a way through the ceiling and somewhere in the distance a steady dripping sound could be heard. Evidently it was audible over the microphone, because a man tiptoed in with a bucket. The drip became louder and then, as the bucket filled, it became more fluid. I could feel hysteria rising, made worse by the knowledge that, as the last line of defence, I could not afford to get a fit of the giggles. The voice in my headphones that told me I could hand over to Melbourne was one of the great lifelines.

However remote you are in Australia on Melbourne Cup day, you will always be aware of the big race. I have seen women spilling out of pubs in Brisbane, a thousand miles from the Flemington race track, done up to the nines for the occasion of watching the race on television as if they were at Royal Ascot. It was not quite like that in Dublin, South Australia, in 1991, when Aggers and I and a couple of other journalists broke our journey to watch the race en route from Adelaide to Port Pirie.

Dublin would be a one-horse town if the horse was still there, so the arrival of a quartet of Poms in the pub was unusual. All conversation stopped as we walked in. We broke the silence with, 'Landlord, do you have four glasses of foaming ale?' and the ice was thoroughly melted as we all gathered round to watch the running of Australia's equivalent of the Derby.

The previous year, my first experience of Test cricket in the Caribbean had been dramatic. It was 1990 and the West Indies were still invincible. Tony Cozier wrote in an article before the First Test in Jamaica, relishing the alliteration, that an England win would be 'a calamity too catastrophic to contemplate.' Much was being made of England's previous Sabina Park Test, when an uneven pitch and Patrick Patterson had proved far too hot to handle.

On the first morning of the match there was an exceptionally tense air, especially amongst those players I saw in the hotel breakfast room.

Making a broadcasting debut with *Test Match Special* was the recently retired Michael Holding. I had first seen him in action in 1976, when the West Indies came to England. I watched him then from square on in the match against MCC at Lord's and saw frightening speed. He was playing for Tasmania when I went to Australia in 1982 and I went there to get an interview with him. Eddie Hemmings, the England off-spinner, reassured me. 'He's really very nice … for a fast bowler!' And so he proved. When I first arrived in Kingston, I gave his home a call to confirm the details of his working on *TMS*.

His wife answered. 'Ee hon de street,' she said.

'I'm sorry?'

'Ee hon de street.'

'Oh, he's gone out?'

'Yeh, man. Ee hon de street.' It was my first real encounter with Jamaican speech.

When the Test started it was business as usual for the great opening partnership of Greenidge and Haynes. Then Gordon Greenidge played a ball down to long-leg, where it was fumbled on the boundary by Devon Malcolm. They ran on the misfield and the throw was rifled in. Greenidge was out by a yard. Malcolm's former Derbyshire colleague, Holding, was called on for a comment. 'They forget,' he said. 'He's the worst fielder … with the best arm!'

From that small incident the Test match turned England's way. We came to the rest day with England on the brink of a victory that hardly anyone in the world – probably no one outside the England dressing room – could have expected. But ominously, late that evening, torrential rain swept down on Kingston from the Blue Mountains and the fourth day was washed out. Now the jovial Holding was entertaining us in the commentary box with his version of a rain dance.

We need not have worried. The job was completed on the fifth morning, with Wayne Larkins scoring the winning runs. The interviews with the captains afterwards were both rather sticky. Graham Gooch seemed resentful at everyone's surprise at the victory, while Viv Richards appeared to be reasserting the pride that had helped to make his team so great.

This had been the first Test for two men who would go on to captain England – Nasser Hussain and Alec Stewart. Interviewing the coach, Micky

Stewart, the day before the match, I had tried to get some sort of fatherly reaction to his son's first cap. Micky always tried hard to divorce that relationship from the job in hand, but after a long pause, he just said, 'His mother will be very pleased.'

We moved on from Jamaica to Guyana, a twenty-four hour journey that involved a flight to Trinidad via Puerto Rico, Antigua and Barbados, then an overnight stay in a collection of shacks that purported to be the airport hotel in Port of Spain, before a dawn flight on to Georgetown. The journey was made slightly less enjoyable by seeing, as we backed off the stand at Kingston, my suitcase sitting on the tarmac. There were a few others with it; one of them, it turned out, belonging to the man in the seat in front of me. His name was Viv Richards, so I left it to him to make the not-unreasonable query about British West Indian Airways' plans for that luggage. It would catch up with us in twenty-four hours, we were told. After a sticky day and night, so it did. Fortunately, with that overnight stop, I had made some provision in my hand luggage.

Life in Guyana would become very much easier over the next few years, but then it had its problems. One of them was that there were only eight international telephone lines out of the country. To call London you just had to keep dialling and dialling and, once in about ten attempts, it would connect. Thus it was infuriating when Allan Lamb came across to the commentary box one morning, asked, 'Can I borrow your phone, Bartex?', and got through to his family in South Africa first time.

Georgetown is below sea level, so the drainage canals around the city have a crucial role to play when it rains, but in those days their maintenance had been rather neglected. When the predictable rain fell, the system overflowed and the ground flooded. The Test match was abandoned and a one-day international played on what would have been the last day.

During that tour we shared with the local commentary in some places, but the advice I had received was that this would not be such a good idea in Guyana and Antigua. I followed this plan, but it did bring me into some political conflict. In Guyana, when we could not get through, I was told many stories, including that we had made no line bookings, but mysteriously the Guyana Broadcasting Corporation's commentary on the one-day international appeared on a line in the control room in Broadcasting House in London.

There was more drama in the next Test in Trinidad, where England got themselves into a winning position, needing 151 for victory on the last day. Two things prevented this. First Graham Gooch, the captain, was hit on the hand by Ezra Moseley and had to retire hurt. Then the afternoon was ruined by rain. When that stopped, England were anxious to get going again – the West Indians, including the groundstaff, less so.

Bulletins on Gooch's ability to return if needed were, it seemed, upbeat as play resumed. The West Indian bowlers were keen to make it clear that the conditions were unplayable. Bowlers walked back to their marks increasingly slowly and the light began to fail, to the extent that eventually the chase had to be abandoned.

Walking down the ground to get close-of-play interviews in the pavilion at the far end, I was struck by the fact that the bowlers' run-ups did, indeed, seem to be a quagmire. In the forecourt of the pavilion, I waited for Gooch to do his television interview and heard him say that his injury was a break. He was out of the rest of the tour.

Knowing that, back in the commentary box, CMJ was busy doing all his close-of-play pieces, was frustrating. In those days before mobile phones, I could not give him the news until I got back to find him packed up and ready to leave. He was not pleased with the news I brought.

In Barbados we found ourselves embroiled in a diplomatic incident during the Test match. In the closing stages of the fourth day's play, I had gone down to the visitors' dressing room to get an interview with England's best bowler, Gladstone Small. The England innings had just started as I came into the passage outside the dressing room and became aware of a huge shout from the middle. The door opened and my interview target emerged, padded up to go out as night watchman. The man he was replacing, Rob Bailey, was the next to appear up the steps from the ground, saying as he passed me, 'Would you bloody believe it?'

To find out what had happened to deny me my interview I had to return to the commentary box. A ball from Ian Bishop had flicked Bailey's hip and been taken behind the wicket. The umpire, Lloyd Barker, had been handing the bowler his cap after that last ball of the over, when he looked up to see the West Indies captain, Viv Richards, charging down the pitch, arms twirling, in full-throated appeal for a catch behind. Belatedly Barker raised a finger.

At the close of play Christopher Martin-Jenkins was recording a 'think piece' to be used on Radio 4's *Today* programme next morning. His theme was the players' responsibilities to the game. 'Both sides,' he said, 'have cheated each other in the matter of over-rates.' He went on to add, on the general subject of player conduct, that, 'Today a previously good umpire was pressured into changing his decision.'

Our close-of-play reports and interviews would all appear late at night in London in one Broadcasting House studio and the tapes would then be distributed to the programmes for which they were destined. But the World Service in Bush House had a feed of the line from Barbados, so that they could use any relevant piece. Unfortunately, this weighty editorial appealed to them.

Many West Indian radio stations rebroadcast items that they pick up from the BBC World Service and this piece, that had been crafted carefully for Radio 4, was on the air in Barbados first thing next morning. This was the rest day of the Test, so I was late to surface, but when I switched on the radio it was to find outraged discussion building on VOB (Voice of Barbados), the very station with which we were sharing commentary. It was being referred to as 'The Martin-Jenkins Affair'.

I went with Christopher to the rest-day press conference at the England team hotel and there he joined in a discussion programme on VOB with Erskine King, one of our fellow commentators, but now one of the leaders of the campaign of condemnation. The word 'cheat' had been included in a piece which also mentioned the West Indies captain and a Barbadian umpire. Thus the inevitable connection was being made.

I was due to meet members of the Caribbean Broadcasting Union at lunchtime and tried to play the diplomat, but by the time I returned to my room and the radio, the level of hysteria had been racked up a few notches and the Barbados Navy, it seemed, was being called on to sail up the River Thames. I listened to a phone-in, in which a man inappropriately called 'The Moderator' incited his callers to be even more extreme than they had been when they initiated the call.

I could not imagine how we could join forces with VOB again in the morning. Sure enough, while I was having a quiet evening meal, I was called to the phone by the head waiter and it was the station's managing director saying much the same. So next day I had to get our own commentary up and running, with help, ironically, from the VOB engineers. Tony Cozier joined us, but there were other locals who declined, as we described a West Indies victory which levelled the series with one to play.

I answered one knock on the commentary box door to find a large man, with

'BAILIFF' written on a card on his lapel, asking for Mr Martin Jenkins. 'He's on the air,' I said, but later he did manage to serve a writ on CMJ on behalf of the umpire. It was settled out of court by the BBC two years later on the advice that, while there was no case to answer, he could not hope to win in Barbados.

The final Test was in Antigua, the other place where it had been recommended to me that we should do our own commentary. Early on it became clear that there would be no local help for us in that enterprise. On the first morning of the match, when I had set up a commentary position on the front desk of the press box – in which our writing colleagues, recognising our problem, were unusually understanding – the leading light of the local commentary team was still arguing with Cable and Wireless that we had no rights to do any commentary and there-fore they should not connect our line. The C & W official, while sympathetic to us, was not inclined to risk making the final connection.

Two overs of the Test match had been bowled before I was able to involve the American executive with whom we had made our rights deal and he could confirm the position and silence the opposition. The Cable and Wireless man, hovering on the edge of the discussion, spoke into his walkie-talkie and by the time I got back up the stairs we had London on the line.

There was one other strange incident during that Test, when West Indies took the field on the second morning while their captain was still in the press box, wearing T-shirt and jeans, and remonstrating with one of the English journalists who had written something critical. Viv Richards had a stroke of good fortune when a brief shower soon after the start enabled him to rejoin his team discreetly and be there when they retook the field.

On our next visit to Antigua, four years later, a very diffident Viv was part of our commentary team. He came to me on the first day to ask for the pass which I had assumed he would not need.

'But there's a stand named after you over there,' I said.

'They forget,' was his sad reply.

I gave him my one spare, which Trevor Bailey had left with me when he went home. So Viv entered the ground for the rest of that Test with Trevor's picture hanging round his neck. No one queried it.

In my early days of doing the job, it seemed unthinkable that we would find ourselves on a cricket tour of South Africa, but in November 1995, for the first of what seemed so many times, I was landing in a Johannesburg dawn. On that occasion I was flying immediately on to catch up with the tour in Kimberley, which gave me what may have been an unfair impression of a country stuck in a 1960s time warp, after their years of social and sporting isolation.

Though England were beaten 1–0 in the Test series, the most remarkable innings was played by Mike Atherton to save the Second Test in Johannesburg. He batted for the best part of two days for 185 not out to save a game which had seemed irredeemably lost.

Christmas on that tour at the Somerstrand Inn in Port Elizabeth was memorably bleak. It is one of the downsides of cricket tours that we celebrate Christmas on the eve of a Test match on a regular basis at least every other year in Australia and South Africa. Sometimes the day surprises you by being successfully convivial, as it did in Calcutta in 1984.

In Zimbabwe, in 1996, I discovered a number of relations and enjoyed a Christmas dinner in Marondera, about fifty miles from Harare, with a party of ten or so all sharing the surname Baxter.

I think of that tour of Zimbabwe whenever there are any news stories of that troubled country and I am glad that I saw it while it was still a wonderful place. It was an inglorious cricketing trip for England, remembered more for the coach's claims that 'we murdered them' after the drawn match in Bulawayo. Zimbabwe won the one-day series comprehensively and, with two drawn Tests, could claim to have had the better of the tour on the field, although England's poor image off the field was more damaging.

I was writing a book on the tour as a joint diary with David Lloyd, then the England coach. With Aggers covering the New Zealand leg of the winter, the three of us put together *Out of the Rough*, a book which was something of a well-kept secret. As he was an employee of the Test and County Cricket Board, I had to put David's part of the book past the authorities and when the man deputed to read the manuscript finally responded, his reaction was not welcoming.

'We've got a few problems.'

'OK,' I said. 'What page?'

'Well, let's start with page one. It says that the team were given one little bus from the airport.'

'They were.'

'Yes, but we don't really want to talk about the Zimbabwean facilities. Actually we'd rather not mention Zimbabwe.'

'It is a book about the tour, you know.' In the end David eased the passage of the book through the Board.

While that 'little bus' had been collecting the team at Harare airport, I had been picking up the hire car that I was to have throughout the tour. Five years later, when I returned for a one-day series, the hiring of a car at all was effectively impossible. On this occasion, though, the man showed me round the vehicle and pointed out the spare wheel in the boot. It was as shiny and smooth as a Formula One racing slick.

'It's not overburdened with tread,' I said.

'Oh, no, sah,' he said proudly.

After England had been defeated by Mashonaland in Harare, I left a day ahead of the rest, to drive down to Bulawayo to recce facilities at the two venues where England would be playing. After four hours on the road I arrived at the Bulawayo Athletic Club, where the match against Matabeleland would be staged. Not a soul was to be seen, but eventually I heard a buzz of conversation from the bar area of the clubhouse. So I headed in that direction. All conversation stopped as I entered and about twenty pairs of piercing eyes were fixed on me from leathery faces used to the African sun. 'Hello,' I said, 'I'm from the BBC.'

Fortunately, the response was entirely welcoming and I found myself having to decline most of the offers of refreshment if I was going to be capable of working at all.

It was the other ground – the Queen's Club – that would stage the one-day international and the Test match and eventually I found where they intended that we should site our commentary position. A low rostrum, no more than a foot high had been placed at the boundary's edge, but that was where it ended. After some appeals a canvas roof was put over it and then, when it became clear that this platform would house *Test Match Special*, Radio 5 and Radio Zimbabwe, a stack of large wooden boards arrived. I contacted the local telecom people who provided eight twisted wires for me to sort out.

With the aid of lengths of duck tape and string and a great deal of trial and error I did achieve three commentary positions and contact with the outside world on the wires and even found a source of electricity to power our equipment. I always regarded getting on the air in Bulawayo as one of the triumphs of my career.

I saw England off to New Zealand at the end of that tour and went off on a wonderful trip right round the beautiful country to celebrate my fiftieth birthday.

Since then, of course, the BBC has been declared persona non grata by the Mugabe regime. We negotiated to get into the country in 2001 for a one-day series and at the end of 2004 we were due to go again. England's tour of South Africa that year was starting with two warm-up games in Namibia and then – to appease the international cricket community – a one-day international series in Zimbabwe.

We had put in our visa applications in good time and had been assured by the Zimbabwean cricket authorities that all would be well. The day after England's second game in Namibia, I was to fly with the team and press to Johannesburg, meeting Jonathan Agnew at the airport and carrying straight on to Harare. But, as we were all packing up for the last time on the verandah that served as a press box at the Windhoek Sports Club, the team public relations man came to us with a missive from Cricket Zimbabwe, sent via Lord's. It was a list of the media organisations that would not be allowed to send a representative into their country. Of course, it was headed by the BBC, although the selection of newspapers that were out of favour seemed remarkably random.

Back at the team hotel that evening, I found myself in the unusual position of giving press conferences to the players on the current situation. Aggers was already on his way to Johannesburg, so we kept our appointment – but at a Sandton hotel, rather than the airport.

The impasse was broken by the action of the players themselves. They were always reluctant to go to Zimbabwe anyway, but refused to do so at all if half the press corps was banned, so they also left Johannesburg airport for an hotel, rather than continue their journey. For a welcome change, too, the ICC supported England's position. After forty-eight hours, when Aggers and I had booked our flights home, things started to move and suddenly we were granted admission.

The two of us got onto the evening flight to Harare, eighteen hours ahead of the team and the rest of the press. Heartened by being met by a British diplomat, we presented ourselves to the immigration desk, where the official looked dubious. Aggers spotted our names on a list on the wall behind the desk and cheerily pointed this out to the man. 'That's good news,' he said.

'No,' said the uniformed official, who was noticeably being shadowed by a sinister character in a dark suit. 'It is not good news.'

No word of the ban being lifted had reached the airport. While the two behind the desk discussed putting us in a cell before the first flight back to

Johannesburg in the morning, we made contact with the local cricket board. They had not expected us to arrive yet, but someone would come to the airport.

For the next hour we managed to argue successfully against the cell option that seemed most popular with the officials, and the arrival of the Cricket Zimbabwe man, with a revised list of those to allow into the country, saw us united with the luggage that we had been able to watch going round the carousel in the distance. We were welcomed at our hotel by the chairman and vice-chairman of the ECB, who themselves had spent several days in diplomatic discussion to save the tour.

Next day Aggers and I were back at the airport to report live on the team's arrival, before I had an interview in a government office with a charming, but frightened official, who insisted that if we used our satellite communications system to broadcast we must pay two thousand US dollars a day. After I had assured him, in that case, that I would not use it, he was nervous enough to ring me in the hotel a couple of times for reassurance that I was really not going to do so. As it was likely that the plainclothed policeman based in the corridor was going through my room in my absence, I made sure the equipment stayed where it was – and fortunately found another set to use.

On the whole, what we saw on that trip was quite sanitised, but one evening the British press corps was given a drinks party by senior members of Zanu PF, President Mugabe's governing party. These, for the most part, were a chilling collection of individuals, doing a little to appear welcoming, but missing no opportunity to tell us of the failings of Tony Blair and the rest of our country.

My final cricket tour for the BBC was the ninth World Cup in 2007 in the West Indies. That was a much criticised tournament – with some justification. But away from the problems with the quality of the cricket, there is something wonderful about any World Cup and the way we meet up with old friends from all round the world. I remember when South Africa first returned to the fold for the 1992 competition, having dinner in Auckland, New Zealand, with a mixed bunch of broadcasters from various countries. Among them were the much-travelled South African commentator, Gerald de Kock, and his producer, Gawie Swart, who was on his first overseas trip.

Gerald said to me quietly, 'Gawie's eyes are out on stalks at the way you all know each other so well.' It has been one of the privileges of the job, to have made so many friends worldwide.

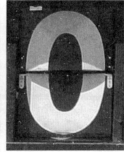

FOREIGN FRIENDS

At the end of February 2007 I set off for the ninth cricket World Cup. I had worked on the first in 1975 and while this 'complete set' of World Cups was not unique, it was at least a rare achievement. Each one has been a challenge to present on the radio, but one of the most delightful features has always been the meeting with the international family of friends that has built up in the broadcasting of cricket.

Back in 1975, the Australian Broadcasting Commission, as it was then, did not send a commentator. The legendary Alan McGilvray kept his powder dry until the four-match Test series which followed the tournament, so when Australia reached the final we recruited Graham Dawson, ABC Sport's Melbourne man, who was on holiday in Britain with his English wife. 'Smokey' Dawson subsequently became a very much more flamboyant sports commentator on a Melbourne commercial station, his outrageous manner making him a great favourite with Radio 5 Live producers looking for a 'typical Aussie' view during various Ashes Test series and he delights in playing up loudly to the outrageous stereotype.

But it was Alan McGilvray who was the main ABC commentator for most of the forty years after the Second World War. He had started radio broadcasting in 1935, when the ABC asked him to do close-of-play despatches from their studios on Sheffield Shield matches in which he was playing, when he had just been made captain of New South Wales. These summaries led to him being asked to take part in a remarkable piece of broadcasting history, known as the 'synthetic' Test commentaries.

In 1938 broadcasting lines from England were unreliable and frequently of unusable quality, so for the Ashes series there the ABC decided to put a commentary team in a Sydney studio overnight, armed with a large photograph of each venue and backed up by a sound effects man. They were supplied with a succession of cryptic cables from their man at the match on the other side of the world, on which they elaborated to create the commentary on the game and the scene, ball-by-ball, just a few minutes after it had happened. Famously, the sound of bat on ball was alleged to be made with a pencil on a block of wood.

That was enough of an experience to encourage Alan McGilvray to take up the real thing after the war. In 1948 that meant accompanying Bradman's invincible side to England.

Early in that tour, McGilvray overheard a less than appreciative comment about him made by John Arlott, which meant that the two men never really got on in all the years they worked together. Indeed, one of the first things I was instructed when preparing a commentary rota, was that I must never schedule McGilvray straight after Arlott, because he would pick holes in much of what John had said. Possibly as a result of this, I am not sure that Alan ever cared much for Poms in general, but he was always greatly appreciated by the *Test Match Special* audience. Commentary being a competitive business, it may well be that he raised his game considerably in England when flanked by the likes of Arlott and Johnston.

In Australia, Alan was untouchable in an ABC commentary team which would normally be made up of himself, a visiting commentator and the local general sports commentator, whose principal sphere of expertise might well not be in cricket. That position of security may have encouraged him in December 1960 to leave Brisbane ahead of the end of the First Test match with the West Indies, which appeared to be heading for a dull draw. He was met by his wife at Sydney airport where he just confirmed the result with her.

'I don't think "draw" was the word they used,' she said. 'I thought they said "tie".'

'No,' said Alan, 'that's wrong. Ties don't happen in Test cricket.'

But a tie it was. And the commentators who did stay got themselves in such a muddle when three wickets fell in the last over that they had to come back the next day to record a dummy commentary for posterity.

Having been sent to England for the 1948 tour, Alan left the ABC fold for a time, so that the 1953 series was covered by Bernie Kerr, later to be ABC's Head of Sport, and the 1956 series by Michael Charlton, later to join BBC television as presenter of *Panorama* and other current affairs programmes. But from the late 1950s through to his retirement in 1985, ABC coverage was synonymous with Alan McGilvray.

My own relationship with him was very good. On the second night after my first arrival in Australia, he summoned me to his room at the hotel he was staying in next door to mine in Perth, so that he could welcome me to the country. He took the top off the whisky bottle and threw it away, with a favourite saying of his, 'We won't be needing that again!' I am relieved to say that he did summon help to dispose of the contents. I was also greatly honoured towards the end of the tour to be invited to 'a function at my unit', discovering after a moment's hesitation that this translated as 'a party at my flat'.

He was less upset than many in the ABC that we had decided for that 1982 tour to mount our own commentary. Over the previous few Ashes series in Australia he had been considerably irritated by having to build the commentary rota around CMJ's need to be available for telephoned reports to Radio 2.

I remember those commentaries for the wonderful relationship between Alan and his regular summariser, the former Australian captain, Lindsay Hassett. Lindsay was the nicest of men and shrewdest of summarisers, with whom my first contact came when I used to get in touch with the ABC box from London at the end of the lunch interval, often finding him the only one there for a chat. Thus, when we had the Centenary Test match at Lord's, I was delighted to persuade Lindsay, along with Keith Miller, to join us in the commentary team.

The McGilvray style was confidential and detailed. He would place an elbow on either side of the microphone stand on the desk and observe the action through his binoculars. Those binoculars carried a small typed warning, underlined in red for the unwary, that the focus *must not* be adjusted. If more needed to be said about a delivery or a shot, he would introduce it with, 'I'll go back on that.' This was just one of the trademark phrases with which we grew familiar. Another favourite, as he might be looking at the way a match was panning out, was, 'That's for the future'.

Should anyone get on the wrong side of him, they might be warned, 'Don't take me too far.' Henry Blofeld suggested at Old Trafford in 1981, when a crucial Australian wicket fell, 'that might be the last nail in Australia's coffin.'

A loud grumble came from the back of the box: 'We're not dead yet.' Alan followed that up with a few terse words to Henry, which prompted a highly amused Brian Johnston to comment, 'Blowers took McGillers too far!'

That was probably a sign of the fact that Alan really did care deeply about the fate of Australia's cricketers and on that 1981 tour he had already seen them have victory snatched from them at the last minute at Headingley and Edgbaston.

He might have been passionately patriotic, but he was never blind to faults he might see in the conduct of some Australian teams. The 1977 team in England were among those who incurred his displeasure, not least for their normally scruffy appearance. That was the tour on which news of the start of Kerry Packer's World Series Cricket broke and that was an upheaval of which he thoroughly disapproved.

Ironically, however, late in his career, it gave his profile something of a boost. In the face of the revolution of television cricket coverage by Australia's Channel Nine, the ABC examined their own strength and decided it was Alan McGilvray. Their counter to the hype from the opposition was a ditty:

'He's everything to cricket,

'Cricket's everything to him, you know,

'The game is not the same without McGilvray.'

All was resolved by the time Alan came to England in 1985 on his last tour. This time the ABC decided it was sensible to send an experienced producer and broadcaster, Alan Marks, to hold his hand and, importantly, to guide him through the close-of-play reports and spare him the need to do any interviews with the players. Again, he was unfortunate in having to cover an Ashes win for England in a memorable series. It might not have been kind of me, in retrospect, to have put him on at the end to describe the moment when Les Taylor caught and bowled Murray Bennett to win the Ashes for David Gower's side. He did that last commentary as matter-of-factly as ever, ending with, 'Well, that's my story.' He was overwhelmed by the huge pile of mail for him in the commentary box, wishing him well.

With the headquarters of the ABC being in Sydney, we all expected to see Jim Maxwell, also from that city, coming to England on the next Australian tour, but it was Alan Marks, the man who had accompanied McGilvray on his last tour, who made the decision to pick someone whom he thought would appeal more to the *Test Match Special* style. His choice was Neville Oliver.

Post-McGilvray, the ABC had assembled a very strong Test match commentary team, which did not need to rely on the presence of an overseas commentator. The trio were Jim Maxwell, Neville Oliver and Tim Lane. All three were versatile, Jim also doing rugby commentaries on television and radio, Neville, based in Tasmania, having dealt initially with his own sport of rowing and Tim, living in Melbourne, dividing his year between cricket and Australian Rules football.

Neville came to England with the 1989 Australians. Mike Gatting's team had defied all the pre-tour hype to retain the Ashes down under in 1986/87, winning two one-day tournaments for good measure, so England were favourites for a change when Alan Border returned to these shores. The comprehensive Australian win, by 4–0, made something of a hero of the man who conveyed the news to his listeners. He was popular with British listeners, too. They enjoyed the larger than life presence of the man nicknamed 'Big Red' in Tasmania and his colourful range of similes. (We did not inflict on our audience Neville's other Australian nickname, 'Bubbles'. Apparently in his early broadcasting days another presenter thought the name Neville Oliver 'sounded like a fart in the bath'.)

Neville, for his part, fitted happily into the *TMS* family, where Johnners nicknamed him 'The Doctor'. This came from my practice of putting up the commentary rota with initials against the timings. Brian, looking up to see who was following him, saw the legend 'NO' and announced that it would be 'Doctor NO'. The name stuck to the extent that by the end of the tour he had received some requests for medical advice.

With the endorsement of the success of the 1989 tour in both cricketing and broadcasting terms behind him, Neville was soon appointed head of ABC Radio Sport, commuting from his home in Tasmania to Sydney, when necessary. He did, however, continue to tour with the cricket team to South Africa and twice more to England. Returning home after the 1997 series, he found himself on a collision course with ABC management over policy and resigned. I was delighted to encounter him in Hobart just before Christmas the following year for a convivial lunch, and he was to make an appearance at the Sydney Olympics, doing rowing commentary.

Following the departure of Neville, it was Tim Lane who was selected to cover the 1999 World Cup for the ABC, calling Australia home in the final at Lord's, as they completed an overwhelming victory over Pakistan. He did admit in his commentary that some of the world's cricket followers might sometimes find his countrymen a little arrogant – a concession that says more about the self-effacing Tim.

A few days earlier in the commentary box at Edgbaston I had had to make a delicate decision about whether he or Gerald de Kock should describe the end of the semi-final between South Africa and Australia. In such circumstances, a producer usually tries to put on the commentator from the winning country, but this one was getting a bit too close to call. I went for Tim and it proved the right choice – just – as Allan Donald hesitated fatally over what would have been the winning run and the match was tied. Tim described the chaotic scene perfectly and knew that the tie put Australia through, by virtue of having won the previous encounter between the two sides.

Incidentally, that day had started with a certain amount of chaos in the commentary box. Just before the scheduled time for going on the air, I received two distressed phone calls. The first was from Aggers: 'Backers, you'll have to start with someone else; the M6 is jammed solid and I'm in the middle of it.' Then, minutes later, came a panicked call from Simon Mann saying that he was lost in the lanes of Worcestershire, trying to find his way from our hotel. I looked around for foreign support. Behind the commentary box Tim Lane was broadcasting on his mobile phone to ABC and Gerald de Kock was doing the same service for SABC. The summarisers, it seemed, were also lost in traffic. I was on the air on my own. Fortunately, after I had discussed the teams and the toss with myself for a bit, both Tim and Gerald ended their respective calls and joined in the anticipation of what became a wonderful day's cricket – eventually also enjoyed by Agnew and Mann.

The tour of 2001 was shared between Messrs Lane and Maxwell and shortly after that, Tim Lane was finding it hard to decline the offers from television stations to leave the ABC to become exclusively an Australian Rules commentator. Love and the opportunity to spend a little less time away from home won the day, but it was a delight to persuade Tim to rejoin the *TMS* team for a couple of Tests during the Ashes series in Australia in 2006/07.

Jim Maxwell first took part in a *TMS* broadcast during the 1983 World Cup in England, in which Australia did not distinguish themselves, bowing out after defeat by India, the eventual winners, at Chelmsford. He proved himself a good member of the team, with a bit more of the brash Sydneysider than we know today. By the time he was confirmed as the undisputed number one in Australian radio commentary, he had mellowed considerably. He had weathered the disappointment of not immediately taking McGilvray's place in the commentary hierarchy philosophically.

This is not to say that he is not persistently certain that Australia will always prevail on the cricket field. We are used to being told in the final words of any match forecast, 'These guys are just too good.' I suppose on that basis we did rather enjoy 2005 in the *TMS* commentary box, but we would have to concede that, despite a lack of recent practice, Jim was gracious in defeat. He was able to appreciate the quality of the cricket and even the excitement of his hosts, as against all the odds, England recovered the Ashes.

It was not a result to dent his general confidence in Australia and he seemed to join the rest of his countrymen in expecting the recapture of the Ashes to be as ruthless and overwhelming as it turned out to be. Even with all the potential pitfalls of a World Cup, Jim, for two successive tournaments, has planned his itinerary on the basis that Australia would win every game, without making any back-up plan. He has not been disappointed. When he commentated on Australia winning the eighth tournament in Johannesburg, he continued an intriguing piece of radio history, in that the conclusion of all eight World Cups to that point had been described on BBC radio by a different commentator. The continuation of that little record was inevitably going to end in Barbados in the 2007 World Cup, when all the available commentators had done one finish. In the end, the chaos that surrounded the end of that tournament made it seem not such a bad thing.

(For the record, the eight were: 1975 Brian Johnston; 1979 Tony Cozier; 1983 Christopher Martin-Jenkins; 1987 Henry Blofeld; 1992 Peter Baxter; 1996 Jonathan Agnew; 1999 Tim Lane; and 2003 Jim Maxwell.)

There was a time when Tony Cozier might have had the same confidence in the performances of the West Indies. He is a thoroughly professional journalist, of course, but he has felt the decline of the game in the Caribbean sorely. I remember an evening in an hotel in Bristol in 2000, when Zimbabwe had just beaten West Indies in the first ever floodlit one-day international in England. Over our late supper, Tony Cozier, Viv Richards and Donna Symmonds became more and more agitated as they discussed the deficiencies in the West Indian performance. Interestingly, it was Tony and Donna, the two Barbadians, whose patois became increasingly incomprehensible to the rest of us.

Tony's father, Jimmy, was also a great man of West Indian journalism. On my first trip to the West Indies, I had the great pleasure of talking to him and hearing about the early days when he had to send dispatches by Morse code. Now Tony's son, Craig, is making it a third generation in the business, editing the *Caribbean Cricket Quarterly* and working for television stations covering the game around the world. The new media centre at Kensington bears three names of Barbados journalism – Coppin, Cozier and Short. We were able to tease Tony during the World Cup by asking him which Cozier it referred to.

It is a great measure of the regard in which Tony is held that he is employed by television stations to commentate, when the current practice is, almost exclusively, to go for former international players. He is extraordinarily well informed, having read everything in the papers and heard everything on the radio and he is without doubt in the top flight of radio commentators of all time.

Tony first appeared on *Test Match Special* for one Test in 1966, because Roy Lawrence had to go home to Jamaica for a couple of weeks as that island prepared to stage the Commonwealth Games. Roy was a delightful, easy-going man, who was very welcoming to me when I first took a hand in *Test Match Special*. He settled in retirement in Harrogate in Yorkshire, which meant that he would always visit us in the commentary box during a Headingley Test.

Other commentators from the Caribbean have included Reds Pereira (whose name was somehow always a bit much for Alan McGilvray, who introduced him to listeners as 'Reg Pieera'). Reds has moved round the Caribbean from his native Guyana and ended up in St Lucia, where he was part of that island's planning and preparations for their unexpectedly large part in the 2007 World Cup.

I first came across Donna Symmonds during the 1994 England tour of the Caribbean, when she was a feisty part of various local commentary teams. Her commentary role had increased by the time we returned in 1998 and, sneaking a listen to her, she sounded a very competent describer of the game. So, for a couple of the Tests in that series, we introduced her to a British audience. She provoked a great deal of interest – and praise – with the result that we invited her to join our World Cup commentary team in 1999 and the team for the

Test series of 2000. That led to her becoming part of the television commentary team for the 2003 World Cup in South Africa. How she has fitted all that in with her legal practice in Barbados is, I suppose, another example of woman's ability to multi-task.

For the 1994 England tour of the West Indies, I decided that we would have in our commentary team a local expert summariser. Not just a West Indian, but a native of the particular island we were in. In Jamaica, we had the old West Indian wicket-keeper, Jackie Hendricks; then the former fast bowler, Colin Croft, in Guyana; and a current, but injured, fast bowler, Ian Bishop, for his home island, Trinidad. In Barbados, I was overwhelmed to be able to secure the services of Sir Everton Weekes. My first proper bat at the age of nine had been a size four 'Everton Weekes' autograph, so this was a huge moment, for me at least. Quite apart from having been one of the greatest batsmen (Trevor Bailey, assessing the three Ws, once said to me, 'Worrell was the most graceful, Walcott the most powerful, but day in and day out, give me Everton.') there was a wonderful wisdom about him, born of rich experience and a delightful twinkle in the eye. The following year, it was splendid to get him to join *TMS* for the Oval Test match.

From one great batsman, we moved to another. Viv Richards was my man for Antigua. Well, who else could it have been? There were doubts expressed to me about whether the great man would give us full value, but these underestimated his commitment to any agreement. He has subsequently also been a regular on *TMS* for series in England. The way he cares passionately for West Indian cricket was demonstrated on a tense Saturday evening at Lord's in 2000, when England had bowled West Indies out for 54, to leave themselves a potentially awkward 188 to win against Walsh and Ambrose. At 149 for seven, the tension in the commentary box was tangible, with Viv, as Aggers said in his commentary, 'pacing up and down like some caged pacing thing.'

Nobody moved from the box as Dominic Cork – apparently nerveless – took England home by two wickets. It was also an occasion when I was so glad I had been difficult with the architects and the MCC over the installation of the only opening window in the media centre, as we appreciated in full measure the low murmur of excitement and anxiety while thirty thousand people seemed to hold their collective breath.

Commentators do try to be neutral. The word 'we' is banned from the commentary. That is easier, probably, in your own country, surrounded by your fellow countrymen. Overseas, you may well be the sole representative of the visiting team in the commentary box and you are expected to keep your end up. There are no fears on that score with New Zealand's Bryan Waddle. In recent years, his natural patriotism has been held in check by the presence in the commentary team for New Zealand's visits of the former Kiwi captain, Jeremy Coney, a man of great even-handedness – and a delightful wit.

I drove Coney once to the wonderful country house hotel that we used for matches at Trent Bridge, Langar Hall, where the approach is between fields of sheep. Acting up to the stereotype joke about New Zealanders' sexual habits, he commented that they were looking nervous at the arrival of a Kiwi. He is something of a perpetual student, whose arrival at Heathrow on the eve of the 1999 World Cup prompted a call to my office from the immigration service, who were clearly unconvinced that this casual character with no more than a rucksack could be a BBC cricket expert. But by the time I had jumped through the required Home Office hoops, he had charmed his way into the country. I experienced his enquiring mind at that tournament when, as we left Nottingham one evening to drive to Leeds, he opened with, 'Tell me about the Wars of the Roses.' By the time we arrived at our hotel, as the result of continuous prompts along the lines of, 'What next?' I think I had covered six hundred years of the kings and queens of England.

Bryan Waddle shares with his predecessor, Alan Richards, a more down-to-earth approach, though in every other respect they had nothing in common. With a background in radio disc-jockeying, Bryan is a very professional and smooth operator. With no back-up on tour, he is accomplished at making the best of things. I recall his turning his hotel bathroom in Lahore into a studio during the 1996 World Cup, because the phone in there was the only one he could dismantle to attach the necessary leads. He was a fine sight, sitting on the pedestal with his broadcasting equipment arranged round the basin.

In that tournament, the first match was England v New Zealand in the less than glorious situation of Ahmedabad. I had suggested to Bryan that he should get his station to book their broadcast circuits from London to pick up the commentary in which he and Richard Hadlee would join us. This seemed to work very satisfactorily for everyone, and in New Zealand a full *TMS* operation, particularly describing a win for New Zealand following a Nathan Astle hundred, went down very well. Bryan was told that, on the strength of that, they wanted commentary on every New Zealand game. Their next was against Holland in Baroda, where the facilities were more limited and Bryan talked himself hoarse on the solitary press box telephone. A week later, I found myself in Faisalabad covering New Zealand v South Africa and wandered round to the commentary box to see how he was getting on. He had managed to rig a microphone mixer to his telephone line and no sooner had I put my head round the door than I was handed the microphone by a wild-eyed Waddle, in desperate need of a break.

His predecessor, Alan Richards, had also known the odd awkward moment in Pakistan. On one tour he had secured agreement that he would join the local commentary team, which seemed like a happy arrangement to all concerned. On the first morning of the First Test, the opening Pakistani commentator did his twenty-minute spell and then handed, with a gracious introduction, to Alan. He did his twenty minutes' commentary and was handed a note with the name of the next commentator, whom he duly introduced. That gentleman thanked him warmly in English, but then launched into Urdu for his twenty minutes. With no warning about this, the radio control room in Wellington was given a nasty shock.

Alan Richards was the last overseas commentator to share a joint Test match commentary in India with All India Radio. Their policy changed in the 1970s after he had suggested that some of the local umpiring left a little to be desired. When Christopher Martin-Jenkins went to India for the first time in 1976/77, I was told very firmly by AIR that he would not be invited to join their team. In fact, we only mounted commentary on that tour on the culmination of the Third Test in Madras, when Tony Greig's team clinched the series by going 3–0 up – a remarkable performance. That match became more remembered for the Vaseline-impregnated gauzes with which John Lever, whose swing bowling had done so much to win the series, tried in vain to prevent the sweat running into his eyes. India, desperate for an explanation of their downfall, leapt on this as evidence of sharp practice.

The fact that English commentators were not included by AIR was given some justification when CMJ suggested that an lbw decision against an England batsman was 'slightly surprising'. Alongside Christopher, the former Sussex captain, later to be President of MCC, Robin Marlar, exploded at that. 'Slightly surprising! Slightly surprising! It was an absolutely disgraceful decision!'

When I first took over *Test Match Special*, Pearson Surita was the visiting commentator from India. He was very much of the old school, an urbane resident of Calcutta, where Henry Blofeld and I visited him on one tour to find that, if the days of the Raj had passed, the news appeared not to have reached his Chowringhee apartment. His cutglass accent would not have been out of place in the drawing rooms of Mayfair and his status in Calcutta society was reinforced by his position as a racecourse judge. His name is still remembered there in an annual race.

With all this pedigree, I was somewhat embarrassed on one occasion to support him as he reported for the World Service from Chelmsford on Essex playing the Indians. In those days, we had no commentary box there and I had to connect some self-operated equipment to a point on a telegraph pole on a grassy bank. We spent a cool May Saturday at a card table on the boundary, but for all the Heath Robinson nature of the operation, he was gracious and grateful.

That same year, Robert Hudson did a deal to secure a splendid Indian summariser. I was summoned one afternoon to his office to meet the Maharaja of Baroda. He had been a power in the Indian Cricket Board and a manager of the team on previous tours. Conscious of needing to conform to his country's abolition of princely titles, he made a request to me. Could he be introduced as 'Fatesingh Gaekwad, the former Maharaja of Baroda'.

I agreed to this as part of the opening announcement, but with a glance at Bob, who was rolling his eyes, suggested, with due respect, that we might find a shorter version for use during the commentaries. 'Certainly,' he said. 'It would be sufficient to address me as "Prince".' So we did, despite constant enquiries as to whether we had a dog in the box.

The former Lancashire and India wicket-keeper/batsman, Farokh Engineer, also brought panache to the commentary box. His excitement at India winning the 1983 World Cup had us almost having to restrain him from leaping out of the Lord's commentary box window to join his compatriots mobbing the pavilion below.

On two tours of India in the 1980s we invited Ashis Ray, the Indian broadcaster and journalist, to join the commentary team. He later moved on to join the CNN organisation, without ever quite losing that hankering to be back on the cricket circuit. In the meantime, I was alerted by Alan Marks in Australia to the great promise of the commentator who had joined the ABC for an Indian visit down under. Harsha Bhogle was first heard on the BBC during the 1992 World Cup in Australia and New Zealand, fitting in with the banter and in-jokes with remarkable facility for a lad from Bombay, although one evening in

Dunedin, Bryan Waddle did manage to convince him that dinner at the home of the veteran New Zealand commentator, Iain Galloway, was an occasion for the best suit. He took the sight of the rest of us casually attired very well.

The list of radio commentators in India can be extensive, which means that the matches are shared out thinly amongst them, but Harsha's career was extended by a move into television. This has given him great celebrity in India and we have known as many fans at the commentary box door clamouring for his autograph as for Sunil Gavaskar's.

Sunil himself, apart from being one of the all-time great cricketers, is a superb summariser. He is fully au fait with our sense of humour and trades easily in the subtleties and ironies that make it up. When he was captain of India, I often had to interview him and he was always extremely helpful, though I do remember approaching him outside the dressing rooms at the Wankhede Stadium in Bombay at the close of play, and feeling the muzzle of a policeman's sub-machine gun pressed into the small of my back – to Sunil's huge amusement. These days he is in such demand by the ICC and others that pinning him down for radio duties is difficult, but always rewarding.

From Pakistan, since the days of Omar Qureishi, which was just before my time, we have not had a ball-by-ball commentator in the team, so the representation that we always try to achieve has been in the form of expert summarisers. For a long time that was a role filled by Mushtaq Mohammed, that wonderfully talented batsman from an extraordinarily talented family. Apart from his glittering Test career, Mushy had been a long-time favourite at Northamptonshire and followed retirement from first-class cricket with a lengthy career with Old Hill in the Birmingham League. We discovered that he was not over-keen on dogs. During the 1983 World Cup, Michael Carey was among the commentators and was frequently accompanied by one of his friendly old Labradors. One day, in the tiny box at Old Trafford, his dog was stretched out under the commentary desk, apparently well out of the way. But his head had come to rest on Mushy's foot and was causing his contributions to the commentary to sound increasingly anxious. Eventually, when asked for his opinion of a shot, all that came was a wail, 'He's licking my leg!'

That 1983 World Cup in England was the first one in which I mounted a full ball-by-ball commentary on every match. That meant trying to find someone to represent every team in the commentary box. Zimbabwe were making their debut and as it happened they had a commentator who had some experience of working in South Africa. Bob Nixon's day job was as a dentist in Bulawayo and he had also won an independent seat in the Zimbabwean parliament. His moment of glory came very early in that tournament, when Zimbabwe, under the leadership of none other than Duncan Fletcher, beat Australia in the first match. Nixon's commentary on the atmosphere – 'And you would believe that this was either Harare or Bulawayo with this crowd. Well, it isn't. It's a Nottingham crowd!' – celebrated the result that launched a very successful three weeks. He so nearly had another day to rejoice in a little later, when the Zimbabwean fast bowler, Peter Rawson, brought India to their knees at Tunbridge Wells. At the last gasp, it was Kapil Dev who played an innings of pure genius – 175 not out – to set up victory for the eventual winners of the cup.

Sadly for Bob, the opportunities for further commentaries were very limited. He came to live in Suffolk, but eventually retired to South Africa.

We also had to find a commentator for Sri Lanka. Lucien Wijesinghe was a man with commentary experience in his native island, who was living in Birmingham. He, too, had a moment to celebrate, when Sri Lanka beat New Zealand at Derby and we were treated to his distinctly plummy tones declaring, 'Well played, Sri Lanka!' He returned to our fold for the 1999 World Cup, when he reduced Mike Atherton to a state of mystification, starting with a joke. 'Have you heard of the man who passed out in an Indian restaurant? He fell into a korma!' (It has to be the way you tell it.) Then he described himself as 'just a small-town boy'.

'Where do you come from?' asked Atherton.

'Colombo,' was the reply.

There was a thoughtful pause before Mike's laconic comment, 'It's not exactly a village, is it?'

More recently, our Sri Lankan commentator has been Roshan Abeysinghe, a Colombo businessman who started his own cricket club, which has brought on a number of promising players. Simon Mann and I visited that club in 2002 for a prize-giving evening when we were made very welcome. Like several other broadcasters in his position, Roshan is hampered by the reluctance of his home radio organisation to finance him accompanying Sri Lanka on tour. This sometimes means that the well-travelled Ranjit Fernando, frequently heard on Sky television and also sometime manager of the national team, is occasionally pressed into service for radio as well.

Ranjit was manager of Sri Lanka when they were in Australia early in 1999 for the triangular one-day series. One night in Adelaide, the Western Australian umpire, Ross Emerson, called Muralitharan for throwing and he had a real crisis on his hands. Up to that point, the travelling British press, remembering the line from the old Abba song, 'Can you hear the drums, Fernando?' had christened Ranjit 'Drums'. After the incident in Adelaide, the previously approachable manager became less ready with a quote. Now the credit for his nickname was moved to Jim Reeves, as he became known as 'Distant Drums'.

There was one other little side effect of that incident. The Sri Lankan captain, Arjuna Ranatunga, had reacted to the throwing call by taking his team off to the boundary. I was putting the finishing touches to a book on the history of the World Cup at that time and I had interviews with all the winning captains except Ranatunga. He had been making himself very elusive as we went round Australia, but early on the morning after the floodlit events at the Adelaide Oval, my hotel phone rang. 'Peter, it is Arjuna. We can do that interview now.' He seemed to need a friend. We did the book interview, before I tried for something more topical for radio on the current crisis. With a smile, he declined to comment.

The ICC referee charged with the problem of sorting out that fracas was Peter Van der Merwe. I remembered listening to his magnificent South African team's performances in England during my last summer before joining the BBC in 1965. The SABC's commentator then, and for most of the post-war years to that point, was Charles Fortune. Of course, listening to him then, none of us could know that he would never again describe a Test series in England. The two sides were playing each other for the last time for twenty-nine years.

During that period the old former schoolmaster, Fortune, would visit the commentary box on occasions, always welcomed by Johnners. His distinction was the way he tied his tie, without the final tuck under, in the manner of a cravat. Later in that isolation period, we would be visited by Gerald de Kock, who would come over every summer to cover Wimbledon for SABC and never missed the opportunity to look in on Lord's.

It is difficult to imagine the emotion he must have felt on 24 July 1994 when he joined *Test Match Special* as of right in that pavilion commentary box to watch Hudson and Kirsten step through the gate on their way out to reopen South Africa's Test cricket in England. The fact that the visitors registered an historic and overwhelming victory must have helped his euphoria.

Two old friends who would have loved to have witnessed the resumption of Anglo-South African cricket were absent. Charles Fortune was to die in November that year and Brian Johnston had died in January. Had he been there, I don't think Brian could have welcomed the man who was our guest on 'A View From the Boundary' – Peter Hain. Touchingly, our South African summariser, whose Test career had been so curtailed by the campaigning that Hain led, found to his surprise that he got on with him very well. Like me, Peter Hain had been in awe of the wonderful batting of Barry Richards, whose broadcasting career was launched at that Test match.

An accomplished broadcaster, who for a time harboured an ambition to play cricket for a living, Gerald de Kock was eventually wooed by television in South Africa, which was a major loss for SABC radio that they could ill afford. The year after that Lord's return, Gerald was back in the box the day before the start of Wimbledon. He had come straight from the airport after commentating the previous day on South Africa winning the rugby World Cup in Johannesburg. We just had to set up a surely unique achievement, so we put him on the air to commentate on an over of England v the West Indies. The next day he was live from Wimbledon. Three different major sporting events in as many days.

Gerald has sometimes been blamed for South Africa's premature exit from their own cricket World Cup in 2003. It is claimed that he advised the captain that they were ahead of the asking rate on the Duckworth-Lewis chart in a rain-affected match against Sri Lanka in Durban. In fact it was rated as a tie and that was enough to put South Africa out in the first stage of the tournament. The team have denied the claim, but the reason that he was in a position to advise them was because of his job then as their media liaison manager. That is an unforgiving task and he may have been unique in having held the respect of both the press box and the dressing room.

The South African Broadcasting Corporation's commentary is going through a settling-down period. More than any other sports broadcasting, cricket commentary demands the best of the English language and the many tongues that make up the Rainbow Nation are dictating a few awkward policy decisions on this front.

Back in 1987 the fourth cricket World Cup was launched in Delhi and the night before the chaotic opening ceremony there was a dinner at the Taj Palace

Hotel for all the teams, administrators and journalists. The scale of the operation these days would make such an evening impossible, but then it was a surprisingly intimate occasion and an embracing of the family of cricket.

A few weeks later, by some quirk of planning during the hectic criss-crossing of the subcontinent that we were all involved in, most of the teams again found themselves in the same hotel for one night, before everyone split up to redistribute themselves around India and Pakistan. Many great yarns were told and it was a very precious twenty-four hours, not least for the international broadcasting family that surrounds cricket. I have always treasured those connections. With every season and every tour it is like another trip to, or visit from, well-loved friends and relations.

MUDDIED OAFS
AND OARSMEN

THERE I WAS IN CALCUTTA, DISCUSSING TECHNICAL arrangements for broadcasting the Calcutta Cup rugby international of 1982. I might be on my first tour with the England cricket team, but I was also rugby union producer, a job I had done – in parallel with the cricket – for eight years. I went to the Calcutta Club, who donated the trophy to England and Scotland for their annual match, to make a radio feature for the occasion, but it was becoming rapidly apparent that if I was to start producing *Test Match Special* on tour, I was going to have to give up the rugby.

In fact, throughout the 1980s, I also produced the coverage of the Boat Race. That did not get in the way of the cricket until I first went on a tour of the West Indies, where England's tours always run well into April, and these days even into May, encompassing that springtime event on the Thames.

In my time as rugby producer the game was still amateur and, while the Five Nations championship (as it was then) was still a big occasion, it had not quite achieved the status of today's Six Nations competition. We did cover some club rugby and commentaries on events like the county championship and the university match. For most of my time doing that job, the rugby correspondent was the former Scottish and British Lions centre three-quarter, Chris Rea. Chris had a fine broadcasting voice, with a pleasing Perthshire accent and a great facility as a commentator and correspondent. He would get intensely involved in the commentary he was giving, seeming to prefer our circumstances at a ground like Murrayfield, where he could stand and move about. (Mind you, it was usually so cold there, in the open in January or February, that moving about was a good idea.) On one of these occasions, as his hand habitually moved in and out of his coat pocket in his excitement, I became aware that it was going in and out of mine, as I stood next to him.

One of the advantages you get from producing rugby, that does not attend the production of cricket, is the regular trip to Paris. Chris had a favourite little hotel quite near the Madeleine, the Hotel Roblin. It was a delight. The first time we went there, he was extolling its virtues and telling me what a warm welcome we would get. Indeed, as I checked in, I did. Chris stepped up to the desk in my wake and gave them a charming smile, which faded abruptly when they denied any knowledge of a booking for him. Following Scotland's first nuclear explosion, it took a while to sort out, and he took a while longer to return to his original view of the hotel.

One event from Chris Rea's broadcasting career gave him nightmares for years. Early in 1975, England's cricketers were on tour in Australia. I was in the *Test Match Special* studio and had the athletics and tennis commentator Norman Cuddeford with me as presenter, introducing the programme and holding the fort if the line went down. One of his duties was to slip out to the *Today* programme studio for the sports bulletin, to do an update on the Test match. This was considered by the programme's producers to be less risky than getting a live telephone report from Australia. How wrong they were to be on this occasion.

Chris Rea was *Today's* sports presenter on this particular morning. He started his round-up with the Test match. 'Let's catch up with events in Sydney. Norman Cuddeford has been following the action. Can you give us the latest, Norman?'

Now Norman had been a broadcaster for many years and he knew that when you go into a studio, you always give the studio managers behind the glass a few words of your speaking level, so that they know what to expect. What apparently had not occurred to him was that the *Today* studio is live on the air for three hours, and therefore that is a procedure that has to be dispensed with. So, in answer to the question, 'Can you give us the latest?' Norman said, 'No, I'm frightfully sorry, I can't.'

By the time he looked up to enquire of a stunned studio, 'Was that all right?' Chris was doing an impression of a goldfish, gaping with incredulity and gesturing to Norman to speak. The programme was being presented that day by John Timpson, who had his head in his hands, trying not to laugh, and Desmond Lynam, who had decided it was safer to leave the studio and tried to do so before taking his headphones off, thus nearly throttling himself. Behind the glass, the studio manager was opening and closing every fader on her desk, in the vain hope that there might be something happening somewhere.

At last Norman – remaining surprisingly calm in all the circumstances – did part with the information. Later, he turned up in the Head of Sport's office to apologise. The man in charge then was Cliff Morgan. Norman added to his apology the hope that it would not affect his chances of being sent to cover the Olympics in Montreal.

Cliff's response was immediate. 'Montreal? You'll be lucky if you get to the Albert bloody 'all!'

Chris was a very conscientious correspondent and scrupulously fair. On the eve of a Scotland v Wales match at Murrayfield, he tipped Wales once as the likely winners. Needless to say, he was personally overjoyed when Scotland came out on top. When we returned to the hotel after the match, we ran into one of the Scotland selectors who had evidently heard Chris's preview. He was incensed at what he perceived to be Chris's disloyalty in tipping the opposition and simply could not get into his head the concept of impartial journalism. He just kept repeating, 'Scotland made you!'

I remember having a conversation with one of New Zealand's top rugby commentators, who expressed the opinion that radio or television commentary should be biased. It is certainly not an approach that I could ever favour, although I think it is becoming more prevalent, even on Radio 5 Live, and especially on local and regional radio stations. It is something I would never have tolerated in *Test Match Special*.

After leaving the BBC for a varied career in rugby journalism, Chris Rea popped up in the cricket world, when he was appointed Assistant Secretary (Marketing) of the MCC, in which capacity, bizarrely for both of us, I found myself dealing with him on an official level, not least over the construction of the new media centre at Lord's. We enjoyed several occasions when well-meaning people introduced us to each other.

During my time as rugby producer, my number one commentary team for an international match was Chris Rea and Peter West doing the description, with Ian Robertson as expert summariser.

Peter West will be remembered by many (of a certain age) as the presenter of BBC Television's cricket coverage and was involved with their commentary team for over thirty years. He also commentated on rugby on television and presented many other programmes, among which was *Come Dancing*. This latter part of his CV did bring him some irritation, when it was repeatedly thrown at him in the environs of rugby matches. Like so many television presenters of his era, Peter had started on the radio and even – for two Tests in 1958 – been a commentator on *Test Match Special*. But I always believed that radio rugby commentary was the thing he did best. He became rugby correspondent of *The Times*, though he was frustrated at the limited chances he had to go on England or British Lions tours, because of his cricket commitments.

He did at least, in 1986/87, realise his ambition to cover an Ashes cricket tour. The *Daily Telegraph* was in something of an interregnum between cricket correspondents, so they invited Peter to follow Mike Gatting's eventually hugely successful tour of Australia. Peter wrote in a way that was typical of him and his bluff, matter-of-fact approach. It was instantly recognisable as his style. Unfortunately, his sports editor apparently wanted something different, which begs the question of why he was asked in the first place. The subsequent arguments did take some of the gilt off the gingerbread for his tour, but he was determined to enjoy the experience.

To a generation of television viewers, there was something reassuring about his appearance on the box, usually having only just stuffed a long-stemmed pipe in his pocket. I certainly found his presence in a radio rugby commentary team reassuring, too, even if the pipe was perhaps not so popular in the small box at Twickenham.

The third member of that dream team, Ian Robertson, has more of a tendency to cause his producers anxiety, not least because he has the habit of speaking at a lunch on a rugby international day, which means a worrying disappearance between his preview of the game and a sometimes finely-judged appearance for the commentary. Through most of my time as rugby producer he was used as an expert summariser, having played at fly-half for Scotland, but he was always hankering to do the commentary.

He and I went to Otley, in Yorkshire, in 1979, to see the famous victory of the North of England over the All Blacks, but again he was the summariser. The commentator was Don Mosey who, as it was on 'his patch', had also had the job of picking the site for the commentary position. On a small ground, the only solution had been to build a scaffolding tower to look over the hedge which ran down one side. We encountered one problem, when it became apparent that there seemed to be more people with tickets than there was space in the ground. A potentially dangerous number of those who could not gain access started to climb our scaffolding, which gave a few uncomfortable lurches, until I asked for some police assistance in the interests of safety.

'Typical of you BBC people,' I was told by one irate ticket-holder. 'I bet you haven't paid to get in. You lot never do pay!'

Robertson, too, displayed some irritation that day as Don Mosey's commentary, which was never quite quick enough for a fast moving game, struggled to keep up with the pace of this historic occasion. Robbo was champing at the bit to seize the microphone, but restricted himself dutifully to his comments.

On that occasion he would clearly have been better employed commentating and ever since then he has proved himself a brilliant exponent of the art, but in his days as summariser we did get more of the enjoyment of his humour – and he is a very funny man. He was, however, once the butt of an on-air misunderstanding. He was presenting the *Today* programme's sports bulletin at a time when the Montreal Olympic Games were under the sort of threat that always seems to attend the run-up to such events. Would the facilities be ready? Mayor Drapeau of Montreal had taken personal charge and Robbo had him on the telephone for a live interview.

After discussing the various problems, Ian was bringing the interview to a close. 'So, it must all be quite a nightmare for you, then,' he said.

There was a slight pause before the Mayor replied. 'Nightmare? I am ze Night Mayor. I am ze Day Mayor. I am ze only Mayor!'

Robbo also came within an ace of making a real fool of me on the air. I was reading the racing results one day and before I went into the studio with the latest batch I was checking the names of the horses. Ian knows a thing or two about racing, so I asked him about a horse called 'Iledoitmiway'.

'Do you know this one?' I asked. 'Is it pronounced as if it's French: *Il y doit miway?*'

'That's right,' he said.

The red light was just about to go on when he put his head round the door. 'I can't let you do it,' he said. 'It's "I'll do it my way!"'

Rugby international weekends always had a wonderful buzz about them, even if they involved fighting your way through the fans who would clog the foyer of the Angel Hotel in Cardiff. Chris Rea was always keen to dine the night before with Bill McLaren, the wonderful television commentator, who would call for a steak, 'Well done … and when I say well done, I want it "burrrnt". When you think it's done, put it back in and do it again.' Then he would retire early to work on 'the big sheet', his crib for the players in the match.

After giving up the full-time production of rugby, I did play a further part in a couple of seasons, first when the England tour of India in 1988 was cancelled after the hosts' objections to players with South African links. I offered my services and enjoyed a splendid Five Nations tournament, always doing the second favourite match on each Saturday and seeing generally the better game. Then in 1991 I played a part in the production of the second rugby World Cup, concentrating my attention on the games in Wales. That country had a bad time of it. I can remember walking into the National Stadium in Cardiff with one of my Welsh radio colleagues who was confident about the game with Western Samoa. 'These players are only there because they couldn't get into the All Blacks' side,' he said.

'You reckon Wales can beat the New Zealand second fifteen, do you?' I asked.

After a comprehensive win for the opposition, my friend was gloomy. 'It wasn't even the whole of bloody Samoa.'

A broadcasting era ended in 1979, when John Snagge commentated on his last Boat Race. He had done his first in 1931, when the technology must have been at full stretch, with a receiving point for the wireless transmission in Harrods Depository, just by Hammersmith Bridge. With his retirement, the radio producer of the event for the last few years, Dick Maddock, who was based inconveniently in Birmingham, decided that this was a good moment for him to pass on the baton, too. I was invited to take on the production.

John Snagge had joined the BBC in 1924, so had been something of a great

24
Allan Lamb uses the TMS box in Guyana in 1990 to contact the family.

25 ABOVE TOP
Geoff Boycott teases Aggers in Jamaica in 1994.

26 ABOVE
A furtive broadcast from Harare Airport in 2004. The equipment is on a luggage trolley for a quick getaway, as Aggers awaits the England team's arrival in Zimbabwe.

27

Another day at the coalface. Aggers on the
air from my hotel balcony in Barbados.

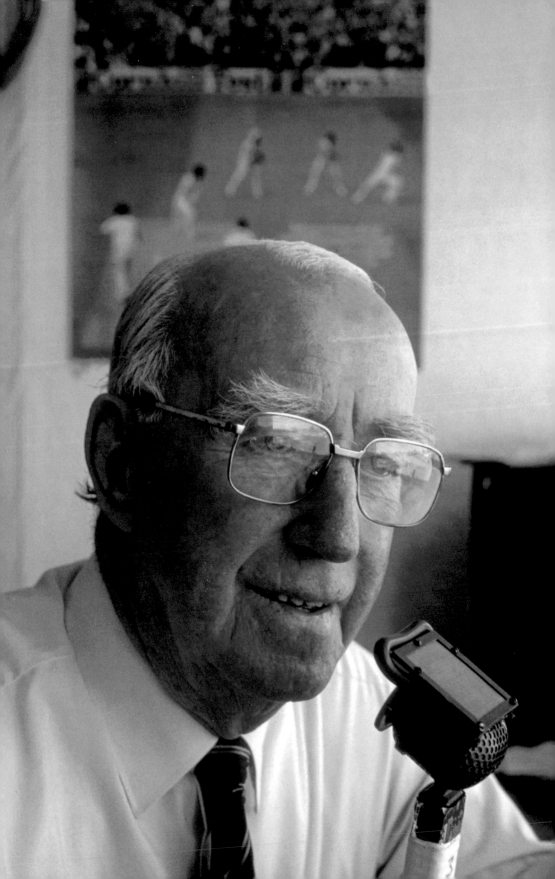

28 OPPOSITE
Alan McGilvray – the voice of Australian cricket for a generation. (*Eagar*)

29 ABOVE TOP
Jim Maxwell in the TMS box in Melbourne 2006.

30 ABOVE
Inzamam leads his 2006 Pakistan team in lunchtime prayers behind the commentary box at Headingley, before the forfeited Test at the Oval.

31 ABOVE
Champagne Moment. PB makes the
presentation to Monty Panesar in 2006.

32 OVERLEAF
'Outside the Box': The only opening
window in the Lord's media centre
provides a frame for Graham Gooch and
Jonathan Agnew, with Tim Lane, Henry
Blofeld and Bill Frindall in the box. To the
left are the engineers, Brian Mack and
Andy Leslie, with David Lloyd and Paul
Allott commentating for Sky on the other
side and the press box below. (*Eagar*)

33 OPPOSITE
Not all commentary rotas are as scruffy as
this one for the second half of a one-day
international. (*Eagar*)

1.45	TC	1.45	V JM
2.10	SM	2.15	WWD
2.30	CMJ	2.45	V JM
2.55	SM	3.15	WWD
3.20	TC		VJM
3.45	CMJ	3.45	
4.10	SM	4.15	WWD
4.35	CMJ	4.45	VJM
5.00	SM		

CAKES

34 ABOVE TOP
Aggers' birthday cake in Antigua 2007.

35 ABOVE
TMS Anniversary cake – Old Trafford
2007.

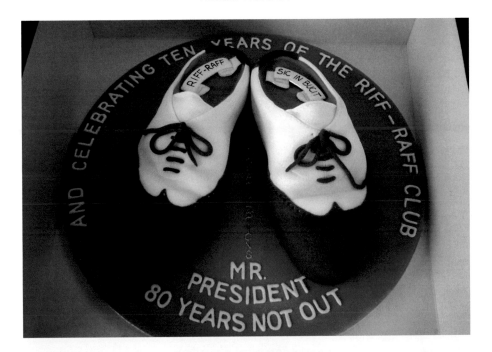

36 ABOVE TOP
Johnners' co-respondent shoes cake from the Riff-Raff Club 1992.

37 ABOVE
The Royal Cake – 'Not personally made, but specially' and presented by Her Majesty The Queen in 2001.

38 OPPOSITE ABOVE
Lord's 2001. At least Blowers and Aggers
seem more interested in Her Majesty than
the cake she has just presented to us.
(*Eagar*)

39 OPPOSITE BELOW
Lord's 2005. Australian Prime Minister
and 'cricket tragic', John Howard takes his
View From the Boundary at last with
Jonathan Agnew. (*Eagar*)

40 ABOVE
The Oval 2005. 'Balconies and rooftops all
round the ground started to fill up.'

41 ABOVE
The Ashes regained. Trafalgar Square 2005. 'Like a pair of schoolboys we took each other's pictures holding the Waterford Crystal trophy.'

42 OPPOSITE ABOVE
2004 Barbados. The tables turned, as it's England who set the umbrella field.

43 OPPOSITE BELOW
Lord's 2007. PB enjoys a joke between Mike Selvey and Jonathan Agnew, while Bill Frindall keeps his concentration. (*Eagar*)

44 ABOVE TOP
The 2007 World Cup is over. Time for a
relaxing cigar in Barbados.

45 ABOVE
The last Test and a presentation from the
ICC delivered by match referee Alan
Hurst at the Riverside.

radio institution, principally as an announcer, with his wonderful, deep, fruity voice, but also as a commentator on various events. I worked with him on the Queen's Silver Jubilee in 1977, when we had a commentary position over-looking Temple Bar, at the Fleet Street entry to the City of London. There, below the window of the empty office in which we were stationed, a little ceremony would be played out as Her Majesty arrived in her procession. The Lord Mayor would offer her the sword of the City and she would touch the hilt. Then, to give the Lord Mayor and his party time to get to St Paul's Cathedral for the service which was the main event, the royal party would have to linger for a few minutes before they could set off again.

Two days before the great day, very early on a Sunday morning, there was a full undress rehearsal. Appropriately, it was a grey, gloomy morning, with even a hint of drizzle. The troops lining the route, who would be in their scarlet tunics on Tuesday, were in khaki today. The carriages of the great and the good were represented by carts, and there were people on horseback, with placards around their necks bearing legends suggesting they were Lord This or Field Marshal the Earl of That. None of which prevented Alun Williams, based in Trafalgar Square and the commentator before us on the processional route, letting his imagination flow. It reached its height when he described 'the Queen Mother, looking radiant with that wonderful smile'. When she reached us, she was a sack of sand in an open cart.

So we groaned when again Williams let himself slip into eulogy about the golden Coronation Coach, which was to be used for the first time since the Coronation. A few minutes later, though, I could see something of a glow in the street just beyond St Clement Danes Church. Then, round the slight bend it came. It really was the Coronation Coach and on that drab morning it lit up the whole scene in a way that took your breath away. It was one of those privileged moments that has lived in my memory over all the intervening years.

It seemed that the vehicle, having not emerged for twenty-four years, was being given a test run, just to make sure it could make the trip, which was anyway a bit further than it had had to go to Westminster Abbey in 1953. It is of course a completely over-the-top creation, but that morning it captivated me, and I could see from the look on John Snagge's face, it had the same effect on him.

When I was invited to produce the Boat Race coverage, I was given a fairly free hand, but asked to 'refresh' the commentary, which had suffered for a few years from races that turned into processions almost from the start. First, I decided that Brian Johnston should be the main commentator in the launch, following the race. He and I went down to Dorney, near Windsor, to see John Snagge and for Brian to interview him for our lead-up to the race. The next time I was to see John was when I was making the *Sport and Verse* programme with John Arlott. We had selected a Victorian ballad called, 'The Oarsman's Farewell to his Oar' and I wanted John to record it. His sight was poor and his hand was unsteady in his failing health, so I had written the poem in large letters on cards. It sounded very poignant as he read the lines, although he did it so slowly that in the editing process I had to cut out the middle verse.

Having selected Brian in the launch for the race, I managed to recruit Dan Topolski, the hugely successful Oxford coach, as his expert comments man. Then I set about finding some commentary positions down the winding course, to cover the possibilities of either a one-sided race, or – almost as likely – something happening to the launch to prevent it keeping up with the crews. I contemplated a position on Chiswick Eyot, an island on the crown of the long Surrey bend, which is the home of many water birds. At low tide I could walk across the mud to the island, but for various reasons it was evidently going to be unsuitable. Instead, I chose a spot on the river wall a bit further downstream, near Chiswick's Black Lion pub, where Tony Adamson, later to become the BBC's golf correspondent, could commentate on the race and talk to the spectators, for whom this was a popular viewing point.

The finish is just below Chiswick Bridge and a commentary point here can be important, particularly if the winning crew is a long distance ahead. For many years this had been Johnners' position, so now I put a couple of men there in case they had to hold the fort for a time. Tom Boswell was the rowing expert and with him was Christopher Martin-Jenkins to describe the scene.

That basic plan stayed with me throughout my ten years producing the race, but that first year I also had a broadcast point in the practice tank at the Quintin Boat Club, where the crews come ashore after the finish. We set up a large television screen in there for the two second crews, Isis and Goldie, whose race always finishes just before the start of the main event, to watch and react to the progress of the race. This turned out to be a mistake, because leaving the atmosphere of the river was too much of an interruption in the flow. As it happened, my first race in charge was quite a close affair, so picking the moment to go to that boat house position was tricky, and I think I probably got it wrong. I never tried it again and subsequently I have always felt that producers considering that sort of clever complication in any coverage should usually give it a second thought.

The BBC lost rights to cover the Boat Race on television and unfortunately, in its pique, also surrendered the radio rights. Predictably, with ITV pulling out in 2009, the organisers must have realised that they were hasty with the race's long term future. However, there would be some who controlled the purse strings in the BBC, who might feel that it was just as well. It is an expensive operation, particularly in the hire of the very specialised launch. Throughout my time we used one called *Arethusa*, which had to be able to move pretty quickly to keep up with the two eights. One producer of *Sport on 2* did ask me one year to try to do without the launch. 'Couldn't you use a cabin cruiser?' he asked.

I told him the crews would be out of sight by the end of the Fulham Wall.

Then he suggested that we might do the commentary 'from a couple of tall buildings'.

I told him we would need to build the tall buildings, which might make more of a dent in his budget, but I did take an engineer down the four-and-a-half miles of the course to see what might be possible. We drew up a list of a minimum of nine shore-based positions, which would be on the limit of binocular vision. Commentating off the television was also suggested, and in refuting that idea I was aided in the next race by television themselves, who were on a long shot from their helicopter at the moment that one of the Cambridge crew 'caught a crab', his oar catching in the water and all but stopping the boat dead. So their shore-based commentator missed it, while on the *Arethusa* it was spotted immediately.

All too late, I discovered that with the Boat Race production went Henley. The Henley Royal Regatta was a great social occasion to attend, but something of a bind from which to organise a broadcast. The stewards were not over keen on the media and seemed intent on being as obstructive as possible. I was not too disappointed when rescheduling of the Test cricket calendar meant that it started to clash with my day job. But I did meet a gentleman who was to earn a bit of fame. The BBC World Service asked for an interview with one of the winners. I asked around who might be a good candidate.

'Try that chap who's just won the Diamond Sculls,' I was told. I found him in the boat tent, where he told me a bit about his ambitions. But I don't think that Steve Redgrave included in that list five Olympic gold medals and a knighthood.

My time with the Boat Race was ended by my first cricket tour to the West Indies in 1990. The football commentator, Peter Jones, who also covered many other events, had taken over in the launch. As chance would have it, I was reporting on England's game against Barbados on the day of the Boat Race and the *Sport on 2* producer had me on standby for another update as soon as the race had finished, so I was listening with interest to the closing stages.

Something was wrong. The commentary was coming entirely from Chiswick Bridge off a television monitor. My conclusion was that the engine of the launch had failed. Sometimes a polythene bag round the propeller can be enough to slow it to the point where it cannot keep up. Later that afternoon I got a call to tell me what had happened. Peter Jones had suffered a massive heart attack while commentating, and by the time they could get him ashore to an ambulance, it was too late to save him.

I had worked with Peter quite a bit for more than twenty years, quite often as his producer at football matches, and in the studio when I was doing shifts producing the Radio 2 *Sports Desk*. He was always very easy to produce, in the sense that he would do anything you asked him. You could feed anything into his headphones and it would come straight out of his mouth. We shared a small commentary booth in the lofty areas of Westminster Abbey for the wedding of the Duke of York to Sarah Ferguson, and I remember pointing out to him something that we could see, as the couple prepared to process after the signing of the register. The new Duchess was peeping through the altar screen to have a look at the assembled congregation beyond. It was a very human moment, which Peter introduced to the commentary with his trademark, 'I like that. I like that a lot.'

In mentioning Peter Jones, I am reminded of Desmond Lynam. These two were the main presenters of sport on radio in the 1970s and 1980s. They were entirely different: Peter with the more flowery language; Desmond more laconic, understated, and possessed of a razor sharp wit. He could save the life of a producer who had messed up his timings, but where Peter would not have turned a hair, Desmond, having just been brilliant, would let the producer know about his failings. In the spring of 1974 I took him down to Lord's to interview the Indian touring captain, Ajit Wadekar. Not being a great cricket follower, he asked me to brief him in the taxi on the way from Broadcasting

House. I thought I had prepared him with all sorts of questions to make him sound knowledgeable, but the first question he asked was about food. 'England players always seem to have trouble with the food in India. How do you all get on here?'

Wadekar seemed charmed by a rather different sort of question. With a smile he said, 'There is an Indian restaurant on every corner.' They got on famously.

It might surprise some of my later colleagues in the BBC, who remember my antipathy for the game, that I produced Peter Jones in soccer commentaries. It was not just him. I even stood in for the football producer for a couple of months in the early 1970s when he went on his long-service leave. Leading up to that, I had frequently helped out on Saturday afternoons, looking after the BBC Arabic Service's weekly football commentaries. These were almost invariably in London, indeed, whenever possible, at Arsenal.

The same two commentators were on duty every time, the younger one always late because – his senior colleague used to tell me – he was always having trouble with his wife (or maybe wives). Otherwise, it was a happily simple afternoon's work. They arrived not long before kick-off, did their ninety minutes of commentary in Arabic and left at the final whistle. No hanging around for interviews and reports for them. I just had to make sure they had their commentary position and got on the air.

In fact, my first broadcasting was on football. Following the 1966 World Cup, my colleague in the radio booking office, Paul Wade, was offered the weekly job of reading the English football results for the Dutch station, Radio Hilversum. He did this for a couple of years, before needing the occasional Saturday away. I was invited to step in as his replacement a few times during the season, gradually doing it more and more and then taking over completely by 1969.

Every Saturday evening, as the day's programme of football matches was coming to an end, I would go to Henry Wood House, a BBC building just across the road from Broadcasting House, where there was a room that housed several self-operated studio booths for the use of foreign broadcasters. At that time on a Saturday, I would almost always have the place to myself, as I wrote down the football results from the start of *Sports Report*, with the back-up of a television monitor tuned to *Grandstand*.

Then into the booth, where Hilversum would already be on the line. The programme was, of course, in Dutch and my Dutch had been limited to learning to count from one to twelve (we considered that, even on a lively day in the Scottish League, twelve should cover it) and a brief selection of introductory phrases. The instruction to the studio in Holland was that, whatever they said in the build-up to my piece, the last words must always be my name, so that I knew when to start.

I would sit looking out across the rooftops at the tower of the Senate House of London University – a building that still makes me remember that wait for the cue, at the end of a long stream of Dutch of which I understood not one word: '... Peter Baxter'. Then I would start with: 'An de top van de League liggen, een Leeds United, twee Liverpool, dree ...'

Then to the results, or 'En nu de resultaaten van de eerste diviesie.' The Dutch, I had been told, took their results in a slightly different style. First the two teams involved and then the result. 'Manchester United, Arsenal – nul – een.'

After the results, I was allowed forty seconds or so to mention some highlights of the day's games, and fortunately the command of English in Holland was considered good enough that I was permitted to do that in my own language.

At the end of 1969 a South African rugby team visited the British Isles and I was asked to include their tour scores in my results. Those tended to exceed the numbers I had learned, so I would consult with Holland before going on the air. It was a start, but a far cry from Test match commentary.

NEWBURY TO MUNICH

FOR TWO OR THREE SUMMERS IN THE EARLY 1970S, I stood in on occasions for the racing producer at various meetings. I was shown the ropes one day at Newbury, when the charming Michael Seth-Smith was the commentator. I mastered it easily enough, but was warned by the old producer who was my guide, 'Michael's easy, but Bromley can be an absolute bugger!'

In fact, although tales of our long-time racing correspondent, Peter Bromley, being outrageously difficult were legion, when I did work at race meetings with him, he was always his brilliant professional self. As a genius of a commentator, he was probably entitled to some idiosyncrasies and I know he drove a succession of racing producers mad.

My first outing with him came a few weeks after my initiation and was again at Newbury. I had brought my new wife down in my Mini Moke – my first and much loved car. Peter saw us arrive and promptly insisted on paying for her entry to Tattersall's, so that she could enjoy the racing at closer hand.

The production job at a race meeting involved having an open telephone line to the Exchange Telegraph Service (known as Extel) to get the latest pre-race odds, reading them on the air whenever the commentator called for them, and then, as the race finished, swiftly writing a card to put into his hand, labelled 'YOU SAID'. This would be the first three horses as the commentator called them. It was a vital aide-mémoire.

Bromley's homework was prodigious. He insisted on several days' notice of which races on a card he was going to have to commentate on, so that he could have all his notes up to date, and he would refuse point-blank to describe any race for which he had not been given that notice. The fruit of that research was that any delay to the start of a race was barely noticed by the listener, because he had so much to tell us about the horses. He also depended on some splendid ex-Naval ship's binoculars, which were so large they had to have a special mounting. I was well aware of the furore created when the binoculars – or more likely the pole on which they sat – did not make it to the relevant meeting. Fortunately, that never happened on any of my outings with Peter, who, for all his foibles, I regarded as one of the truly great radio commentators.

I have two main memories of my two or three summers occasionally standing in for the racing producer, before my own duties of being cricket producer kicked in. The first is of a horse. This was the heyday of Brigadier Gerard. I am no judge of horseflesh, but this was a real beauty. He seemed to be on duty whenever I was – and he always seemed to win.

The other memory is of the tortured pronunciations of the man on the Extel line, giving me the odds. With Bromley clicking his fingers impatiently for me to be ready to call the odds, I could still be trying to find an animal on the race card that would vaguely match what he was offering. 'Copper Knickers' for Copernicus is an old favourite, but there was one that nearly caused me to miss my cue to voice the betting.

'Four to one, Leako Dior,' said my man.

'What?' I pulled him up.

'Leako Dior,' he said and repeated it with increasing impatience.

'You'll have to give me a number,' I said, as I could see Peter looking round to see if I was ready.

He gave me the horse's number and I discovered it to be 'Le Coq D'Or'.

In my early days in the Radio Outside Broadcasts Department, it had a dual role, with its own programmes to produce, and also the responsibility to help other departments in the matter of outside broadcasting expertise. That all helped in my own grounding in the business. Amongst the missions over my time in that office, I was sent to Brighton to get two warring union leaders, Jack Jones and Hugh Scanlon, to the studio at the Dome during the TUC conference, for a discussion in *The World Tonight*; and to the House of Commons on Budget Day to get three MPs across the road to the Westminster Abbey studio for Radio 2.

That latter experience introduced me to two people who were to go on to lead their respective parliamentary parties. Labour were in government at the time and their representative in the triumvirate was a backbencher, George Cunningham. The Liberal was David Steel and the Conservatives offered their shadow on Education and Science, one Margaret Thatcher.

My immediate impression was of her authority. When I met her and Mr Cunningham in the lobby, it was she who darted back into the Chamber to hurry David Steel along. Then, as I shepherded them over to the Abbey crypt and settled them in the cosy little studio, it quickly became apparent that the two men accepted unreservedly her understanding of what the Chancellor had just delivered. The political spin from each of them only came when the microphones were open.

When I joined the BBC, there were two household names on the door of the office set aside for the staff commentators. Brian Johnston's was one and the other was Raymond Baxter.

Raymond was – I should say right from the start – no relation, though thereby hangs a tale. He had been the main motor sport commentator on BBC television, competed himself in many motor rallies, often broadcasting on them the while, and was also just starting then as the main presenter of a television science programme called *Tomorrow's World*. He was to fulfil that role for another twelve years.

My first personal memory of him in the office came in the approach to my first Christmas as a BBC employee. The departmental party was an informal affair in the commentators' office and I remember Raymond staggering in under a large case of wine, chuckling that he had just encountered the Director General in the foyer and hoped that he had not noticed the alcohol he was carrying. Over forty years on, it might seem surprising, both that such a star turn as Raymond Baxter should fetch the booze, and that he should be concerned about the Director General's disapproval. Some of those who consider themselves stars today might learn some of that humility.

In early summer the following year, I was sent down one day to the Farnborough Air Show, probably more for the experience than for anything useful that I was going to contribute. Raymond led the radio broadcasts. He had flown Spitfires in the Second World War and provided radio and television commentaries on aviation events, which were covered then much more than would be imaginable now. I remember clearly Raymond's television commentaries on the maiden flights of the VC10 and Concorde.

Now at Farnborough he was clearly under pressure, preparing for broadcasts and operating around – but clearly not in harness with – the serious and long-serving news air correspondent, Reginald Turnhill. When the time came for me to return to London, I was offered a lift to the station by one of the engineers, driving the cab section of the articulated studio truck. All the way down the road this man regaled me with tales of 'your dad'.

For the life of me, I could not imagine how or why he knew my father, and the penny only dropped, when he left me at Farnborough station, that he assumed the shared surname was no coincidence. Thereafter, whenever I met Raymond, I would greet him as 'Dad'.

In fact his *Tomorrow's World* duties meant that Raymond went freelance soon after that and we saw little of him in the corridors of Broadcasting House. He would attend reunions and retirement parties and was interesting on the subject of the Association of Dunkirk Little Ships of which, as an owner of one himself, he was Honorary Admiral for twenty-four years. But he was also a frequent radio commentator of state occasions over the years and I did act as his producer in 1979, when we shared a small commentary hut in Whitehall for the coverage of the funeral procession of Lord Mountbatten.

On that occasion I saw a nervous trait, which I gathered from older producers who had dealt with him more, was familiar. Listening to the commentator preceding us on the description of the funeral cortège's progress, he grabbed my arm. 'This is a disaster; he's using all my material!' It seemed he was not to be reassured, but when the moment came and the gun carriage bearing the coffin approached, followed by the poignant sight of the charger with the boots reversed in the stirrups, Raymond shook off any real or imagined worries and was magnificent. He was, after all, one of the great broadcasting professionals.

Whenever I was involved in non-sporting events I was grateful for the lessons I had learned from Robert Hudson on the necessary preparations. Even on radio it is all too easy to say too much and on many occasions the sounds of the event will carry you along.

For instance, Bob pointed out that the commentator in any religious service, such as the three royal weddings that I worked on, only needs to add a word of stage direction if it is not obvious. Sometimes action happens during a hymn and then you should pick the least significant verse and time your words to take exactly the length of that verse.

That meant that on all these occasions the rehearsal on the day before was crucial. Bob would always be there for that, stopwatch in hand, and when I had to produce a pair of services at Canterbury Cathedral without him, I did just the same.

In 1987 I had to put on the air the memorial service for the victims of the *Herald of Free Enterprise* disaster, following the capsizing of that cross-channel ferry in which 193 passengers and crew lost their lives. That was an extremely emotional occasion.

Five years before, however, the moment had been one of celebration of a remarkable event, as Pope John Paul II came to Britain. On that occasion, I had been with the BBC's religious affairs correspondent, the delightfully eccentric Gerald Priestland, the previous morning in Westminster Cathedral, when the Pope's arrival in the country was marked with a Catholic mass.

It was my first visit inside that great church and my first experience of a Catholic service. My impression was of barely suppressed chaos. We headed for Canterbury straight afterwards in order to catch the rehearsal, but when I asked Gerald if he was coming along to that with me, he said, 'Oh, no, I don't think so. I shall have a shower to wash all that incense out of my hair and see you in the pub afterwards.'

When I pitched up in the selected watering hole armed with timings of pauses in the action, durations of hymn verses, and suggestions of the moments when a word from Priestland would be required, he seemed barely interested. It was going to be very different from Hudson. This time we would wing it.

The following day, there were a couple of occasions when I nudged Gerald to speak and found him happily conducting the music with his microphone. One of these was when the Pope, greeting the great semi-circle of Bishops of the Church of England, arrayed behind the altar, stopped for a special word with old Archbishop Ramsey, who had started the moves to get a visit here from Rome. The assembled clergy broke out in applause. 'You'll need to explain that,' I hissed to Gerald.

'Oh yes, I suppose so,' and as always, he found just the right words.

Like most of the great cathedrals, Canterbury is divided by the substantial choir screen, so that the only place from which you can see the magnificent full length of that wonderful building is on top of that screen. Happily, that was our commentary position.

Doing the job I have done for more than forty years has given me moments that have sent a tingle down my spine and that Saturday morning in Canterbury Cathedral, the enormity of the occasion that I was witnessing was one of those.

In the sporting world, I have enjoyed the diversity of events that I have covered. These include hockey, which I think I tumbled into because at one time there was an annual Easter international tournament staged at Lord's. There would be one pitch in front of the pavilion and another at the Nursery End of the ground and, while Radio 2 might take the occasional report, the other countries involved, notably always Holland, might well be requiring help to mount a full radio commentary. This tournament ended when all internationals started being played on artificial surfaces.

When England were having their troubled cricket tour of Pakistan in 1987, the Dutch national hockey team were also in the country engaged in a five-match series of internationals. As we went along, I saw in the papers that they had won the first two matches comfortably enough, but then the artificial pitch for their next game in Lahore was strangely not available and the third match would have to be played on the grass of the Gadaffi Stadium, the cricket ground. Pakistan duly won, and the Dutch did not see another artificial pitch, losing the series 3–2. When we arrived in Karachi for the final Test match of that tour, their players were staying in our hotel, having just lost the fifth match. They had been following the trials and tribulations of the Gatting/Shakoor Rana affair, and we shared a few wry comments.

Lawn bowls is another game that is now played at the highest level on an artificial surface, but I covered the national championships once on grass at Mortlake in London, where the smell of the yeast from the old Watneys Brewery provided – for me at any rate – a delightful atmosphere.

Then there was the Horse of the Year Show at Wembley and the Dunhill International Christmas event at Olympia, both of which I worked on quite a few times, with the excellent and delightful Raymond Brooks-Ward. I can still recall the look of shock on the face of Anne Moore, the Olympic silver medallist, when I told her that I really knew only that a horse had a leg at each corner and a head and a tail at opposite ends.

I worked on one golf tournament at a newly laid-out course at Abridge in Essex, providing information from the further reaches of the course for the regular team of Tom Scott and John Fenton. I shared an office in Broadcasting House for several years with John, so I think I must have been doing him a favour that day.

Although I never went to Crystal Palace for football or athletics, I did go there for swimming, which I found very boring, and the World Cyclo-Cross Championships, which I think I found rather bewildering.

In 1970 I was sent on two substantial missions to handle the planning and allocation of broadcasting facilities. The first and more straightforward was the World Cycling Championships at Leicester. Cycling then seemed to me a peculiarly Continental sport and none of us could have imagined that Britain would become the foremost track cycling nation. My office was in a caravan in the car park at the Velodrome and, as much as anything else, it was interesting to lift the veil on the inscrutable mysteries of sprint races in cycling, in which the contestants would frequently stand stock-still on their pedals. Luckily, our main commentator on the sport at the time, a Yorkshireman called John Burns, was both helpful and entertaining on the subject.

The Championships ended with the road race conclusion at Mallory Park motor racing circuit (and I had the greatest fun taking my Mini Moke for a couple of laps around that). The day of the race was particularly windy and the commentary positions we had set up were on a tall scaffolding structure alongside the track. An attempt to shield the broadcasters with tarpaulins nearly ended in disaster, as the whole construction started to sway like a gigantic sail, and I remember a South Asian correspondent looking anxiously upwards and saying, 'I would rather go to Vietnam than go up there!'

The other event was the Commonwealth Games, held that year in Edinburgh, centred on the newly built Meadowbank Stadium. Bob Hudson had a reputation for being excessively careful with budgeting and he had booked the BBC team into a colourful hotel in Queen's Gardens, called the Abercrombie. (There was to be more significance in the address than we initially realised.) Most of us had to share rooms there for the duration. I was billeted with the chief engineer from the Glasgow control room, a man with a snore that would not have disgraced a tugboat on the Clyde. Fortunately, Glasgow was not so far distant that he could not have the odd night at home during the fortnight.

The Abercrombie was an old and elegant building with elaborate décor in several rooms, notably the dining room, where the flamboyant wallpaper was quite an awakener over the breakfast orange juice. On Friday and Saturday evenings, though, the old place really came into its own, as a number of exquisite young men would move in. Fur coats and bouffant hair abounded, to the extent that we were involved in any number of double-takes and quizzical looks. One of our number even got some distance into a chat-up at the bar before he realised that his target was not female – to the huge amusement of those of us looking on and making bets as to when the penny would drop.

During the course of the games I got to know three people whom I was to see much more of over the ensuing years.

Trevor McDonald was covering the games with reports for BBC World Service's Caribbean Service and rather feeling his way, but was an amusing and friendly companion. I am not sure that I could have picked then that there was a knighthood on the way for him, and the status of being the guardian of the English language.

Jasdev Singh, the permanently crisis-beset Hindi commentator for All India Radio, also went on to win great honours in India, becoming something of a national institution himself for his coverage of big events of state. Cricket was one of the sports on which he used to commentate, so I saw plenty of him over the years, even driving out to Heathrow to meet him at the start of one Indian tour of England.

'Can I take you to your hotel?' I asked then.

'That would be most kind. The Savoy. I did not know any London hotels, but someone in Delhi told me it was quite good.'

'Not a bad pub,' was Robert Hudson's reaction, when I told him later, also passing on Jasdev's insistence that he must see the Director General.

'I hardly ever see the DG,' said Bob. 'He'll have to make do with me.'

And he did – as well as moving pretty rapidly out of the Savoy, to keep nearer to All India Radio's budget.

At Meadowbank, we had supplemented our technical staff of OB engineers with studio managers, whose usual duties – as the name implies – were to run the technical aspects of studio-based productions. One of these was a feisty young lady called Jenny Abramsky, who was to go on via production and editorial roles in the Current Affairs Department to be the Head of all BBC Radio, and later to become a Dame and chairman of the Heritage Lottery Fund. That was one success story I might just about have spotted.

As a knock-on from the Edinburgh games, Bob Hudson gave me the job of running the radio Commonwealth Pool at the 1972 Munich Olympics. This meant handling all the broadcasters from the Commonwealth, with the notable exception of the Canadians, who chose to go it alone. Bob made it clear that my German A level qualification had played a part in my getting this trip.

I drove to Munich from London in my Mini Moke, listening, until the signal faded, to *Test Match Special* from the Oval, little imagining as I did so that I would be the cricket producer for the next Test match in England. After a night in a camp site at Reims, the second half of my two-day journey was in filthy weather, which was something of a challenge in a Moke, and I remember driving into Munich in the dark, after leaving a storm-tossed autobahn, and asking directions to my billet in the Presse Stadt from a soldier steward. That was when I found the massive difference between the 'hoch Deutsch' from the north that I had learned at school and the strong Bavarian version of the language. It was as if a German's first landfall in England was in Newcastle.

Bob's faith in my command of German remained until a couple of weeks later, when he took me along to the central radio control room for the Olympic Games, to sort out some problem with our international broadcasting lines. Faced with an engineering crisis that I scarcely understood in English, I found the translation hard going. 'I thought you had a German A level,' he said, as we left.

'Oh yes,' I said, 'and I'm red-hot on Thomas Mann and Friedrich Hebbel, but international telecommunications wasn't in the curriculum.'

As with the Commonwealth Games, I had an office in amongst the studios, but this time we were one element in the huge International Broadcasting Centre. Every day, I would go to the office in the central building to negotiate the needs of all the radio broadcasters of the Commonwealth. The staff there had been recruited for their expertise on the radical new idea of doing everything on computers. Unfortunately, shortly before the start of the games, it had been realised that the computers were not up to the job. So that idea was scrapped but the staff remained, and they may have been computer experts, but they were not experts on broadcasting.

Fairly early on, my old friend from Edinburgh, Jasdev Singh, came to see me. With him was his colleague, Surajit Sen, who was the English language commentator. Their first concern was the coverage of the hockey. A few days before, the Indian Sports Minister had stood up in Parliament in Delhi to reassure the House that all India's hockey matches in the Olympics would be carried live on All India Radio. (He could do that, because AIR is a government organisation.) Singh and Sen (as they became known to us all) were just checking that all was well.

I went to see the Germans.

'Some of these matches cannot be done,' I was told. 'There are no broadcast facilities at the outlying grounds.'

I explained the problem that might cause in Indian Government circles.

'You are thinking we Germans are inflexible,' said the smart blond-haired young man I was dealing with.

It was exactly what I was thinking, so I said, 'No, of course not. Not in the least.'

In my office a mournful pair did not take the news well.

'Mr Peter, this cannot be so. You must do something, Mr Peter,' said Singh.

'Heads will roll!' wailed Sen, with the air of one who is pretty sure his will be among them.

Fortunately, my Aryan friend succumbed after a couple more visits from me, and agreed that special lines would be laid to the outlying ground to solve the problem. 'But this is not a precedent,' he insisted. After that, I always found him very willing to try some of the improvisations that are the life-blood of outside broadcasting.

The 1972 Olympics were being staged only twenty-seven years after the end of the Second World War. They were, inevitably, quite a political and national statement. West Germany was telling the world that they were not a militaristic nation, and all the security guards were dressed in powder blue, with baggy white caps that seemed to have come straight from Carnaby Street. Pastel colours were everywhere. Orange and lime green were side by side, in what was very much the current fashionable mix. The stewarding and security at the athletes' village was done by a squad of people in orange tracksuits. As they checked the competitors in and out, they earned the provocative nickname – mostly from the American athletes – of 'The Orange Gestapo'. After all their efforts, that stung them.

Thus, when some of these security men saw a few young people apparently getting back to their accommodation via a short cut under the wire of the compound, they decided against making a scene. What they had witnessed was a group of Palestinian terrorists from an organisation called Black September entering the village to take Israeli athletes hostage.

Mundanely, I was handing in washing at the laundry on our campus, when I heard that there had been a shooting incident in the Israeli camp, news which I interpreted as some sort of accident in the shooting team. In the office, though, I found bedlam, as sports reporters turned news correspondents for the day. The urbane equestrian commentator, Raymond Brooks-Ward, was outstanding with live updates on the situation at the athletes' village. Speculation and rumour were rife throughout the day, which was to end tragically with eleven Israelis, five terrorists, and a German policeman dead after an airport shoot out.

The next speculation was over the future of these Olympics. Cynically, one would have to say that simply too much had been invested in them to abandon the event and, probably even more than the desire not to be defeated by terrorism, that meant we carried on, after a day's break and a moving memorial event at the Olympic Stadium, although without the full enthusiasm that we had previously enjoyed.

Robert Hudson found himself an unwitting tester of the new security atmosphere when he drove as usual into the Olympic Park the day afterwards. The man in the powder-blue suit and the white mod cap now had a gun.

'You cannot come in this gate,' he declared.

'But this is the gate I always use,' insisted Bob.

'Things are different now. I am in charge!'

As time goes on, one becomes so specialised – or is perceived to be – that one never gets asked to do anything beyond one's subject. So it became with me and cricket. Indeed, few of my younger colleagues remembered that I had ever done anything else.

Princess Diana's funeral was such a large operation that I was asked to man a commentary point along the route, and did so with the Radio 4 presenter, Robin Lustig. It was an extraordinary day, on which the raw emotion of all concerned went beyond all logic. High profile as it was, all those involved received rapturous letters of praise afterwards. I reflected that the far more remarkable success of getting *Test Match Special* on the air from Bulawayo had never received a word of praise.

On the radio front, while most things went very well, there were signs of a new era which does not, in my humble opinion, handle the coverage of the biggest state occasions with anything like the accomplishment of their predecessors.

2005 AND ALL THAT

On the evening of Wednesday 20 July 2005, Jonathan Agnew and I went to have a quiet dinner in St John's Wood High Street, as was our custom on the eve of a Test match at Lord's. As we walked back to our hotel, we found several hundred people settling down for the night on the pavements by the turnstiles of the 'Home of Cricket'. There was a feeling of excitement in the air and these people, mostly young men, with a few young women among them, told us how much they were looking forward to the next day and they wanted to make sure of getting tickets.

Such enthusiasm could not fail to stir even cynical old hacks like us, but surely we could never have imagined that the thrilling Ashes series that was about to start would exceed even its wildest expectations.

We had had an interesting taster in the one-day matches that had been played. First there was the Twenty20 international at the Rose Bowl – the first one ever played in England. The evening before, Shilpa Patel and I had met Jim Maxwell, just arrived from Australia, in a pub in Botley, near the ground. If it would be lese-majesty to describe Jim as 'cocky', he was certainly confident that he was not going to see any reversal of recent form on this tour.

At the Rose Bowl it was new commentary boxes for us and a new experience for me, mounting a commentary on this form of the game. There was also a great deal of interest from many different programmes round the

BBC, so that fulfilling all the requests for reporting space at the ground presented its own problems. As happens all too often, the ground authorities had spent little time discussing their building plans with those who were going to use the facilities, which presented a few practical problems.

Test Match Special had a new scorer, too. Bill Frindall had announced that he would make this his last season doing the one-day international circus and that he would start by relinquishing the task for the Twenty20. We did not have an entirely new face to replace him. Malcolm Ashton had come to me to score county matches twenty years before, had stood in for Bill on Saturdays, during the two-year spell when he was cricket correspondent of the *Mail on Sunday*, and then scored for BBC Television, Channel 4 and on tour for England, in which capacity his title metamorphosed into 'Analyst'.

On this day, Malcolm's biggest problem came when the interval between innings was abbreviated and the queues for the Portaloos made a comfort break impossible. We watched him anxiously through the second half of the game. Fortunately, he would not have to wait too long, as Australia were to be dismissed inside fifteen overs.

There had been a little gentle pressure on me to go down the Radio 5-style route for the coverage, even perhaps handing the production to a new producer. They had been doing the county Twenty20 Cup since its inception, but I felt that this was different. It was the first international encounter of an Ashes summer. After a bit of thought, I felt that the 'oohs and aahs' of Henry Blofeld would go down well alongside Agnew and Maxwell. To represent Australia in the summariser's chair, we had Darren Lehman. Chris Adams and Chris Cairns had each played in the curtain-raiser match and now moved into the commentary box. I did learn that that was too many personnel for a Twenty20.

As for the cricket, we were not at all sure, with the formidable top seven batsmen that Australia had on display, that England's 179 for eight was going to be enough. As it turned out, it was more than enough. The five England bowlers were all superb and Australia were rushed to defeat by an extraordinary hundred runs.

A Twenty20 World Cup was still more than two years away. This was meant to be the fun side of the game. It was cricket with a smile on its face. But, while Australians could laugh it off in those terms, this was a huge result. If Ashes fever had been just a glow, this had fanned it into a flame.

There were still two one-day series to go before the First Test. As I was getting myself set up at the Oval for the start of the triangular series, involving Bangladesh, I was hearing of Australia having run up 342 in the fifty overs of their warm-up match with Somerset. Hayden and Ponting had even been confident enough to retire. But later, I heard the news that Somerset had reached their target with three overs in hand. By the time we met up with Jim Maxwell again, this was being referred to as defeat by 'the hired guns' of Somerset. I suppose Graeme Smith and Sanath Jayasuriya are not exactly horny-handed sons of the West Country soil, but whatever the opposition, the Australian attack had not been able to defend 342.

As we headed from England's straightforward ten-wicket win over Bangladesh at the Oval to Cardiff, where Australia were to play Bangladesh, it is just possible that all the members of the *TMS* team were not as sympathetic to Australia's plight as we might have been. Cramming ourselves into our cosy little commentary box at Sophia Gardens that Saturday morning – never suspecting that in four years' time this would be a Test match venue – news came from the Australian dressing room that Andrew Symonds had been left out of the side for disciplinary reasons. With only Bangladesh to beat, they must surely have felt that a show of firmness was easily affordable. Incredibly, some seven hours later we were describing a Bangladesh win over the world champions.

Even as Jonny Saunders called them home ('That is one of the most extraordinary moments in cricketing history. Bangladesh – lowly Bangladesh, some people call them – have beaten the world champions, Australia, here at Sophia Gardens.'), Australians in the media were still laughing it off as a quirky result that happens sometimes.

Twenty-four hours later, in Bristol, I detected more tension in Jim and the former Australian fast bowler, Geoff Lawson, who had now joined us, when Kevin Pietersen rescued England from the position of needing 93 from the last twelve overs, with six wickets down, to record a three-wicket victory with two-and-a-half overs to spare. It was an unbelievable situation. After the first round of games in the triangular NatWest series, England were top and Australia bottom, with two defeats.

As we embarked on the sort of tour round the country that puts a strain on the laundry arrangements, we did not really expect things to stay like that. England duly fell well short at Durham's Riverside ground, to give Australia their first win in the competition at the half-way point, and two days later they were ruthless with Bangladesh at Old Trafford.

By way of Leeds, Birmingham and Canterbury, we made our way to Lord's and the expected final between the old enemies.

They had reached the final having beaten each other once and had the third match abandoned. If we expected that level situation to be resolved at Lord's we reckoned without a tied match. Even that, though, kept us guessing, with Australia recovering from 93 for five to reach a still vulnerable 196. With Lee and McGrath tearing into England, they were quickly 33 for five, and it looked as if they were not going to get close to challenging that. It took a splendid partnership from Collingwood and Geraint Jones to keep them in the hunt, which came down to Ashley Giles and Darren Gough needing to make ten off the last over from McGrath. Gough was run out off the penultimate ball, leaving Giles the task of making three off the last ball. A misfield by Lee allowed him a second leg-bye and the scores were levelled.

It was impossible to say where the balance of power now lay, but all appetites were thoroughly whetted for the Ashes. Bizarrely, however, we had to wait a bit more for the main attraction, as we embarked on yet another one-day series, which was superfluous to all but marketing men and television executives.

This was the three-match NatWest Challenge, just involving England and Australia this time, presumably needed in case Bangladesh had made the NatWest series final. It enabled us to make another trip to Headingley, where a Trescothick hundred saw England home, though the day was more notable for the hourly news bulletins that we were carrying on a terrorist outrage in London. It was 7 July 2005. We could scarcely believe the details of explosions on tubes and a bus as they built up.

All the way down the M1 motorway that evening, I saw the huge matrix signs carrying the warning that London should be avoided following bombs there. The capital was palpably on edge during the two games that followed. Approaching the Oval for the deciding game, two days after Ricky Ponting's hundred had squared the series at Lord's, the sound of police sirens seemed to fill the air.

But I did enjoy one moment of peace, the afternoon before that Oval match, sitting in front of the pavilion to record an interview with the umpire David Shepherd. It was one of the most delightful of tasks, though sad that it was to mark his retirement. I used it in the interval the following day, and at the end of the game the players gave him a guard of honour as he left the field for the last time.

By then, Australia had scored a comfortable victory, and this time it was as if the world champions had had enough of the nonsense. A total of 229 had not seemed a stiff enough target set by England, but it was demolished by Adam Gilchrist with just over fifteen overs to spare, to send an obvious warning. There would be many – not least in the Australian corner – who would now feel that normal service had been resumed. Plenty of others built the anticipation of an upset on those few cracks that had been seen earlier in the impregnable Australian edifice.

A couple of days before the First Test a splendid dinner at Lord's celebrated fifty years of the Primary Club. This charity, with the mission to help sporting activity for the blind and visually impaired, has long been closely associated with *Test Match Special*, so this was an evening very dear to the hearts of all of us. As part of a feature on the club for one of the lunch intervals, I had been earlier in the summer to Dorton House, in Kent, the specialised school which has long been a beneficiary of the club, and where the infants section is named after Brian Johnston. At the Lord's dinner, Richie Benaud's speech pulled us back to the expectations being built up for Thursday.

At last, on the remarkably late date in the summer of 21 July, the Ashes series started. Already, thanks to our previous evening's encounter with the would-be spectators bedding down for the night, there was a great feeling that this was something beyond the norm, even for old sweats like me who might have worked on a few hundred Tests. Nonetheless, the preparations were standard.

On the previous afternoon, I had installed the various bits and pieces that turned the empty commentary box into our office for the coming week. There was the indicator that sat in front of the commentators to remind them what networks they were talking to. (I had tried years before to get one made up with lights that could be controlled from behind, but that had defeated the boffins, so I had run this up in the garage one Sunday afternoon with bits of wood and wire.) There was a folding table, one of two which I carried around for the boxes that were inadequately furnished. This would be quickly covered in cakes, used tea cups, and correspondence. Then there would be a laptop computer with printer and a digital editing machine, on which I would be preparing the various recorded elements of any features that we might be using in an interval, or before the start of play. Most important of all, I would have what Simon Mann christened my 'Mary Poppins bag' in which would reside pens, pencils, scissors, screwdrivers, pliers, glue, sticky tape and – yes – probably even a birdcage and a standard lamp.

For some Test matches, particularly since the summer schedule had become more hectic, I would also be transporting the four heavy steel cases that carried the radio-link equipment used by our roving reporters for live reports and interviews around the ground.

I would give the engineers the mini-disc recording of the *TMS* signature tune, 'Soul Limbo'. This familiar music from Booker T and the MGs was BBC Television's opening theme for a long time, before they lost the broadcasting rights in 1999. Aggers was keen that we should take it over immediately after that, but I was reluctant to be picking up the crumbs from the television table. However, in the West Indies in 2004, when TalkSport had managed to secure the live commentary rights, I felt we needed something like that for our *TMS Report* highlights programme. It was the right sound and it sent out the right message that we were there. After that, it was inked in. It seemed, anyway, that most people had imagined it had always been the *TMS* theme.

There would be a little work to do on that, mixing a clip of commentary, or maybe at the start of a series, a snatch of an interview, with the music. There was an eighteen-second opportunity over the music that worked perfectly. On this occasion it was the voices of the two captains, Michael Vaughan and Ricky Ponting, that provided the introduction, with their anticipation of the greatest encounter in cricket – the Ashes.

On this tension-fuelled morning I was in the commentary box by 8 a.m., but by then Radio 5 Live's *Breakfast* programme was in full swing in their separate box, with a plethora of producers and editors. Aggers emerged to do a live piece for Radio 4's *Today* programme. Then, since the hotel we were using was only across the road, he slipped away for some breakfast while I completed my preparations. There was the commentary rota to construct, and the set-up in all our boxes, including the crowded Radio 5 one, to be checked. (Radio 1, the World Service, the BBC Asian Network and Radio Wales all had to be found space.)

That breathing space, before the commentary team began to assemble, was always very precious to me. And it always disappeared very quickly. Henry Blofeld was the first to arrive. A breakfasted Aggers returned. Bill Frindall panted in with another heavy briefcase, to join the bags he had left the previous evening. Shilpa bustled in, clutching her mobile phone and a bacon sandwich ('Do you want me to get you one, Backers?'), and then set about trying to pin down our Australian summariser for this match, Merv Hughes, an Australian selector and also guide to a group of Australian supporters. Mike Gatting rang from the Tavern to say that he was hosting a breakfast, but would be there in good time. Jim Maxwell entered in mid-mobile phone conversation with the ABC in Sydney, which apparently changed suddenly into a live broadcast. Finally even CMJ appeared ahead of time. This must be a big day.

Greetings were exchanged with the invaluable Andy Rushton, the announcer and studio manager in Broadcasting House, and all too soon he was closing the fader on *Woman's Hour* and welcoming listeners to *Test Match Special*. '… Let's join Jonathan Agnew at Lord's.' The familiar staccato beat of 'Soul Limbo' was playing and, on the radio microphone in the middle of a buzzing Lord's, Aggers was greeting listeners worldwide.

Australia had struck the first blow by winning the toss, but it soon became apparent that their top order were not in for a comfortable morning. Justin Langer was hit on the arm by a fired-up Steve Harmison in the opening over. He tested the grille on Matthew Hayden's helmet, too, before Hoggard bowled the Queenslander, and then Ricky Ponting received a blow on the cheek that drew blood. The Ashes series was on and Australia looked a little rattled. Five wickets were down by lunch. Jim Maxwell could scarcely believe what he was describing, when he reported Simon Jones' having Damien Martyn caught behind with his first ball. There was incredulity in his voice: 'Australia are four for sixty-six – yes, four for sixty-six!'

The wicket of Adam Gilchrist, twenty minutes after lunch, had Aggers describing Flintoff, 'yelling. He's like a man possessed. He's baying. He's bellowing. He's screaming at his team-mates.' In mid-afternoon they were all out for 190 and we imagined all England taking their chance to tune in for the astounding but heart-warming news. There was a note of caution, though, in Blowers' commentary on the final wicket.

'It would be a brave man who would be prepared to bet on what the English score would be when we all go home this evening,' he said.

When the stumps were drawn that first evening, England were 92 for seven. A familiar old enemy had hit back. Glenn McGrath had taken five of them.

Interestingly, a young man was still in overnight for England. He was playing his first Test match, having appeared in a handful of one-day internationals. His name was Kevin Pietersen.

For all the unpromising situation, Pietersen relished the moment on the second morning, as he took on McGrath, hitting him for a straight six and driving through cover for four and a half-century. As Aggers said in his commentary, 'You can only say watching this, that it'll be the first of many. And he'll convert these fifties into centuries. And he's lapping up the applause.' There was to be no century this time, though it took a Champagne-Moment-winning catch by Martyn to end his innings. He had restricted Australia's lead to 35.

By the end of the second day they had stretched that lead to 314, with three wickets in hand, and on Saturday morning their tail wagged to take it beyond 400. Shortly before lunch, with the last Australian pair at the wicket, I was keeping a look-out for our guest for the 'A View From the Boundary' feature that traditionally occupied the interval on Saturdays. I had started this in 1980, after hearing an interview on the radio with the great farceur, Ben Travers. In the course of this, he had mentioned his love of cricket and the fact that he had gone round Australia in 1928/29 with Percy Chapman's side, even sharing a bath with the captain on occasion. That had got me thinking and quickly drawing up a list of celebrities who were devoted followers of the game.

Twenty-five years later, it was still going and today's guest was none other than the Australian Prime Minister, John Howard. He had visited the box before, when we had been in the more convenient location for VIPs of the Lord's pavilion. With ten minutes to go and a certain anxiety building in me, I received a slightly garbled message that he would not be able to come, as the news of his appearance had been leaked to photographers and they were massing. Extraordinarily, in the last over of the session, he arrived in a great rush, with accompanying security men, came straight along the balcony behind the commentary boxes towards me, and explained the situation in person. Then he said, 'But, if we can get it sorted out, I'll come back at tea.' I accepted that, hugely impressed by this personal approach. Then I turned to how we were now going to fill the interval. Fortunately, I always carried in my kit a few spare recorded features which could be used in such an emergency.

By the time Jonathan did sit down with Mr Howard, who described himself as 'a cricket tragic', Trescothick and Strauss had knocked off 65 of the 420 that England had been set to win. He was very content with his country's position in this match, and by the time the rain swept in late in the afternoon, half the England side was out.

The rain was still there on a very bleak-looking Sunday morning. But, as I was about to find out to my cost, the new Lord's drainage system could handle just about anything. In mid-afternoon, when we had long since given up talking over emails and the like in the commentary box, Andy Rushton contacted me from the studio. He wanted to check on conditions, to see whether I judged it safe to get into Radio 4's Sunday afternoon drama. If he did that, they would have to stay with it to the end. On these occasions, I would assess the possibilities if the rain were to stop immediately. How long would it take to get things going again? Usually, after that amount of rain, it would take the groundstaff at least an hour to remove the covers and mop up. Andy went to the play, the rain stopped, and a quarter of an hour before the play was due to end, the Test match resumed. I registered that blunder, in case I was ever in the same situation on this ground.

Geraint Jones' wicket in the second innings was not heard by Radio 4, though we were on for our digital listeners and the ABC, who all now heard McGrath and Warne sweep Australia to a four-day victory by a surprisingly large 239-run margin in an hour's play. We were a little stunned. Jim was unsurprised. Yes, it had been a rough first morning, 'but these guys are just too good.'

In the ten days before the Second Test match at Edgbaston, England's chances were largely being written off. In an interview on the radio, Glenn McGrath, the man of the match at Lord's for his nine wickets, said that he expected Australia to take the series 5-0. A great deal of attention focussed on Ashley Giles. The left-arm spinner, who had had such a big effect on the West Indies series the previous year, had failed to take a wicket in an expensive eleven overs.

The Edgbaston commentary box is small, a fact which made me keen to keep to a tight commentary team there. The route to the Radio 5 hut on the roof, known to us all as 'the potting shed', where Pat Murphy held sway, was tortuous, involving a choice of precipitous ladders. For over a quarter of a century, the word had been that the whole building would be redeveloped soon, so there was no point in making radical changes.

The box does have the advantage of being lower than most others and, as we gathered in the cramped conditions, we were close to the teams' practice routines on the outfield. Close enough, in fact, to be well aware of the moment when Glenn McGrath stepped on a stray ball which had been rolled back to the Australians. It was immediately obvious that he was in serious trouble, confirmed when he was taken off on one of the groundsman's vehicles. Torn ankle ligaments was the eventual verdict.

Mike Kasprowicz was McGrath's replacement, but the change in his attack did not turn Ponting from his chosen course of putting England in to bat when he won the toss. His theory was presumably that England would be down after their batting decline at Lord's, and I wondered later if he felt that he could not say to his dressing room that he had changed his mind after McGrath's injury, because they were not quite as good a side as they had been half an hour earlier.

The crucial piece of bad luck was to be compounded by this critical decision. Trescothick and Strauss reached their hundred partnership in only the twenty-third over of the morning, a milestone greeted rapturously by a crowd which was to give England colossal support throughout the four days. Jim Maxwell chuckled his way appreciatively through the final over before lunch, in which Marcus Trescothick took eighteen runs off Brett Lee, the fastest of the Australian bowlers. He could scarcely credit that 132 runs had been scored in the session, after being put into bat.

As a keen rugby fan, he was delighted that we enticed the retired England captain, Martin Johnson, to cram his enormous frame into our cubicle in the tea interval. Aggers commented that his guest of the week before, John Howard, had not looked overjoyed to be handing him the rugby World Cup in 2003. Martin agreed, but added that 'it didn't spoil my day'.

Not a huge follower of cricket, he was nevertheless appreciating the tempo of the batting, which persisted through the day, though there were many who were saying that evening that, while running up 407 in the day was a great achievement, being dismissed in eighty overs was not. It might well be that England had not made enough, and would regret their millionaire batting next day. Twenty-four hours later, however, Australia had been dismissed for 308, a crucial 99 runs behind, and Ashley Giles had answered his critics by taking three good wickets.

Most of the commentary team were staying in delightful country surroundings just outside Birmingham at Brockencote Hall, which I always found well worth the half-hour drive through Worcestershire villages into the south of the city. So Veuve Clicquot, who provide the vital ingredient of the Champagne Moment, chose that venue to dine us all. A lot of excellent fizz was enjoyed that night and so was the discussion on the match situation.

One can get very cynical about emotions of excitement, when following the sport is your daily occupation, but now we had certainly caught the mood of the Edgbaston crowd and the nation.

That mood became one of great tension very quickly on the cool Saturday morning, when Lee reduced England to a very vulnerable 31 for four. Pietersen counter-attacked, but Warne had the last word and at 75 for six, the match seemed to be Australia's for the taking, with England only 174 ahead. The bright eyes of our lunchtime guest were taking it all in with relish. Nigel Havers, the actor, took his 'A View from the Boundary' with Blowers, the two very much at home with each other.

Forty minutes after lunch, the ninth England wicket went down, with the lead still only 230. But now Andrew Flintoff, as he had the previous summer on the same ground against the West Indies, decided that the long handle was needed. Then Blowers had enjoyed describing the ball hit into the Ladies' Stand, where it was almost caught by Flintoff's father. This time he hit Lee over the pavilion: 'You won't see a bigger six in a hundred years!'

Flintoff's 73 contained four sixes, but more importantly for England, it helped add 51 for the last wicket and just make Australia's target a little stiffer. They would need 282 to win and leave England with a monumental task if they were to regain the Ashes. The dream would have all but vanished for another couple of years.

With the last England wicket falling within half an hour of the normal tea interval time, that refreshment was taken before the players emerged for what would be a long final session on this third day. (Knowing the many regulations governing the timing of the tea interval is just one of the bizarre qualifications for being cricket producer, so that you can anticipate the rearrangement of rotas and other plans.)

Andrew Flintoff had finished the first innings with two wickets in as many balls, so he was on a hat-trick, but was not called on by Vaughan until the twelfth over, by which time Hayden and Langer were making great headway. The hat-trick eluded him, but the second ball was played onto his stumps by Langer. The rest of the over was a torrid examination of Ponting, who was caught behind off the last ball. Indeed, such an over was it, that we awarded it the Champagne Moment. It had fired up the crowd and the team, and it seemed now that there was no holding England.

With seven wickets down by the scheduled close and keen to maintain the momentum, England claimed the extra half hour that is available to either side if there is a realistic chance of them finishing the match on any of the first four days. That was not to be, but Harmison did bowl Michael Clarke in the last over of the day, with an outrageous slower ball at the end of a very rapid over, to leave Australia 174 for eight at the end of the day. As we dined in the village pub at Chaddesley Corbett, all of us were certain of an England win early next morning.

Shane Warne had taken ten wickets in the match, he had hit Australia's only two sixes of the game, as against sixteen from England, and now on Sunday morning he proved that he was not a pushover as a batsman. In forty minutes' batting he began to sow some seeds of doubt in English minds, enough for there to be relief when he trod on his stumps. 'That's just about the game here,' said Jim in his commentary. But it wasn't.

Over the next eleven overs the Australian fast bowlers, Brett Lee and Mike Kasprowicz, rattled up another 59 runs, to have England frustrated and the crowd – and there was a crowd, despite the possibility that it might have been over in two balls – anxious. There was anxiety in the commentary box, too, not least from the producer. As the target came closer and closer, it seemed likely that Jim Maxwell, in harness with his fellow New South Welshman, Geoff Lawson, would be describing an extraordinary Australian win.

Lawson's 'Wow!' when the catch down the leg side off Kasprowicz' glove was taken by Geraint Jones off Harmison, was the letting-off of the pent-up emotions that had been building. England had won by just two runs and there in front of our box we saw the devastated figure of Brett Lee, hunkered down in his disappointment, consoled by his opponent, Andrew Flintoff.

The series was all square.

THE RETURN OF
THE ASHES

IF WE DIDN'T KNOW IT BEFORE, WE KNEW NOW THAT this was going to be a tremendous series. Australia had been only three runs away from virtually killing off the rubber and now it was all square with three matches to play. Surely those three could not come close to that excitement.

There was little time to grab a breath between Tests. Had Edgbaston gone the distance and not finished before lunch on the fourth day, we would have had only two days. It was still soon enough that I was setting out again up the M1 and M6 for Manchester. Old Trafford never looks in its first flush of youth, but the broadcast boxes were rebuilt for the 1999 World Cup. After the last of our meetings with the architects and the club, however, not all the finishing touches were carried out as agreed, so that acoustically, the boxes echo like bathrooms. The other main problem can be the placement of the ever-growing number of television cameras that gather in front of the *TMS* window. The day before a Test match at Old Trafford can be one of negotiation with TV producers. That apart, there is plenty of space, even if a couple of the commentary team are sitting at the back, writing their newspaper pieces.

It was a great relief to all England supporters that their better batting form of the first innings at Edgbaston continued here. Jim Maxwell seemed to get the best of the commentary highlights that first day. He was on to describe

Vaughan being dropped by Gilchrist and McGrath's response next ball: 'He's bowled! Oh! No-ball!' He seemed then to follow the England captain, calling his fifty, his hundred and his 150. But the moment he really wanted came in mid-afternoon, when one Australian magician grabbed the centre stage, although Shane Warne's six-hundredth Test wicket was perhaps more messy than might have been ideal, as Trescothick tried to paddle him away and was caught behind. 'Oh, a jumble of pad and glove,' said Jim. Still, it looked unlikely to be surpassed as our Champagne Moment for the match.

England's 341 for five overnight might have been the base for an even bigger total than the 444 that was reached shortly after lunch next day. Warne, as CMJ commented, was already on his way to seven hundred Test wickets. His four in this innings had taken him to 603. By the end of the day, he would be batting, with Australia in some discomfort.

It was the post-tea session in which the damage was done, starting with Simon Jones having Ponting caught at gully with the first ball after tea. That reinforced a Maxwell theory, which he was still expounding after the mid-session drinks break: 'First ball after a break is the one to watch, more and more ... Flintoff bowls ... and Katich is bowled! Clean bowled! He didn't play a shot ... and it's hit the off stump ... and it's flattened it. And I'm going to get out of here.' Commentators do harbour the superstition that some days they are going to get all the wickets.

That was the fourth wicket, and by the end of the day there were seven down. The score on the board by then was 270, but the next morning it had increased by four, as a result of some unsignalled byes. This caused Bill Frindall some agitation, although he had had his doubts the previous evening, and may even have taken the wise precaution of recording the close-of-play score in pencil. We were needing such diversion that Saturday, because Manchester was living up to its reputation for rain.

There is a corridor behind the Old Trafford commentary box, equipped with round port-hole-like windows, which face the direction from where the bad weather traditionally approaches. The Lancashire dressing room is similarly blessed, and it was there that the old saying, 'It's looking a bit black over Bill's mother's' originated. (Who Bill was, no one seems to know.) On days like this, we try to keep the chat going in the commentary box. I always reckon that a discussion trio is ideal. Then the talk can be refreshed by the occasional replacement of one of the three, without the flow being interrupted too much.

The arrival of email has made such discussions much easier, and more lively, and Aggers is a great encourager of such correspondence. I also managed to harness the technology enabling us to run our own phone-ins at the drop of a hat, with our own equipment at the ground, and the same telephone number wherever we are. Previously, a specialised studio and a team of telephonists had to be booked in advance.

When it rains on a Saturday, the guest on 'A View from the Boundary' can either find himself doing an extra-long stint, or arriving at the ground when the unequal struggle to talk has been abandoned. On this particular day, our guest was a lady, Michelle Veroken, who had been director of ethics and anti-doping for UK Sport. Jim Maxwell was the only one of the commentators who had covered an Olympic Games, so I allocated him the interview, and he had a great deal of fun with it. At one stage, they used the power of radio to suggest that he was giving a urine sample – by pouring water from one glass to another in front of the microphone. Michelle may have been chasing drugs cheats professionally, but she is a very keen follower, and player, of cricket.

There was very little play that day – and no wicket for the England bowlers – who took an hour and a quarter on Sunday morning to wrap things up, with Warne falling ten runs short of his first Test hundred. The Australian deficit was 142 and they knew very quickly that England were after them, with the positive approach of Marcus Trescothick, and then a splendid stand of 127 between Andrew Strauss and Ian Bell. Strauss got his century and Bell, who had not had a happy series so far, was selfless in his approach, even hitting McGrath for six. As CMJ said in his commentary, 'Well, well, well. Ian Bell driving Glenn McGrath for six. Talk about balances of power shifting.'

There was another sign of the times, and the wonderful spirit of the series, when Strauss was out for 106. This from Jonathan Agnew: 'Shane Warne has broken away from the celebrations to shake him by the hand ... and so too Brett Lee, who hit him on the head earlier on today. He went running up to Andrew Strauss.'

The declaration came forty minutes before the close, with a lead of 422, but the light prevented more than ten overs being bowled. So effectively Australia were left the last day to bat to save the match. Not a position they were familiar with in recent history.

The scenes approaching Old Trafford on Monday morning were remarkable. Thousands were heading for the ground in the hope of seeing England going one-up in the series. Aggers and Vic Marks started *Test Match Special* standing on the outfield, describing the atmosphere all around them. Geoff Lawson commented that he had never seen anyone getting, as Hoggard did: 'A standing "ove" for the warm up. But,' he added, 'it was an outstanding warm-up!'

England were cheered onto the field with the sort of noise that would not have disgraced the less-important Old Trafford just up the road. It even impressed Sir Bobby Charlton, who visited our commentary box that day.

Two wickets fell by lunch, and three more by tea, which still left quite a bit of work to do. For the third innings in a row, Warne made useful runs, but it was Ricky Ponting who was England's stumbling block. In a long last session, he passed a hundred and 150, falling four overs before the end – the ninth man out. Somehow, Lee and McGrath repelled everything that England could hurl at them in those four overs. Their celebrations, and those on the balcony, must have been extremely rare for any Australian cricketers who had only achieved a draw, but that fact was all the consolation that England could take to Trent Bridge ten days later.

Trent Bridge is a favourite venue for *Test Match Special* and has been for a long time. In the days when we had a tiny box slung on the front of the pavilion, I used to find life at the ground something of a nightmare, just for lack of space, but since the new stand was built at the Radcliffe Road end, it has become a great deal easier. A cluster of four good-size commentary boxes with a small engineering control point, all served by a short private corridor, make it easy to manage one's space, which is just as well, as this is the ground where rival pork pie manufacturers try to tempt us with their spectacular offerings. The other delight was always staying at Langar Hall. A friend of Christopher's had put us onto this more than fifteen years before, and it was always like coming home to drive up the avenue of trees, between the sheep fields, to the fine old house that joins onto the village church. Some sort of tradition had been started that I always got the same room, with a four poster bed, an enormous bath, and a glorious view across the fields. The twenty-minute drive into Nottingham on a fine summer morning was as good as any journey to work could possibly be.

Trescothick and Strauss gave England another good start, but the highlight of the innings came on the second day, with the batting of Andrew Flintoff. Our Australian summariser for the last two Tests was the former Test wicket-keeper, Rod Marsh, who had just relinquished his role as an England selector and director of the national academy. After Jim had described Flintoff's hundred ('This man is a colossus!'), Rod paid his own tribute, born of his personal dealings with Freddie.

'I just love him. I reckon he's so good for the game of cricket. He's a fantastic young man. He plays the game in the right spirit … and boy, can he play!' Later he was to add of the ball that dismissed Martyn in the second innings, 'I reckon he's too good for Australia, this bloke.'

Flintoff and Geraint Jones put on 177 together for the sixth wicket. England's 477 was looking very good by the end of the second day, when Hoggard had taken three of the five Australian wickets to fall before a hundred was on the board. Half an hour before lunch on Saturday, they were being invited to follow on, 259 runs behind.

On some evenings of a Trent Bridge Test, people arriving to dine at Langar Hall might see, as they pass the croquet lawn, the sight of a former Middlesex and England seam bowler playing a guitar. Mike Selvey usually inhabits the chalet there, and on a fine evening likes to sit out on his porch to entertain the sheep and the rabbits. That guitar was pressed into higher service on the Saturday of this Test match. Our 'A View from the Boundary' guest was Hugh Cornwell from the Stranglers. Our engineers love a bit of a sound challenge and before play they were testing microphone set-ups, so that Hugh could perform 'Golden Brown' for us during his interview with Aggers. Whether Selve's guitar has sounded as good as that before – or since – is another matter.

The afternoon was enlivened by a bit of a spat involving the Australian captain. He was playing his part in fighting Australia back into the game. At 155 for two they were only just over a hundred behind, and nervous Englishmen could imagine problems with Warne on a fourth or fifth day pitch. But then England's substitute, the Durham player, Gary Pratt, ran Ponting out with a direct throw from cover, which had to be referred to the third umpire. Rod Marsh in the commentary box was quick to spot that Ponting had spat out quite a deal of vitriol, which, reckoned Rod, could get him into trouble with the referee. Members in the pavilion were treated to a bit more of it, the tenor being that England were overusing a specialist substitute. It is common practice to release the man left out of the team on the morning of the match, and use players not involved in county matches as substitutes if needed. Although I think that we all felt the comings and goings of players during Test matches were certainly being overdone. Ponting's furious reaction, though, was enjoyed by England's players and the crowd as a sign that he was rattled.

By Saturday evening, Australia were still 37 runs adrift, but had lost only two more wickets. The talk in the Martin's Arms at Colston Bassett that night was of whether we should be checking out of our hotel in the morning. On the whole, we felt that would be tempting providence.

It did turn into a tense Sunday, too. There was only one wicket in the morning, but soon after lunch came a stunning flying catch from Strauss to dismiss Gilchrist and win himself our Champagne Moment. Australia batted till tea, leaving England 129 to win and all of four sessions to get them. Time was not the problem. Warne and Lee might be. Warne was on for the sixth over, taking a wicket with his first ball and another in his second over. Seeds of doubt were planted. At 57 for four, that doubt had taken root. Pietersen and Flintoff got it to 103 for four and surely it was in the bag. But at 116 for seven, it was looking like a remarkable Australian victory. I put Vic Marks and Rod Marsh on together to accompany Aggers. There was anxiety in the commentary box, but Ashley Giles and Matthew Hoggard were the men whose nerve held, and when Giles turned Warne through mid-wicket for two to win the game, the shout of relief from Trent Bridge must have been echoed by listeners and viewers throughout the land.

In all my time in the job, there was nothing to approach the build-up to the Fifth Test match. Everyone seemed to want a slice of the pie. It is easy to get a little resentful of the fair-weather cricket supporters in those circumstances. My phone was ringing off the hook with requests for this and that. Radio 5 had decided to expand their coverage beyond their usual set-up of Pat Murphy and an expert summariser. They would even, it seemed, be doing some of their own commentary. The number of passes I was being asked to sanction for their operation made me wonder if their box would be big enough.

One distraction was the *Daily Mail* running a story about how disgraceful it was that Henry Blofeld had been dropped from the *TMS* team for this crucial last Test. It started as a mischievous diary item and within a few days had been beaten up into a full page feature, which culminated in the opinion that if the BBC did not appreciate Henry, it did not deserve to have *Test Match Special*. Feeding the *Daily Mail* anything would not normally be my practice, but on this occasion I was stung enough to tip their diarist the wink that Blowers was not doing the Oval at his own request. As I have mentioned earlier, it had been one of the matches I had offered him at the start of the season.

Shilpa Patel had set in motion a bit of a *TMS* tradition over the previous few years. On the eve of the final Test of the summer, we would have an outing to a show in town. Shilpa's partner, the news presenter Chris Lowe, was always very skilful at picking out the right performance for us. A couple of years earlier, when we had been to see *The Rat Pack*, we had gone to the pub across the road from the theatre afterwards and noticed the actor we had just seen on stage playing Dean Martin. Simultaneously, he realised he was confronted by the *Test Match Special* team. It turned out he was a huge fan, so it was mutual congratulations all round. This time Shilpa and Chris had chosen *The Producers*, which was right up our street.

It was obviously going to be essential to get early to the Oval on 8 September, for what was to be the latest Test match in the year ever staged in England. Even at 7.30 a.m., an hour before the public would be admitted, the place was buzzing. Television news crews were everywhere. On the balcony of a flat just behind the new Vauxhall End stand, I could see that some network's breakfast show was being broadcast, and I poked my head round the door of the box I had allocated to Radio 5 to see an appropriate level of chaos reigning.

Balconies and even rooftops all round the ground started to fill up, as the start of play approached. I harboured an unworthy thought: wouldn't it be terrible if so many hopes and expectations were thwarted. England had not held the Ashes for sixteen years, and some of us had even begun to fear they might not do so again in our lifetime. A draw would be enough to win them back, but if Australia could win and square the series, they would retain them.

Late the previous year, I had been contacted about a bust of Brian Johnston which had been cast about fifteen years before by Neil Andrew, a sculptor whose father, Keith, had kept wicket for Northamptonshire and England. It was owned by the BBC, but refurbishments at Broadcasting House meant that it was languishing in a storeroom. I had a brainwave. The radio and television area at the Oval had been named the Brian Johnston Broadcasting Centre after his death. Now we were starting in new accommodation at the other end of the ground, would it retain its name? And if it did, would they like the bust on loan from the BBC? Happily, Surrey loved the idea. On the Sunday of the Test we would have a little unveiling ceremony. In the meantime, it could not be fixed to the plinth yet, so for safety it had been delivered to the commentary box. That meant that there was a familiar face waiting for me when I arrived – albeit in bronze – and since there was a spare pair of headphones lying about, I put them on the old boy. It was good to have him in the box when England might regain the Ashes.

In front of a packed Oval, Michael Vaughan won a crucial third toss in a row. After another good start from Trescothick and Strauss, Ponting again turned early to Warne to weave a bit of magic – and it worked. Half an hour after lunch, he had four wickets to his name and at 131 for four, England knew the Ashes were not secure yet. The contrasting styles of Strauss and Flintoff stopped any rot setting in, with a stand of 143, but both were gone by the end of the day – Strauss for his second century of the series. England closed at 319 for seven.

With such national enthusiasm for the game of cricket (the rather insulting expression being bandied about was that cricket was the 'new football') the question already being asked was how this moment could be grasped best. In the tea interval, we talked to someone who might just have embarked on a new initiative at absolutely the right moment. The Governor of the Bank of England, Mervyn King, had started the 'Chance to Shine' scheme in the spring, to bring cricket into state schools for the benefit of not only the game, but also of the schools and their pupils. Cricket making the headlines was just the welcome ingredient.

One of England's great successes of the series had been to neutralise Matthew Hayden, but after the innings had ended before lunch on the second day at 373, he set out on a mission to change his fortunes. For once it was his opening partner, Justin Langer, who substantially outscored him. They needed good progress to give Australia a chance of saving the Ashes, but now the September skies started to take England's part and bad light prevented any play after tea on the second day. There was rain on Saturday, too, when only forty-five overs were bowled.

Michael Grade, then Chairman of the BBC, was our 'A View from the Boundary' guest, talking to CMJ of the need for any sport to throw up heroes to capture the public imagination. We also had a visit from an England cricket captain who had already secured one version of the Ashes. In the last two weeks, Clare Connor's women's team had beaten the seemingly invincible Australians, and she brought the trophy into the box to which she was no stranger, having been an excellent part of our team on the Champions Trophy in 2004.

Between the rain breaks, the new-look, more cautious, Hayden had reached 70 when Langer was out for 105, but he got to his own century before the close. Australia were still 96 runs behind, but they had eight wickets in hand if they could mount an assault on Sunday.

As it was, they lost those last eight wickets for 86 to Hoggard and an inspired Flintoff, to give England an unexpected first-innings lead. It was only six, but it was a lead. There was only a day and a half to go, so surely the Ashes should be won now.

Still it was tense as Warne came on to bowl as early as the fourth over this time, in poor light, and immediately claimed Strauss. One over later, the umpires offered England the light, to a huge cheer from the crowd. Aggers had anticipated it: 'The light meters are coming out. You'll hear something unusual in a moment, if they do go off. You'll hear an enormous cheer from the crowd. They've called Ricky Ponting over. Michael Vaughan can't wait to get off. Listen to the crowd … People here have paid fifty pounds each to come and watch Test cricket. The players are walking off at twenty past two in the afternoon for bad light and there's a standing ovation.'

That was not quite the end of the day. Another half hour was managed before bad light and rain arrived. Now there was just one day to negotiate to claim the prize, but Monday would start with England only forty runs ahead and Shane Warne did have the knack of making you believe he could take a wicket with every ball.

In the event, Glenn McGrath shared the four wickets that fell in the morning with Warne, but it could so easily have been five when Pietersen was dropped early on by Warne in the slips off Lee. That could have been the final piece of fortune that secured the Ashes for England, although the dismissal of Flintoff, caught and bowled by Warne, made us all feel uncertain. In the afternoon, Pietersen decided to end the doubts in his way. And he was simply magnificent.

He reached his first Test hundred shortly before tea, when he drove Tait through extra-cover for four. Aggers appreciated his sense of timing: 'What a day and what an occasion to pick … And like a gladiator he holds his bat aloft, and his helmet. And he looks around to see everybody on this ground … and those outside it, too … on the balconies, on the rooftops, leaning out of windows … standing and applauding.' That was the atmosphere of the day.

When he was finally bowled by McGrath, CMJ was able to say with confidence, 'He has made sure that England are going to win the Ashes.'

Shilpa had been working hard for a few days to encourage the actor, Hugh Grant, to come and visit us from the box he was inhabiting, and he had said he would rather not until he was sure that the game was safe. In the last tea interval, he felt the time was right, though fans of the singer, Lesley Garrett, might not have been pleased with his feelings about her rendering of 'Jerusalem' at the start of play.

Pietersen had given us a glorious finish to the series, even if the actual moment that the match ended was a little messy, with the players off the field for bad light, just four balls into Australia's second innings. By then Aggers, who had been granted access to the England dressing room with the radio microphone, was commentating on the final removal of the bails by the umpires from that vantage point, describing the scene and persuading the coach, Duncan Fletcher to crack a smile. Then it was to the wild celebrations on the outfield in front of the old pavilion.

It was dark when Aggers and I left the ground and headed for our hotel, where we raised a quiet glass to the coming home of the Ashes. We were staying the extra night because we had another duty for the next morning.

In the early stages of the Test, we had heard that England had been offered an open-topped bus procession through London if they did manage to win the Ashes. It seemed to me – and I am sure to the England team – that such arrangements made in advance were tempting fate. But if it was to be on the day after the match, arrangements had to be in hand, and it would be difficult to keep them wholly secret. Aggers and I had been given space on the top of the bus to broadcast live on its progress, via a radio link with a helicopter hovering overhead.

Early in the morning, I arrived at the Mansion House in the City, and made contact with the television engineers who were handling the link. Two double-decker buses were parked there, and Aggers and I took our place at the rear of the open top deck of the leading one. At last, a very tired and emotional group of individuals emerged from the Mansion House. It looked as if the players had made sure they enjoyed their triumph. The women's team, who were to travel in the second vehicle, looked happy, and in rather better order, but then they had had more time to get used to their success.

We were starting from a quiet side street, but when we turned onto Cannon Street and our route to Trafalgar Square, the crowds and their joyous reaction genuinely took the players' breath away. All the way, past St Paul's, down Ludgate Hill, up Fleet Street and into the Strand, the crowds were several ranks deep on pavements that were not always wide enough to take them. Office windows were open and crowded with celebrating workers. (Though the Australian High Commission, which was en route, had its windows closed.) Down the side roads, as we passed, we could see people running to join the fun. The players might not have been at their sharpest, but they were clearly overwhelmed by their reception.

The top deck was crowded, and Aggers fought his way through the crush to interview all those who were capable of speech – and a couple who were not. They included Gary Pratt, whose efforts as a regular substitute fielder had given him an iconic status, to the extent that Marcus Trescothick was brandishing a banner that said: 'GARY PRATT OBE'.

There was a pause in our progress as we reached the side of St Martin-in-the-Fields church and then we edged forward into Trafalgar Square. If the players had been surprised at the warmth of their reception thus far, the sight that greeted them in the square astonished them. I heard gasps of amazement as they beheld the throng gathered, cheering around Nelson's Column and the fountains.

The players disembarked to address the crowd from a stage in front of the National Gallery. As they did so, Aggers and I were left packing up our kit on the top of the bus. I noticed, lying on the back seat, the Waterford Crystal Ashes Trophy, pointed it out to Jonathan and, like a pair of schoolboys, we took each other's pictures holding it, while below us the crowd cheered the men who had won it.

Maybe, at that moment, the only people who were looking ahead to Brisbane in fourteen months time were the Australians, boarding their flight home at Heathrow. The England team that had played unchanged through the first four matches of this Ashes-winning series would never play together again.

Anticipation of the defence of the Ashes in Australia and the wealth of interest in it meant that, for the only time in the job, I was despatched at the end of the 2006 season for a reconnaissance of our facilities down under. All the build-up seemed damned by the first ball of the series, however, fired by Steve Harmison straight at second slip. Somehow, the 5–0 whitewash that followed seemed inevitable from that moment.

The year 2005 had been an extraordinary experience as far as the cricket went. At the end of the season, I sat back and decided that on the whole *Test Match Special* had been on top form, too. Just after the season had ended, and the preparations for the tour to Pakistan were being made, I was summoned to a meeting of the Radio Review Board in Broadcasting House. Their subject, I was told, was to be *Test Match Special*'s coverage of the Ashes.

Reactions at the meeting were mixed. Those who followed cricket all seemed full of congratulation, but there was a substantial contingent from Radio 5 Live who had an obviously hostile air about them. Something was afoot. A few weeks later, on the eve of the First Test match in Multan, a peremptory email from the Head of Radio Sport spoke of it being time to change the 'style and tone' of *Test Match Special*, accompanying various orders. I was distraught, not least at the manner of such a command being delivered.

It was early next year that I discovered what had gone on. It seemed more likely that it was the success of *Test Match Special* in 2005 that had sparked this approach, rather than any perceived failure. Our driving radio network had been Radio 4, with the programme also carried on Radio 5 Live Sports Extra. Now that emphasis had been switched (though no one had had the courtesy to tell me), apparently with the intention of boosting the take-up of digital radio. In future, the money for *Test Match Special* would come from the news and sports network, Radio 5 Live, who would be keen for more of their own sound to be reflected. They were the last people to recognise that *Test Match Special* was popular with many, precisely because it did not sound like the rest of Radio 5. With televised cricket now only available to those with satellite dishes, there would be some nervousness among our audience that another old friend might be damaged.

Retirement was beckoning for me, which would be popular with those looking to make changes. Were I to stay, I could see myself being involved in many battles which, for the most part, I could not win. The defence of the Ashes and one more World Cup would take us to *TMS*'s fiftieth anniversary. It would be an appropriate time to go.

CHAMPAGNE
MOMENTS

As THE OPEN-TOPPED BUS EDGED ITS WAY TOWARDS Trafalgar Square that day in September 2005, bearing the triumphant England team, I reflected how lucky I have been to witness some amazing events such as that one, to see some great sights, and to meet some remarkable people. In cricketing terms, that particular moment of celebration was to become all the more precious a memory, because of the decline in England's cricketing fortunes that followed that pinnacle. The nadir was the whitewash in Australia eighteen months later, but the build-up to the Ashes victory had given us so much to relish.

That build-up was born in England's success in the West Indies at the start of 2004. It was clinched with what would have once been unthinkable, a win in Barbados. Those who lived through the total domination of world cricket throughout the 1980s by the West Indies have to acknowledge that they have now been dragged back to the status of mortals, but nonetheless, a victory in fortress Barbados is still sweet. I had commentated on a most unexpected one in 1994. It came hard on the heels of two humiliating defeats, first in the Trinidad Test match and then a few days later to a West Indies Cricket Board XI in Grenada. The first was shattering and the second inept.

In Trinidad, England had manoeuvred themselves into a reasonable position, in which they needed less than 200 to win and had just over a day to get them. That was if you reckoned without Messrs Ambrose and Walsh. I was on the air as the England second innings started, and I can remember the horrified fascination of seeing the first two wickets go down in the first over. In fifteen overs before the close of the fourth day England were 40 for eight. It did not take long next day.

The low-key match in Grenada only achieved note because of a horrible second-innings batting collapse, when England lost seven wickets for ten runs in the space of fifteen overs, and lost the game by eight wickets.

So on to Barbados, the Fourth Test match, and the influx of wives, girl-friends and supporters that has become traditional for this part of the tour. That was all the joy most people would have predicted for the visitors, though. The series had already been lost; 3–0 down with two matches to play. But a century from Alec Stewart, and heroic bowling from Angus Fraser, gave England an unaccustomed first-innings lead. A second hundred from Stewart, and useful contributions from Thorpe and Hick, enabled Atherton to declare and this time it was Andrew Caddick, with support from Phil Tufnell, who bowled England to victory.

Only one other visiting team had ever won a Test match in Barbados – and that was fifty-nine years before. But ten years later I saw it again, and in some ways the irony was more stark. This time, England were leading the four-match series 2–0 when the Test started. There was nothing in it on first innings, but what changed the game England's way was a hat-trick by Matthew Hoggard on the third morning. They were three crucial wickets: Sarwan, Chanderpaul and Hinds, and the last of the three looked completely unprepared. Towards the end of the innings, in which the West Indies were dismissed for 94, England were setting an umbrella field of catchers, reminiscent of the days when it was the West Indian fast bowlers who had terrorised the world.

England won by eight wickets, and I remember watching their lap of honour from our lofty commentary box, as beyond them a cruise liner set sail from the deepwater harbour into the sunset over the Caribbean.

There was another more remarkable coincidence after that win. As had happened ten years previously, we went on to Antigua and saw the world record individual Test score broken by Brian Lara. In 1994 he was passing

Gary Sobers' 365. In 2004 the record was held by Matthew Hayden, who had overtaken him in the interim. And this time, in 2004, there was an inevitability about Lara's record-breaking, as he went on to make 400 not out.

England did not win that Test match, but it was the start of a year in which they won all seven of their home Tests. When they completed the clean sweep against the West Indies at the Oval, there were many old players who had suffered at Caribbean hands in the past who relished the moment – among them Jonathan Agnew, who actually prepared the words he would say to that effect, if he was commentating when the England victory came – and he was. But the West Indian side was so changed in pride and ability since its heyday, I was not entirely sorry to see two veteran Barbadian players take them home to the Champions Trophy the following month.

However, that heroic stand between Bradshaw and Browne in the final was not quite the Champagne Moment for me of that particular tournament. That came at Edgbaston, when England overhauled Australia with a bit to spare. It was the first time in over five-and-a-half years and fourteen matches that England had beaten Australia in a one-day international and was all the sweeter for that. Our Australian representation in the commentary box that day was only a part-time appearance from Ian Chappell, who was amused at, and appreciative of, our relief at this change in the old order. A year before the Ashes would be reclaimed, it was, perhaps, a significant reversal.

It was a remarkable year in 2004 for England's Test cricket. That 3–0 win in the West Indies was followed by seven wins out of seven Tests against New Zealand and the West Indies again. Then we were off to South Africa, where a much stiffer challenge was anticipated. The build-up to the First Test in Port Elizabeth was not ideal, but two fine innings by Andrew Strauss gave England a decisive win. Then South Africa frustrated England's domination of the first half of the Boxing Day Test in Durban. Still, I reflected as we headed for New Year in Cape Town, it had been an incredible year. England had been undefeated in Tests, with eleven wins out of thirteen, and for those who had witnessed some fairly poor years, it had been a real treat.

Following that, it was a disappointment to start 2005 with defeat in Cape Town, but that was almost certainly a legacy of the efforts to force a win in Durban a couple of days earlier. In Johannesburg, the Test seemed to be heading for a draw on the final morning, but then a superb burst of swing bowling by Matthew Hoggard in the afternoon turned it on its head. Hoggard finished with twelve wickets in the match and England were one up with one to play.

That was the third Test match I have seen at the Wanderers in Johannesburg and each has had its drama. The previous one had been in November 1999, when on the first morning England found themselves four wickets down with only two runs on the board, and Allan Donald and Shaun Pollock rampant. Michael Vaughan started his Test career in the middle of that debacle, coming in at 2 for two, which soon became 2 for four, but revealing something in his 33 that demonstrated to all of us onlookers that he had the temperament and class for Test cricket.

England were overwhelmed in that Test match, as had seemed likely four years earlier. On that occasion I was privileged to see one of the great Test innings. England were set 479 to win in five sessions, plus a quarter of an hour before lunch on the fourth day, which was the time left when Hansie Cronje made the declaration he had delayed to let Brian McMillan reach his century. That was when Mike Atherton went in. By the end of the day he was 82 not out in a total of 167 for four. With Stewart, Ramprakash, Thorpe and Hick already gone, Robin Smith with him, and then Russell, Cork and the tail to come, the odds were heavily against England surviving on the final day.

Atherton gave a chance to short-leg on 99 and infuriated Donald further with a hook for four next ball. Only Smith fell before lunch, bringing in Jack Russell, who had already had an outstanding Test match by taking a world record eleven catches. He became crucial in the mix that saw the pair bat through the rest of the day. In the two hours from lunch to tea, Russell added just eight runs himself.

In the commentary box we had a feed of the pitch microphones, though we were not using it on the air. We could hear in the morning that Atherton was getting a lot of sledging from the close fielders. It was a little quieter after lunch and completely silent after tea. He batted in all for ten hours and forty-four minutes, facing 429 balls and finished with 185 not out. Cronje only gave up the hunt for the last five wickets when there was one over left. He would agree with the headline in the next morning's *Johannesburg Star*: 'Hero Atherton's never-ending innings'.

If I was able to relish the build-up to the winning of the Ashes in 2005, I, in common with so many who made the trip down under, found the surrendering of them in 2006/07 very hard to take. It was not that it was not unexpected, but the disarray that seemed to have set in was exemplified by that first ball of the series bowled by Harmison. It was just as well that Flintoff was watching him rather than the edge of the bat at second slip, because it was fired straight at him. Ponting said he knew before lunch on the first day of that match that Australia would reclaim the Ashes. Most of us felt fairly sure after that one delivery.

In Adelaide we did have that one glorious piece of defiance, when Paul Collingwood made his double century and England bounced back from the First Test defeat by making 551, but the way they slumped to Warne – even allowing for the genius that he was – was gut-wrenching. In that respect at least, I can tell my grandchildren, should they be interested, that I saw Warne get his six hundredth and his seven hundredth Test wickets. I also commentated on him taking a hat-trick.

That latter event happened at Melbourne at the end of 1994, taking England to the brink of defeat, as they were being bowled out for 92. I can remember having a terrible doubt about whether the third wicket was indeed the catch at short-leg off Malcolm that it turned out to be. It came off the glove and David Boon's substantial frame largely masked the event from me. But I got it right. A few days later, we were in Sydney for the traditional New Year Test, and I was staying in the same hotel as the Australian team. (I became aware of this only when I found my wife trying to teach Shane Warne how to use the restaurant toaster.) It was a golden opportunity to arrange the presentation of the Champagne Moment award to Warne for the hat-trick. The photographer, Graham Morris, had been briefed to take the official snaps of presentations on this tour and he suggested the roof of the hotel, which had a magnificent view of Sydney Harbour, with the Bridge and Opera House in prominent position. We could put this other Australian icon between those two. Shane was far more helpful over this than any England cricketer to whom I have made the presentation has ever been. He offered to go and put on an appropriate shirt, and shared my amazement when we discovered that the magnum of champagne did not bear the usual orange Veuve Clicquot label, but the gold of the vintage product.

The Melbourne Cricket Ground has given me plenty of great memories. I was also privileged to commentate on the end of the 1992 World Cup final there, when Pakistan came from nowhere in the early stages of the tournament to lift the trophy. For more than twenty years I reckoned I had seen there the tightest

Test finish I would ever witness, when England won by three runs. That, of course, was until they cut the margin to two runs at Edgbaston in 2005.

There was another remarkable Melbourne Test match in 1998. Australia had enjoyed much the better of it and bowled England out for the second time for an early tea on the fourth day. It was effectively the third day, because the first had been washed out, which meant that every day thereafter had started half an hour earlier and finished half an hour later. So there were five extended sessions for Australia to make 175 to win. They passed 100 with only two wickets down and Justin Langer and Mark Waugh well set. Then Mark Ramprakash took a fine one-handed catch at square-leg to dismiss Langer off Mullally. Now Dean Headley took over for his finest hour. In three overs he took the wickets of Mark Waugh, Darren Lehmann, Ian Healy and Damien Fleming. Suddenly Australia were 140 for seven, but only 35 more were needed. Crucially, Steve Waugh was still there, batting with the tail, at that moment in the shape of Matthew Nicholson, playing his one and only Test match. Together they added another 21, so that at the official close-of-play time at 7.20 p.m., with only 24 now needed, Waugh claimed the extra half hour to finish it that night. The body language from the middle seemed to suggest that England were not too happy, having been in the field for ten minutes short of four hours since the last break. Their mood improved in the very next over, though, when Headley had Nicholson caught behind for his sixth wicket.

With Aggers in animated commentary for *TMS*, I was on another line at the back of the box, doing a report for the 8.25 a.m. sports bulletin on Radio 4's *Today* programme. In the middle of my live update, which was only forty seconds, Stuart MacGill was bowled by Darren Gough. The sports presenter, Steve May, announced that he was hurrying away to listen to Radio 4 long wave and *Test Match Special*, which received a less-than-delighted reaction from Sue MacGregor. Happily, the other *Today* presenter, Jim Naughtie, recognised the dramatic situation in Melbourne and persuaded the producer to call me up again. Thus, as soon as Gough had Glenn McGrath out lbw, I was back on the air to bring the news of an extraordinary turnaround and an England win by twelve runs.

In the history of dramatic changes of fortune, of course, the Headingley Test match against Australia in 1981 has passed into folklore. However, for the first three days it was tediously one-sided. Our Saturday lunchtime guest, the actor John Alderton, was even bemoaning as much with Brian Johnston. By the close of play on that third day, England, following on 227 runs behind, had already lost the wicket of Gooch. When Godfrey Evans, who used to visit our box two or three times during the day with the latest odds for Ladbrokes, set England at 500 to 1 against, it did not seem unreasonable.

I was among the majority who decided to check out of the hotel on the Monday morning after the rest day. When the seventh wicket fell on Monday afternoon, with England still 92 runs behind, that seemed like a perfectly safe thing to have done. But that wicket had brought Graham Dilley in to join Ian Botham, who, with the cause now lost, was enjoying himself with a merry slog. In the early stages of the partnership Dilley's hitting seemed more scientific than Botham's. He was, anyway, a good straight hitter of the ball, and I can well remember a six driven down towards us in our gloomy commentary box at the top of the rugby stand. All of a sudden, it seemed that the last-gasp stand had moved from being a bit of entertainment to becoming an irritation to the Australians. They were still relying on the quicker bowlers who had done the job for them thus far, rather than offering the temptation of Ray Bright's slow left arm.

The moment came when Botham struck another four and Fred Trueman muttered, 'Australia have got to bat again.' England were only 25 ahead when Terry Alderman bowled Dilley to end the eighth-wicket stand at 117. The resistance had been fun, although we had no great expectations of much more embarrassment for Australia. But now Chris Old, too, showed that he was not really flattered to be coming in at number ten. Alan McGilvray described Botham reaching his hundred in appreciative terms. Runs were continuing to come and it became apparent that Australia were unlikely to win tonight. Late in the day, we were all trying to book back into our hotels. Mine was full and I had to ring round to find another.

With the England lead 92, Old was bowled by Geoff Lawson, but even Bob Willis, the number eleven, was in defiant mood, thrusting the front pad out with a great lunge and leaving the run-scoring to Botham. By the end of the day he had contributed one run to the last-wicket stand of 32. Interest in the series perked up that night and I was asked to gather an extra opinion piece at the close of play for the overnight sports desks, with England now 124 ahead. In the committee room I found Fred Trueman having a glass of wine with Tom Graveney, so I recorded a chat with the pair of them. Even with the lead so slender and the last pair in, they were not entirely dismissive of England's chances. 'If they could get another twenty or thirty in the morning,' said Fred, 'Australia might just find it a bit awkward.'

The twenty or thirty eluded them. It turned out to be another five before Willis fell to Alderman. Australia would need only 130 to win.

There had been little obvious impact from Mike Brearley's return for this match, to relieve Botham of the burden of captaincy that had apparently drawn all his fire, but now he applied some psychology. Botham was obviously 'hot' after his 149 not out, so he was given the new ball. He did get the wicket of Graeme Wood with the score on 13, but Willis did not bowl until the fifth over and then it was initially up the hill. The great transformation came with his switch to the Kirkstall Lane end. From 56 for one and cruising home, Australia slumped to 75 for eight.

The tension in the box grew, as a ninth-wicket stand of 35 inched Australia towards their target. Brian Johnston tried to ease it with a letter he had been sent. 'Who was the ice cream seller in the Bible?' he asked. 'Walls of Jericho.' Then, after a bit of thought, he felt that his correspondent had forgotten 'Lyons of Judah'.

We heard later of the huge audience we had around the country and – less cheery – in the middle of the night in Australia. There were tales of drivers punching the air on the motorway as each wicket fell, and the guard on one Inter-City train to the West Country was tuned in and relaying the news to his passengers on the intercom. Office workers were late back to their desks, as they followed events from amongst excited crowds in pubs.

After an agonising time, in which we began to feel that it had been a good effort, but Australia were going to do it, Gatting took the crucial catch to dismiss Lillee with the target still twenty runs away. Henry Blofeld was at the microphone. 'I wonder how many heart attacks there are around the country,' he said. But there was not too much longer to wait before Willis bowled Bright. 'Willis runs around, punching the air!' cried Blowers, with almost as much excitement, though less of a glazed look in the eyes than the fast bowler. England had won by eighteen runs. It was only the second time in Test history that a side following-on had won and, more immediately, it levelled the Ashes series 1–1.

Nor was that the end of the Botham heroics for the summer. The following week at Edgbaston, Australia again seemed to be cruising to victory, when a reluctant Botham came on to bowl. In the space of 28 balls he took five wickets at the cost of a single run and brought England a win on an excited Sunday afternoon. My fiancée at the time was taking an interest in the cricket to see whether she could really live with someone in this line of work and, jumping up and down in the Edgbaston stands as each wicket fell, reckoned that if cricket was always like this it might be rather a lot of fun. (I decided not to let her into the secret that it was not like this all the time.)

Then, at Old Trafford, Botham took on Dennis Lillee armed with a new ball in the second innings, and scored a glorious hundred which ensured that England retained the Ashes. That memory of Old Trafford, with a television camera man on a cherry-picker hoist seeming to duck as Botham hooked another six, remains sharp, but so does an earlier one of that ground in 1976. That Test match against the West Indies was Mike Selvey's debut and he had a dream start on the first morning, taking three for 6 in his first twenty balls, but it is the Saturday evening that is etched in my memory. Two veteran English battlers were facing the full fury of Andy Roberts and Michael Holding at the start of England's second innings. Neither John Edrich nor Brian Close ever played a Test match again, but they went out with an amazing display of courage. Blowers was commentating when Holding struck Close with a short ball: 'Dear old Brian Close ... he's still not rubbing anything.'

But Fred Trueman was concerned for his old Yorkshire team mate: 'I don't know; I think it hurt the old boy. He buckled a little bit at the knees. It was a nasty one.' The next ball was the fourth bouncer of the over and the umpire, Bill Alley, issued a warning for intimidatory bowling. Close and Edrich put on 54 for the first wicket, but after they were separated England slumped to 126 all out and defeat by 425 runs.

A month later, on a pitch on which Viv Richards scored 291 and Dennis Amiss also made a double hundred, Michael Holding purred in like a Rolls-Royce and took fourteen wickets. This was the tour that earned him the nickname 'Whispering Death'. Richards on that occasion – as on so many others – was imperious. It was a shock that he did not go on to his triple hundred. There are not so many one-day internationals that stick in the memory, but his 189 not out at Old Trafford in 1984 is one, particularly the six that ended up rolling down the platform of Warwick Road station.

With so many Test matches to remember, these are all snapshots of memories. In 1990 I saw one of the most remarkable Test matches at Lord's. Graham Gooch made 333 against India and Mohammad Azharuddin responded to criticism of his blunder in putting England in by making a glorious hundred. But even among those great events, what I remember most clearly was the end of the Indian first innings. Kapil Dev was facing Eddie Hemmings, with the Indian number eleven at the other end and 24 still needed to avoid the follow-on. There were four balls to go in the over and he hit the first three of those for six. In the commentary box it was debated whether he should hit a fourth six to save the follow-on, or push the single to keep the strike.

'I'd take the single,' said Trevor Bailey.

We all laughed at the characteristic Bailey caution, with a chorus of 'You would' from the back of the box. Kapil Dev, however, chose the bolder option, lofting Hemmings back over his head for a fourth successive six. The follow-on was saved and Hirwani was out to the first ball of the next over.

In English domestic cricket I remember with great affection – and some regret that they seem to have passed – the days when the quarter- and semi-finals of the cup competitions were great occasions, with county grounds packed and so much tension attending the chance to get to a final at Lord's.

Although a Sussex supporter since the mid-1950s, I was very pleased for Durham when they won the county championship in 2008. I had covered their first home game as a first-class county, a Sunday League match at the Racecourse ground in Durham in 1992, when I remember being so cold towards the end that the lights shining from Durham gaol looked distinctly welcoming. They enjoyed a narrow win, too, against Lancashire. A week later, I was back again for their debut in the championship. I also reported on their first championship match on the new Riverside ground – the ground where I was to produce *Test Match Special* for the last time.

I suppose it is natural in a job like the one I have been doing that you get a little blasé about meeting the famous. It is strange, then, when you do feel moved by an encounter. Of course, in cricketing terms, that would apply to a meeting with Sir Don Bradman. In the days when Test matches had rest days, the custom in Adelaide was to go to the day-long party for both teams at the Yalumba winery. Bradman was always there and inevitably the centre of all attention. In Australia he was not just the greatest cricketer, but the most celebrated Australian. I met him there in 1982 and subsequently exchanged correspondence with him a few years later.

In 1988 I made a *TMS* feature to mark his eightieth birthday and sent him a copy. As was his habit, he replied by return of post, not so much with thanks, but criticism of the fact that I had included a few words from Bill O'Reilly, who, while a great admirer of his ability, did not care for him over much. Bradman was also not pleased that I had mentioned his knighthood, but not his Australian decorations. I replied, explaining each of these decisions, but then he switched to the BBC's reluctance to buy from the ABC the eight hours of interview with him that they had been broadcasting. I pointed out that the restrictions which had been imposed on its use presented too many problems. The rules that had been set were that there should be no editing and the series of eight one-hour programmes could only be broadcast as they were. The price that was being asked was also way beyond *Test Match Special*'s budget. I told him that I had neither the time nor the money available on my programme to take them.

With that the correspondence ended, but only about a week later I heard from BBC Enterprises, following an approach from the ABC, that they were in discussion about a more acceptable deal, which was quickly concluded. The tapes could be edited to six forty-five-minute programmes for Radio 3, but Bradman would have to approve the editing of each episode beforehand. I was asked by Radio 3 to do that editing, working to a very tight schedule at the start of the 1989 Ashes series, when there was plenty of other work to be done. Happily, after hearing the first two edited versions, Bradman waived the right to hear the rest in advance, which made life a bit easier.

One great Australian cricketer who never seemed to me to lose his aura was Keith Miller. I met him a number of times, once picking him up to take him to ABC Radio studios in Sydney for a live link to London. He had that priceless ability to remember everyone he met and to make anyone he was speaking to feel that they were the one person he wanted to see. It was an enormous sadness, during one of the last Lord's Tests that he attended, to speak to him on the phone but to hear that lively voice say that he was sorry he could not come up to see us, because he could no longer make the stairs.

Miller's old fast-bowling comrade-in-arms, Ray Lindwall, visited the Lord's commentary box in 1993 and the most touching thing was to see Fred Trueman greeting him completely star-struck. He had met Lindwall several times before, but the man had always been his hero and you never quite lose that feeling. My own first cricket hero was Jim Parks, the Sussex batsman who became an England wicket-keeper. A combination of his swashbuckling batting and the fact that he came from Hayward's Heath, where I was at school in the 1950s, gave him that status. Years later he became marketing manager for the Sussex county club and I found myself meeting him over discussions on a change of commentary position at Hove.

Fred also used to treat Sir Len Hutton with near reverence and I can remember having a moment with him when I felt the same. I had met Hutton a few times. Bizarrely, one of the early times was at Scarborough during a one-day international. There was a British Telecom strike in operation, which meant that our normal broadcasting lines had not been connected and I had to deliver a report from a telephone in the secretary's office. While I was doing that, Sir Len was dictating his newspaper copy on another phone. Suddenly, the door burst open, and a man whom I knew to be the landlord of a nearby country pub came in with a booming voice, which rose a few decibels when he found himself in the presence of a Yorkshire legend. Hutton apologised politely to the copytaker and addressed the newcomer in angry terms: 'Be quiet! I am busy on the telephone and this young man [pointing at me] is on the radio. Now go away!'

In the early days of 1988, I was putting together a programme on Hutton's triumphant tour of Australia in 1954/55, and I asked if I might come to his house in Surrey to interview him about it. He was very welcoming; it was a lovely spring morning and we had coffee in the garden. He was wonderful on the subject in question, with his intriguingly subtle sense of humour. After the recorder was turned off, he said, 'They're hard, you know, the Australians. The grounds are hard. Even the stumps are hard.'

Then he surprised me by asking to hear all the details of what had gone on in Pakistan during Mike Gatting's controversial tour that had finished just before Christmas. 'I've been listening to all your reports,' he said. That was quite a shaker. Sir Len Hutton, no less, had been listening to my reports and now wanted my opinions on what had happened. I was overwhelmed.

To meet such people has been one of the privileges of the job, which culminated in 2001 with a small group representing the commentary team being presented to Her Majesty the Queen and, what is more, receiving from her a Dundee cake. It was a rainy afternoon at Lord's and the England and Australian teams had just been presented in the Committee Room in the pavilion. With the weather so bad, the pavilion was packed, particularly with members wanting a glimpse of the monarch. For a moment, having had to sort out what Tim Lane and those left in the box would be doing while we were gone, I was not at all sure that I was going to be able to force my way through the throng to join Messrs Agnew, Blofeld, Martin-Jenkins and Frindall. But I made it just in time. Tim Rice, the President of MCC, introduced me and I presented the others. 'They tell me people give you cakes,' said the Queen, and handed me the wonderfully heavy fruit cake.

Aggers asked the question we were all wondering, 'Was it personally made, Ma'am?'

'Not personally, but specially,' she replied immediately.

It was, I felt, recognition that *Test Match Special* had a small part in the fabric of the nation for which we could all be proud.

Of course, not only have I been privileged to meet the great and the good and to witness some stirring moments, thanks to the job, but to see some wonderful sights. To step through the gateway into the traditional first view of the Taj Mahal, for instance, is breathtaking. Tony Cozier reported on a large West Indian fast bowler, not usually impressed by anything, greeting that sight with, 'Wow!'

It is wonderful to see the wonders that live up to their reputation. Table Mountain was something that amazed me by looking exactly like the postcards. When staying in an hotel near the Cape Town waterfront, I have always felt that the drive to work at Newlands must be one of the most spectacular commutes anywhere. There is a moment on the journey when the road turns to face the mountain and for a minute or two it fills your windscreen. Of course, when it comes to mountains, the Himalayas take a bit of beating and I first saw those at dawn one morning in 1981, from a plane climbing out of Delhi en route to Kashmir.

Sydney Harbour – and particularly the Bridge – has always been a special favourite. On my first trip there, we managed to convince one of the younger members of the press party that if he got down to the harbour at dawn, he would see the bridge open to allow bigger ships in and out. Dining almost in its shadow, when you've just flown in from London, is one of those moments that makes you pinch yourself, in disbelief that you really are on the other side of the world. It was the backdrop for one of those moments that gave me a tingle down the spine. As happens from time to time, a German cruise liner was in Sydney's Circular Quay, dominating the area and the busy ferries that buzz in and out of the five piers to visit the various corners of the harbour. The liner seemed big as it set off for sea again, turning past the Opera House.

Next morning, in a steady, murky drizzle, I went onto the roof of my hotel overlooking the harbour and I had timed it just right. Coming past the Opera House was something that put that German cruise liner in its place. The *Queen Elizabeth* 2 made her way up to the bridge under her own steam and then was towed by three tugs back into Circular Quay. It was the most magnificent of sights.

That was a sign of Britain's footprint on the globe, as is Rorke's Drift, the lonely outpost defended successfully by the South Wales Borderers, as depicted in the film *Zulu*. I went there with my two children on our way to spending Christmas in Durban, before the Boxing Day Test of 1999. In between one-day internationals in Bulawayo, I have also twice visited Cecil Rhodes' grave, carved in the rock of the Matopos Hills. That is another magnificent and lonely spot.

The job has caused me to miss too many Christmases at home, though I have been able to celebrate several birthdays in exotic places. My thirty-fifth, for instance, was in Kathmandu, while on a three-day break from a tour of India. My fiftieth was at Leopard's Rock, at the eastern end of Zimbabwe, and I have enjoyed two birthdays in wineries at the Cape in South Africa. My wife organised a superb party on the top floor of a pub under Sydney Harbour Bridge on my sixtieth birthday. I have been very lucky.

Towards the end of 2006 I totted up the number of nights I had spent in hotels for the job. It came to 186 in that calendar year and I could add to that four nights spent in the air. There comes a time when you hanker for home.

At the start of 2007, in the wake of the tour of Australia followed by the World Cup in the West Indies, *Test Match Special* celebrated its fiftieth birthday. In the midst of the celebrations of this event, I had received an invitation from the MCC to a pre-Test dinner in the Long Room at Lord's. There were a few odd things about it, and the way the invitation had reached me, but I was so busy, I just accepted it. When I arrived at the pavilion, I was taken up to the top of the building where I found all the *TMS* team gathered, with their wives. It took a while for the penny to drop that this was their dinner for me, as I started my last Test series as the producer. We dined in the Writing Room that overlooks the ground. During the course of the meal, Shilpa, as ever with an eye for an opportunity, even enticed Brian Lara, who was attending another function in the building, to join us for a while. It was the start of a number of really touching send-offs.

So standing on the edge of the field of play at the Riverside in June was an emotional moment. Within the next hour, I would leave the commentary box for the last time. It really had been not just a job, but my life. The feeling was as if I was handing my children over to someone else to care for.

Do I miss it? Yes, of course I do, and particularly all the people in the commentary team and around the game. Another question I am asked is whether *Test Match Special* will go on to celebrate a hundredth anniversary. That will surely depend mostly on radio's destiny and the quality of the available broadcasters. I am a great believer in radio's future. Its principal attraction is that you can do something else while you listen, and the best pictures are those created in your head. The game of cricket, I am sure, will sustain the programme. Radio and Test matches in my view are made for each other and I sincerely believe that Test cricket will outlive the Twenty20 craze. This listener will continue to tune in, as he did more than half a century ago.

INDEX

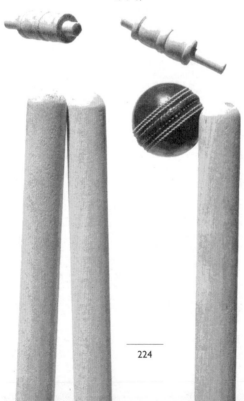